A
Death
on 66

Also by William Sanders

*The Next Victim**

Hardball

The Wild Blue and the Gray

Journey to Fusang

*Pockets of Resistance***

*The Hell-Bound Train***

*a Taggart Roper mystery

**written as Will Sundown

A Death on 66

William Sanders

St. Martin's Press • New York

4-8-96

Production Editor: David Stanford Burr

Design: Basha Zapatka

Library of Congress Cataloging-in-Publication Data

Sanders, William.
  A death on 66 / William Sanders.
    p. cm.
  "A Thomas Dunne book."
  ISBN 0-312-10452-9
  I. Title. II. Title: Death on sixty-six.
 PS3569.A5139D4 1994
 813'.54—dc20   93-43523
              CIP

First Edition: February 1994

10 9 8 7 6 5 4 3 2 1

To

ROGER ZELAZNY

for years of help and encouragement

and

in memory of a certain Baltimore cellar

where you were kind enough

to refrain from shooting the guitar player

Author's Note

Certain liberties have been taken herein with the geography and contemporary realities of eastern Oklahoma. There is no community of Yuchi Park, and Tulsa has no newspaper called the *Courier*. Creek County does exist, and Route 66 does run through it, but nothing in these pages should be interpreted as having any relevancy to the actual personnel or operations of the Creek County Sheriff's Department.

The surviving stretch of Route 66 between Missouri and Oklahoma City does, however, exist as described at the time of writing; and its miles of winding blacktop are commended to off-slab travelers, nostalgia trippers, and students of modern history. Check out the buffalo herd up near Miami.

A
Death
on 66

It was a dark and stormy night. And I *know*, God damn it, but I can't help it; it *was*.

A big late-fall front had been marching unhurriedly across the southern plains for the last couple of days, hammering Colorado and then Kansas with snow and freezing rain, and switching its gray bedraggled tail down over the northern half of Oklahoma. By the time it reached my part of the state, the freezing stuff was gone, but there was still plenty of very cold water and all of it seemed to have decided to come down on the Tulsa area.

It had been raining all afternoon, big heavy wind-driven drops that drummed on the thin metal of my old trailer and turned the world outside to a dull grayish blur. Now it was dark and the rain was falling harder than ever. I couldn't see out the windows any more, but the rattle on the trailer's roof and walls had grown to a steady roar. Big gusts shook the trailer and as the wind passed beneath the floor there was a nasty low moaning that made my teeth itch. Now and then a flash of lightning lit up the soggy world outside.

My dog whined and padded around in nervous circles and finally went back to the bedroom and curled up on the bed, snuffling to himself, and went to sleep. Not a bad way to get through a night like this; I might have joined him, with a fifth of Jim Beam to make a cozy threesome, if I hadn't been working.

At least that was what I told myself I was doing. An uninformed observer, one not familiar with the literary creative process, might have concluded that I was trying to memorize the appearance of my typewriter. Or maybe engaged in some bizarre experiment in psychic powers, seeing if I could stare a hole through a blank sheet of paper.

Characterize it as you like, that was what I was doing around eight o'clock when the phone rang.

I leaned back in my chair and rubbed my eyes and muttered a couple of perfunctory curses, while the phone continued to ring. Should have unplugged the damn thing, I thought, and then made a mental face at myself. Who was I kidding? It wasn't as if my novelistic efforts this evening were likely to suffer from any interruption. . . .

What the hell. Maybe it would be a wrong number and I could take out my frustrations on some fumble-fingered stranger. I jacked myself out of the chair and went over and picked up the phone and grunted into it. A male voice said, "Hello? Is this Mr. Taggart Roper?"

It wasn't a voice that I recognized, not that that meant much under the circumstances. On that cheap little discount-store phone, with the storm making all that racket, I'd have been hard put to tell Mel Tormé from Ross Perot.

I admitted to being me. There was a pause. I could hear

music playing in the background. Jazz; I didn't recognize the tune.

The voice said, "Uh, hey, is this a bad time? I mean, I understand you're some kind of a writer—"

I looked across the tiny living room, at the metal desk and the reams of paper and the stack of reference books and the coffee can full of pens and pencils and the overflowing wastebasket and the floor littered with Michelob empties and wadded-up sheets of bond paper—none bearing more than a dozen typed words—and the big sleek electronic typewriter that sat there in the middle of it all and hummed and hummed and hummed. Some kind of a writer, all right. What kind, I'd hate to have to say. I said, "It's okay."

"You sure?" The guy at the other end sounded genuinely concerned. And now it seemed to me that there *was* something familiar about that voice after all, though I still couldn't couple a face to it.

"Because if you're working on something," he persisted, "I could just as easily call back later. Or have you call me, or whatever."

"No, no." I wondered how long this was going to take. What I really wanted right now was a cup of coffee, but I didn't know if it would be worth making my unknown caller wait while I went and got it. "Go ahead and talk," I said. "No offense, but is this somebody I know?"

There was a quick, slightly nervous laugh. "Oh, no. Far as I know, we've never met. I was given your name," he said, "by a guy named Shelby—"

"Excuse me," I cut in. "Could you hang on just a minute or two?"

I laid the phone down on the little table and went back to the kitchen—or the outhouse-sized alcove that the trailer's designer had somewhat whimsically called a kitchen—and poured myself a cup of black coffee. The pot was cold but I stuck the cup in the microwave for half a minute to warm it up. When the microwave grunted and dinged to a stop I took the cup out and got the Jim Beam from the shelf above the sink and improved the coffee with a dollop of bourbon. *Caffè corretto,* they call it in Italy: corrected coffee. Two of the basic food groups in one drink, not bad. And if this was somebody who'd gotten my name from Shelby, I was probably going to need both.

Not that I had any problems with Shelby, who was merely a small-time Tulsa night-club owner and occasional concert promoter for whom I'd done a couple of minor jobs. It was just that he had a habit of sending people my way, people who needed various things done; and now and then his little referrals had been more trouble than I needed. Whoever my rainy-night caller was, whatever he wanted, I figured I'd better be alert when he started talking.

I went back into the living room and flopped down on the buttsprung couch and took a swig of bourbon-laced coffee and stuck the phone to the side of my head and said, "Talk to me."

The guy at the other end cleared his throat. He seemed uncertain how to begin. They usually are.

"My name's Loomis," he said. "I've got kind of a peculiar problem. Shelby said I ought to talk to you about it."

He paused. When I didn't say anything he added, "Look, it's really not something I want to talk about over the phone, you know? I was wondering if we could get together. Like maybe tomorrow."

I drank some more corrected coffee and looked across the room at the littered desk and the typewriter. A flash of lightning lit up the windows for a second and I wondered if it was a good idea to have the machine plugged in during a storm. On the other hand, if an electrical surge did its worst, at least I wouldn't have to sit there any longer trying to drag a story out of the overpriced, overengineered son of a bitch. Or listen to it hum.

I said, "Mr. Loomis, I'm afraid my time is pretty limited these

4

days. As it happens, I'm working on a novel—" Hah. Well, it was theoretically true anyway. "I hadn't planned to, um, take any other work for the rest of the year."

"This shouldn't take long." Damn it, that voice was triggering recognition signals down in some disused branch of my brain's circuitry. And yet, as best I could recall, I didn't know anybody named Loomis and never had.

"It's one of those things," he went on, "either you'll be able to take care of it right away and without much trouble, or else you won't be able to handle it at all and I'll have to think of another angle." While I was trying to figure out what that meant he added, "If you'll just come and listen to the whole story, I'll make it worth your while. Even if you decide you don't want to get involved, I'll pay you for your time and trouble. Whatever's fair."

I thought that over for a couple of seconds. "Thought" isn't really the word; I was watching my overdue utility bills and auto insurance renewal notices dancing a kind of boot-scoot boogie across my interior stage, partnered with vanishing-point royalty statements and little notes from editors who had *loved* my latest manuscript but were afraid that in today's difficult fiction market it just wasn't quite right for Numnutz House....

I said, "When did you have in mind?"

"Tomorrow afternoon? Say about two?"

"Two's fine." Sure; fits right into my busy schedule. "Where do we meet?"

"You know the Flying Tiger Club?"

I had to confess I didn't. "Yeah," he said a little sourly, "you and a good many other people. Well, do you know the area across the river from the city? West Tulsa, Oakhurst, Sapulpa, along through there?"

"Vaguely."

"Okay, the club's on old Route 66. Let's see, you live in Yuchi

Park, right? So I guess you'll be coming up from the south? You'll see the place, then. Just before 66 runs into the Turnpike."

"I'll find it," I said.

Loomis made an odd noise, like a muffled laugh. "Oh, yeah," he said, "you'll find it, all right. You can hardly miss it." His voice suggested a joke that I wasn't in on. "Tomorrow, then."

My dog had come back down the little passageway from the bedroom, awakened by the phone and curious to see who I was talking to. He looked around the living room with an expression of disappointment, seeing no visitors whose shins he could hump. I put the phone down and said, "Grocery money, Harry."

He made one of those weird back-of-the-throat sounds that cause idiotic dog lovers to say, "Oh, listen, he's trying to talk!" I knew better; he was just yawning.

I said, "Mr. Loomis wants me to meet him at the Flying Tiger Club on Route 66. How about that?"

Harry wasn't impressed. He gave a big wet snort and hoisted his shaggy black ass up onto the couch and went back to sleep. By the time I finished my coffee he was snoring.

I took the coffee cup back to the kitchen and put it in the sink. I didn't have any serious plans to wash it; I just wanted to be able to find it next time. Not that there were going to be many next times if I didn't buy some more coffee. Another good reason to go see the mysterious Mr. Loomis. I wondered why I'd hemmed and hawed around with him. Maybe I just hadn't wanted to admit, to a stranger or to myself, how hard up I was.

Back in the living room, I stood at the desk for a few minutes, looking down at the typewriter, which still going *dnnnnnnnnnnnnnn*. It wasn't supposed to hum; it hadn't made any sound at all when it was new, back when I was a Promising New Author blowing the advance money for my Impressive First Novel. But that was several years and a few book-length manuscripts ago, and it was no longer operating at its original level

6

of efficiency. Of course you could, if you wanted to point out the obvious, have said the same about its owner.

I sat back down and wiggled my fingers like a concert pianist showing off. Before I knew it I had typed:

> Flying Tiger Club
> Route 66
> Loomis???????

Okay, the hell with it; I wasn't going to get anything done tonight. My protagonist was just going to have to wait a little longer for me to get him out of his current situation. Which was a little rough on the poor bastard, seeing that he was ass-deep in a Florida swamp and surrounded by a large number of severely pissed-off Seminole warriors; but hell, he'd been there since Monday and they hadn't gotten him yet. Anyway, I was going to do even worse things to him in Chapter Nine. Assuming I ever got that far.

I switched off the machine and sat back, listening to the boom of the storm and Harry's long slobbery snores. My mind kept replaying Loomis's voice; there was some kind of memory there, just the other side of recognition, and I knew it was going to eat at me all night.

Well, whoever Loomis was, he had a hell of a classy address. . . .

Legends die hard in Oklahoma. Even legends made of asphalt.

Route 66, in its day, was the most famous highway in the United States, maybe in the world. It was much more than just a way to drive from Chicago to Los Angeles without getting lost or breaking an axle, though that in itself was an amazing concept when the road was built. Even in the first days, even before it was finished, it was legend material.

It was part of the national myth, like the Natchez Trace and the Camino Real and the Oregon Trail, with more than a touch of the Yellow Brick Road. Generations of tourists and truckers and thumb-riding drifters, Grapes-of-Wrath migrants and Hollywood-wantabe runaways and college boys out to learn about Real Life: they all knew—as did thousands of others who never left home except in secret fantasies—that when you were on 66, you weren't just going somewhere, you were already there.

When I was growing up back during the Ike-JFK years, the legend was already being overtaken by reality, in the form of new high-speed multi-lane slabs. Little towns, bypassed by the turnpikes and freeways, had begun to dry up and blow away. Bitter-faced men and women stood in front of dying motels and gas stations and diners, into which they had poured their savings and their lives, and watched the traffic roar past on the nearby and hopelessly inaccessible Interstate. A few hundred yards' difference in the placement of an off-ramp could destroy a family's livelihood; a mile's difference in the location of an interchange could make or break a community—but either way, Route 66 was becoming, literally, history.

Yet the legend hung on; long after the old road had passed its glory days, there was a TV series about a couple of young guys having adventures on Route 66, while singers still assured us that there was no better road on which to get your kicks.

Nowadays Route 66 is little more than a vague folk memory; most of the old highway has physically disappeared, though you can still find forgotten stretches of crumbling, half-buried blacktop out on the plains and in the desert, traveled now by nothing faster than lizards and roadrunners. The West has long had ghost towns; now it has ghost roads. On which, perhaps, on a moonlit night, you might see the ragged shades of Jack Kerouac and Neal Cassady trudging along, thumbs forever extended. . . .

And yet, believe it or not, Route 66 is still alive and well in eastern Oklahoma. Nostalgia buffs and time-warp addicts, as well as people who simply don't care to pay the tolls on the faster turnpikes, can drive from Missouri clear to Oklahoma City on 66, which is now just another winding country road. Except for a single hundred-mile stretch in Arizona, which I keep promising myself to go and drive some day, there is nowhere else that the legend lives on.

*   *   *

The storm blew itself out around dawn, leaving behind a couple of hours of cold drizzle and a raw northwest wind. By early afternoon, when I turned my geriatric Camaro onto Route 66, the last of the rain was gone, but the sun was still hidden and the sky was the color of old bullets.

Yuchi Park, where I live, is south of the Arkansas River, so I hadn't had to deal with Tulsa's maniacal traffic. Instead I'd come up by Bixby and Glenpool, picking up 66 at Sapulpa. I'd never been this way before, as it happened. The area had lain a little outside my normal beat during my days as a police reporter for the Tulsa *Courier*, and since then I'd passed through only at speed, on the Turnpike. From what I could see of Sapulpa, I hadn't missed much.

Rolling northeast out of Sapulpa, I felt a faint twinge of disappointment. Route 66 didn't look very legendary here; it was just a wide, well-maintained stretch of blacktop, and except for the little HISTORIC ROUTE 66 markers along the roadside, it could have been any road anywhere. Off to the left, beyond a chain-link fence and a narrow strip of November-brown brush, traffic boomed along the Turner Turnpike, the big semis shuddering in the gusty crosswinds.

The view in the other direction was even less inspiring, considering my present business. The right side of the road was lined with various commercial establishments: auto and RV lots, seedy-looking little restaurants, a couple of truck-driving schools, a discount Western clothing shop. Few of the businesses looked very prosperous; most had a desperate appearance, and several were obviously out of business. A big steak house stood abandoned, half its sign missing. This didn't look like the place to get your kicks; it looked more like Desolation Row. It was all a bit unsettling. If Loomis ran some kind of night club on this stretch of road, I couldn't see how he was going to be a very valuable client. . . .

Then, as I came over the last hill before Route 66 joined the

Turner Turnpike, I saw it. Loomis had been right; you couldn't miss it.

After all, how often do you see a building with a World War II fighter plane on its roof?

The sight was so astonishing that I forgot for a moment what I was supposed to be doing here. By the time I recovered enough to put on the brakes, I'd sailed right past the place, and I had to pull off onto the shoulder and do a little graceless backing up, getting honked at by a passing truck, before I could wrestle the Camaro around and into the parking area.

Then I just sat there for a little while, looking.

The building itself was ordinary to the point of ugliness: a medium-large concrete-block structure, uncompromisingly rectangular, with a low flat roof. The walls were painted flat black, and I couldn't see any windows. Above the front entrance, covering at least a quarter of the front wall, was a black-on-white sign, done in that fake-Chinese style beloved by really corny sign painters:

FLYING TIGER CLUB
DRINKING - DINING - DANCING

Both sign and walls had been painted, or repainted, not long ago; such things weather fast in this part of the country. The parking lot must have been given a coat of asphalt at around the same time, since the Oklahoma sun had not yet begun to crack the black surface. Even so, the whole place had an intangible over-the-hill look about it, like a menopausal waitress wearing a little too much makeup.

None of which mattered at all, because nobody was ever going to take a second look, or even a long first look, at the exterior of the Flying Tiger Club. Not with that fantastic predatory shape crouching on the roof.

From where I sat I could see most of the old airplane, enough to recognize its distinctive outlines: a Curtiss P-40, for God's sake, just like the plastic model I put together from a hobbyshop kit back when I was fourteen or fifteen. It was painted in a blotchy camouflage pattern of dull brown and green, with light gray undersides. The wings and fuselage wore the old-style Army Air Corps insignia of a white star on a blue circle, without the little side tabs; and up front, just back of the big three-bladed propeller, were painted a pair of eyes and a great red mouth with sharp white teeth, giving the nose the appearance of a shark's head.

I got out of the Camaro, finally, and walked toward the building, still looking up at the old fighter. Sitting there against the gray sky, its wings shaking a little in the wind, it seemed to be looking down over Route 66 and the nearby Turnpike, waiting to swoop down and carry off a carload of shrieking tourists. I wondered what it thought of the passing Mitsubishis and Toyotas and Isuzus.

The parking lot was empty except for my Camaro and, parked around at the side of the building, a dark-blue Dodge van. There was nobody in sight unless you counted a coverall-clad figure hosing down a row of trailers at the truck-driving school down the road. I pushed open the front door of the Flying Tiger Club and went in.

Even with the gray day outside, it took my eyes a moment to adjust to the dim light within. When they did, I found myself in a kind of small lobby. To the left of the entrance was a chest-high counter with a large, old-fashioned cash register, plus the usual junk—a bowl of matchbooks bearing the club's name, another bowl of gimme mints, a spike for bills. Beneath the counter's glass top was a display of T-shirts with FLYING

TIGER CLUB printed above a pretty good likeness of a shark-nosed P-40.

On the right was a red-painted door with a small sign reading OFFICE. Straight ahead, no more than a dozen feet from the entrance, was a wide doorway, curtained with strings of little bamboo joints. On the wall beside the doorway was a huge, old-looking movie poster: John Wayne in *Flying Tigers*. As far as I could see, the Duke and I had the place to ourselves.

Then, while I stood there looking around, the music started up beyond the bamboo-curtained doorway.

Not everyone would have called it music; there was no recognizable melody line. Someone was just running through progressions on a piano keyboard, laying down a series of amazing one-hand changes, stacking up the chords until it seemed the structure could go no farther and then, smooth as ice, hanging one last outrageous variation on top before modulating down to another key and beginning a new framework.

Abruptly the sound changed, from piano tinkle to the throbbing tones of an organ. The right-hand chords slipped into a steady slow rhythm and a deep bass line came in, walking into a twelve-bar blues. A soft baritone voice began to sing:

> *"Being a loser ain't much fun*
> > *but at least the work is steady;*
> > *woman stomped out of here this morning,*
> > > *didn't even wait to pack her teddy—*
> > *nothing left to say but shit*
> > > *and I said that already."*

I said, "Jesus Christ."

The right hand started doing something mildly impossible while I walked—I didn't run, but the impulse was there—across the little lobby and through the bamboo curtain.

The Flying Tiger Club looked a lot bigger on the inside than it had from the parking lot. The floor of the main room was sunken well below ground level, dramatically increasing the vertical proportion, while mirrors behind the long bar further added to the impression of spaciousness, and the tables were far enough apart to avoid the sardine-can effect that you get in a lot of small clubs. I'd been expecting something pretty low-rent, but this definitely wasn't that.

All these perceptions were peripheral. At that moment I wasn't paying much attention to the layout. I was looking at the man on the stage at the far end of the room.

The lights were turned low and there was no spot on the stage, so I couldn't see much; just a big, broad-shouldered man sitting behind a large and elaborate-looking electronic keyboard setup. His face was in shadow. The soft light shone on a head of bushy silver hair.

He looked up as I started down the carpeted stairs. "Hey," he called, "are you Roper? Be right with you."

He stood up and flicked off a couple of switches. I could see his face now, wide and snub-nosed, with heavy Norman Mailer eyebrows. He wore a dark suit over a red turtle-necked sweater. The left sleeve of his jacket seemed to be folded up in a strange way.

"Hi," he said, coming down off the stage and walking toward me. No doubt about it, the left sleeve was pinned or sewn up and there was nothing in it. "Just screwing around while I waited for you. Lost track of the time." He stuck out his right hand as he approached. "You *are* Roper, aren't you? I'm Loomis."

Well, if this wasn't a day for legends. First Route 66, then the P-40, and now, by God, Hondo Loomis.

Hondo Loomis. I hadn't even known he was still alive.

He was never one of the really big ones, but there are people who will tell you that he was one of the greats.

Not being qualified to judge greatness—in music or anything else—I'd have to pass on that question. But I don't suppose I could ever be impartial on the subject of Hondo Loomis. Too many memories, for one thing. . . .

The timing was against him from the beginning. He came on the national music scene in the mid-sixties, just when the winds of popular music were blowing at gale force in very special directions. It was all blasting acid-rock bands with wasted skinny faces, or else elegant high-voiced British and pseudo-British groups, with now and then a rare doomed loner like Janis or Jimi; not much demand for a one-off model like Hondo Loomis, with his quirky, understated singing style and his jazz-man's hands.

There weren't half a dozen of us in my high school, back in Coffeyville, Kansas, who had even heard of him. What we lacked in numbers—and social status; if he was out of step with the times, so were we—we made up in fierce loyalty, sitting up till all hours playing his first couple of records over and over, lost in those incredible riffs and chords and that hickory-smoked three-in-the-morning voice.

By the time I got to college he was getting a little more recognition. You could actually find his records for sale in the better stores, and there were fewer blank looks when you mentioned his name in company, though he was still a long way from the superstar echelons. A lot of the memories came out of those years: Hondo Loomis on the stereo, all the albums stacked up on the changer in that dusty apartment, while we drank beer bought on a fake ID and passed sloppily-rolled joints and tried to score with long-legged girls in short skirts who said "Far out" and had brothers named Biff . . . and a lot of nights alone, too, with only Hondo for company against the dark.

As far as I know they never played him on the GI radio in Nam, though events there didn't leave me a lot of time to listen. By the time I got home his career was already in decline. Nobody seemed to know the reason; his last couple of albums were poorly produced and his playing had gotten uneven. Some time in the late seventies he seemed to just drop off the edge of the world. The last time I heard a Hondo Loomis song on the radio, some trio of castrati were doing it in a disco arrangement. Not long after that somebody stole my stereo and all my records and I never did replace them.

Now here he was, standing right in front of me, sticking out his hand. I took it and, to my own horror and disgust, heard myself saying, "I used to own every record you ever made."

He rolled back his eyes. "Oh, my God, a fan." He didn't sound particularly annoyed, but he didn't sound particularly thrilled either. "Used to?" he said, jacking up an eyebrow.

"What happened, you finally throw them out with the rest of the trash?"

"Somebody stole them."

"Damn, talk about crime bringing its own punishment. Well, Roper . . . Taggart?"

"Tag."

"Okay, Tag." He slapped me on the shoulder. "Come on in the office and I'll lay it out for you."

I followed him back up the steps and through the bamboo curtain, trying not to stare at the empty sleeve. So something had taken that rolling-thunder left hand. It was like seeing graffiti sprayed across the ceiling of the Sistine Chapel.

We crossed the lobby and he opened the office door and flicked on the light. The office was tiny but neater than I'd have expected; most of the musicians I've known were spectacular slobs. There was a wooden desk with a basic computer setup, a file cabinet, and a couple of chairs. Loomis went around behind the desk and sat down and opened a drawer and took out a bottle of Wild Turkey. "Drink?"

I nodded. He got out a couple of glasses and poured us each an approximate double. "Need ice, mixer, anything?"

"This is fine." I sat down in the other chair and took the glass and sipped. Regular-strength Wild Turkey, not the high-octane kind. That was okay; I did have to drive home eventually.

He leaned back and tasted his own drink. The light was stronger in here and I had a better look at his face. It was still the face I remembered, but with a lot of miles on it; there were deep lines around the mouth and at the corners of the bright blue eyes, and I could make out the paths of a lot of little blood vessels under the leathery skin. Well, he'd never been a pretty boy; he'd always looked more like a football player or a wrestler than a musician.

And then there was that silver-white hair. All the album-cover photographs had been in black and white, but as I recalled the hair had been pretty dark. But then he had to be . . . Christ, he was at least ten years older than me, that would put him in his early fifties. Hondo Loomis, middle-aged? The thought was enough to make me gulp quickly at my own drink.

He looked across the desk at me with an odd expression. Suddenly he set his drink down and reached across his chest to touch the empty sleeve. "Car crash. If you were wondering, and they usually are."

"Sorry," I said, idiotically. "Um, that's why you, ah—"

"Dropped out of sight?" He made a face that was half grin and half grimace. "Wish I had that good an excuse. Truth is, I just got all fucked up on coke and pills. Hadn't been worth Johann Sebastian Squat for years, even before it happened . . . but hell, I got no right to bitch. Losing the wing made me stop and dig myself and get off the dope. Hadn't been for that, I might be dead by now, like practically everybody I knew in the old days."

"Are you recording again?"

"God, no. I can play enough one-handed to work my own club—I've got a foot-pedal setup now that lets me play a simple-headed bass line—but I'm just diddling around. It ain't only the arm that's gone, you know what I'm saying?"

"You sounded damn good to me, just now."

"Just diddling around," he repeated, and changed the subject. "So you're a writer. What kind of stuff do you write?"

"Historical novels, set on the American frontier. The publishers don't know what to do with them, so they call them Westerns."

He nodded. "I know how that works. The record companies never knew how to market my sound either. God help your ass in this country if the bastards can't stick a label on you."

"I wouldn't mind so much," I said, "but the bottom's dropped out of the Western market lately. And the only historical fiction that's selling is heaving-tit costume romances for women—that and those Stone Age things. I'm thinking of writing a novel titled *Hominid Nurse.*"

He picked up his drink. "I'd guess that's why you do these little odd jobs? Sort of moonlighting to help pay the bills?"

"That's about it," I told him. "I was a cop-beat reporter for seven years, over in Tulsa. Made a few contacts, picked up a few tricks. Now and then somebody wants me to find out something, or locate somebody, or deliver a message. Or whatever."

"Hm." He appeared to consider this for a moment. "Well, that's what I need, all right. Something I need to find out, maybe a message to be delivered too."

He paused and drank some more bourbon. I waited for him to go on, but he seemed in no hurry to get to the point. He said, "Are you from around here, Roper? Originally, I mean."

I shook my head. "Kansas. I've lived in the Tulsa area since—" I realized suddenly that I'd gone to work for the *Courier* just about the same time Hondo Loomis's life and career had gone to hell. "Since the tail end of the seventies," I finished.

"Yeah? We're both foreigners, then. I grew up in Helena, Arkansas, myself. Still," he said, "a guy in the history business, I guess you know a little bit about this area. Route 66, I mean."

He gestured with his drink. "Used to be real hot real estate, along through here. Of course this was farther out of town in those days, but still, it was what was happening. Guy that built this place, right after World War Twice, I bet he figured he had himself a can't-lose proposition. Specially after he got the bright idea of putting an airplane on the roof. Damn if I know where that notion came from," Loomis said, "whether he was in the air force or just a John Wayne fan."

"This place goes back that far? The plane, and all?"

"Oh, sure. Went up back in 'forty-six or maybe 'forty-seven, and it's always been the Flying Tiger Club. And yeah, plane and all. Anyway," he said, "you know what happened. They put in

19

the Turnpike in 'fifty-three and right away all these places along 66 started to die. This one closed down in the late fifties. Every couple of years or so somebody would buy it and try to reopen it—the old joint's been in more hands than a hooker's butt at a Republican convention—but nobody ever made it work. One guy did keep it open for a few years by having tits-and-ass dancers, but even that didn't last."

"That's show biz."

"No shit. Anyway, the last few years—you probably already know about this—there's been this big wave of interest in Route 66. One of those nostalgia trips, I guess. Like this cat I know who's spending every spare nickel he makes fixing up a God-damned Oldsmobile 88." Loomis grinned. "Takes all kinds. Not that I ought to laugh—it's sure as hell been money in the bank for me."

He looked around the paneled walls of the little office. "Last guy that had this place, he bought it about half a dozen years ago, had it figured that this stretch of road was due for a comeback. Spent most of a year, and all the bread he owned or could borrow, giving the old joint a total overhaul. New sound system, new lighting, even a new kitchen. Brought in some good acts, too. And you know, it took off like a son of a bitch. Even though this is a considerable drive from the city, it got to be a real trendy place to go. I mean, you just weren't part of the hip upscale crowd if you hadn't been to the Flying Tiger Club on Route 66."

"If it did so well," I said, "what happened to him? The owner?"

"Far as I know, he just fucked up the finances. Had a basically good idea, but he blew it on the details—spent too much on renovation, for one thing. Got in over his head, had to sell out. I heard about the place from some friends of mine who'd played here," Loomis said, "and I had a little bread put away—they used a couple of my songs in a movie, I got a few bucks off that—and I'd always wanted to own my own club. So I came down from Chicago and, well, here I am. Been here two years now and so far the nostalgia trip, or whatever it is, hasn't peaked out. At least they keep coming and spending their money."

I had a feeling it wasn't just a famous piece of highway and an old airplane that the nostalgia buffs were coming to see. I figured Loomis had already thought of that, though. He didn't impress me as a man who let much get past him.

He knocked back the rest of his drink and looked at me. "Which brings us to the point of this little consultation, Roper. I got somebody leaning on me and I want you to find out who."

I started to speak but he held up his hand. "No, wait, I said that wrong. What I mean is, I need you to find out if it's this certain particular who."

"You want to chase that one by me again?"

He set the empty glass on the desk. "Last year," he said, "not long after I got the place reopened, some people came to see me. People working for a cat named Garvin. Mean anything to you?"

It meant a number of anythings to me, none of them good. For several years Mitch Garvin had run most of the organized rackets around the Tulsa area—as far as anybody could be said to run them, crime being as disorganized as everything else in Oklahoma—though there was some question as to his affiliations at the national level, if any. I said, "Sure."

"Well, then," Loomis said, "you can imagine what kind of visitors these bastards were. Wanted to shake me down for kind of a privilege tax for operating in this area, suggested if I didn't get with the program I'd find I couldn't get liquor supplies or food deliveries, that sort of tired old shit. Then when that didn't fly they got into the straight muscle routine. Like something could happen to this place, maybe even something could happen to me, if I didn't get myself some insurance."

21

"What did you do?" I figured I knew the answer, but I had the feeling he wanted me to ask.

"I told them to go fuck themselves." Loomis's face said that he was still enjoying the memory. "Then later on Garvin came by in person and I told him the same thing. Christ, Roper, I spent my life working in places like Memphis, St. Louis, Chicago. I've seen tougher guys than Garvin bussing tables. And that was as far as it went," Loomis went on, "because, as I'm sure you know, last summer somebody did cosmetic surgery on Garvin with a shotgun. End of that problem. Or so I thought at the time."

"Somebody else is leaning on you?"

"Somebody's doing something, but I can't tell who it is or what they want. About a month ago I started getting these weird little notes in the mail."

"Threats?"

He nodded. "Pretty primitive stuff at first—'Watch your ass, Loomis, you could get hurt,' childish shit like that. One real winner that said, 'Too bad about your arm. Hope you don't lose the other one.' "

"Jesus."

"Uh huh. Then there were some that didn't come by mail. Slipped under the front door of the club, or stuck in our mail slot—one said, 'What if this was a bomb?' and there was another that just said in big letters 'BOOM!' "

He picked up his glass and looked at it, as if considering giving himself a refill, but after a second he set it back down and pushed it away with an impatient motion.

"Anyway," he said, "I figured it was all some kind of practical gag. We get a lot of college kids in here, now and then I have to throw a few out for being under age, and this felt like the kind of half-assed routine they'd come up with to get even. But then it got weird. Phone calls with no voice on the other end, just breathing. Crazy stuff painted on the outside walls, till finally I had the whole place painted flat black. Had to have the sign replaced, too, because some son of a bitch blew holes in it with a shotgun. Just fun and games? After a while you start to wonder."

"Did you report any of this to the law?"

"Yeah. Not that I expected it would do any good, but after the vandalism started I needed the police reports for the insurance. We're about a mile outside Tulsa County, so I had to drive down to Sapulpa to the sheriff's office. Seemed like a reasonably competent bunch of cops," Loomis said, "but they admitted right away that there wasn't much chance of catching the son of a bitch who was doing it. I think the deputies drive by here now and then, but—" He shrugged. "Of course I didn't tell the county mounties anything about the business with Garvin."

"But nobody's made any demands? Just threats and vandalism?"

"Right. What I been thinking," Loomis said, "what if the guy who took over from Garvin—"

"Manzano," I told him. "Garvin's successor is named Freddie Manzano."

I hoped he wouldn't ask for more information, because the name was all I knew. For various reasons, I'd been a little out of touch lately.

"Manzano, huh?" Loomis looked thoughtful, as if trying to remember whether he'd heard the name before. "Okay, well, what if this Manzano has some idea he's going to pick up where Garvin left off? Like maybe this is supposed to soften me up, then one day the boys come around and put the squeeze on and my nerves are so fucked by then I'll be happy to pay."

I gave it a few seconds' thought. "It's possible. I don't know how probable it is, but it's possible."

"Well, what I was hoping you could do," Loomis said, "is find out whether this Manzano is the one behind the harassment. If

23

not, then I'll know I'm dealing with local punks—or some kind of a nut case—and I'll have to come up with some way to put a stop to this shit. Hire a security guard or something."

"And if it is Manzano? Directly or indirectly?"

"Then I'll think it over and decide what to do. Don't worry, Roper, I'm not going to want you to do anything about it. Just find out for me, so I'll know what's going on, all right? I fucking *hate* not knowing." He made a disgusted face. "Back in Chi, I'd make two phone calls and I'd know all I needed to know. Probably St. Louis too, even as long as it's been. Here, I got a bag over my head."

Something occurred to me. "Did you tell Shelby the whole story?"

"Nah. Just happened to mention to him that I needed somebody who could find out something for me, and it might not be anything a regular PI would want to touch. Why?"

"Just wondering." I couldn't imagine Shelby knowingly getting mixed up in anything that might involve the local rackets people, to whom he was perpetually in debt. "And that's all you want me to do? Find out if Manzano's behind the trouble you've been having?"

"That," Loomis said, "plus if you do run this thing down to Manzano's door, you might give him a message to please cut the silly shit and let me know straight out what he wants."

I didn't say anything for a minute or two. It was an interesting job offer but not a very appealing one. As a matter of policy, I try to avoid any involvement with people like Freddie Manzano. They tend to react very negatively, and vigorously, to outsiders inquiring into their affairs.

"Tell you what." Loomis pulled a checkbook from the top drawer of the desk and opened it and began scribbling rapidly. A minute later he tore out a check—not an easy one-hand operation, but he managed—and passed it to me. "How about this for openers? And the same again when you've finished the gig?"

I took the check and read the numbers. Then I read them again, to make sure I hadn't seen them wrong the first time, and then I mentally multiplied by two.

"Why, yes," I said when I could trust my voice, "I think this would do. . . ."

Rita Ninekiller was still at her desk when I phoned. That was good; in the crowded *Courier* office, she'd have to be reasonably restrained. I'd been afraid I'd have to call her at home, where there'd be nothing to stop her from frying my ears, in English and Cherokee, when I told her I wasn't going to be able to make our dinner date. Not that Rita was the bitchy type, but this would be the third date I'd broken this month.

"I'm sorry," I said, "but I'm working again. What can I say?"

"Don't worry about it. You're a writer, I'm a journalist, this kind of thing goes with the territory. You were very understanding when I was working on that air-pollution story."

She'd made a mistaken assumption, but I didn't correct her.

"Hey," she said, "why don't I come over and cook for you tonight? If you've finally made some sort of breakthrough on your novel, you won't want to stop work to fool around in the kitchen. I promise not to talk or distract you."

Ah, hell. Should have known I wasn't going to get away with it. "Rita," I said, "I'm not going to be home this evening."

There was a short pause. My shoulders moved a little closer together.

"Tag," she said slowly, "when you said you were working, you didn't mean writing, did you? You meant," her voice dropped, "the other kind of work you do. One of those jobs."

I waited for the explosion, but there was only a long soft sigh. "Oh, Tag," she said sadly. "Not again."

"The money's good. And I'm damn near broke."

"I know." She didn't sound angry, just worried. "But I wish you could find some other answer. You take these jobs and sometimes things happen to you."

"This one isn't dangerous." I said it so easily I almost convinced myself.

"It's not just the physical danger. You know what I'm talking about."

I did, but I didn't want to get into it over the phone. The previous summer, I'd taken a minor-seeming job that had blown up into a national scandal, and before it was over I'd gotten my head badly messed up. Still, I couldn't see that the precedent applied to this case. I said, "I ought to be done pretty fast. Then I'll call you."

"I suppose you will." Her voice contained a trace of acid now. "And I suppose I won't have sense enough to hang up on you."

"Rita—"

"Oh, don't mind me." She sighed again. "You know, it wouldn't be so bad if I didn't know what you're doing this evening. It's what you almost always do when you start one of these weird little jobs. You're going to talk with Wiley Harmon, aren't you?"

"I guess so."

"Boy, you know how to hurt a woman's self-esteem. Getting stood up is rough enough when you're over thirty. Getting stood up for a foul-mouthed, bigoted, physically *unsanitary*—"

"He's not that bad."

"Yes he is, too. And, quite possibly, the crookedest cop in the Tulsa Police Department. Have a wonderful evening, Tag," she said. "Give my regards to the Toad from Hell."

Wiley Harmon lit a cigarette and said, "I'm telling you, Roper, I don't know what people fucking *want* any more."

It was around eight in the evening. We were sitting at a back-corner table at the Copper Bottom, a Tulsa bar which, as its cute name was meant to suggest, functions mainly as a cop hangout. I knew a good many of the regulars from my days as a police reporter, and I'd been there a lot of times, but it still wasn't one of my favorite night spots. I didn't even know why Wiley Harmon always wanted to meet there. He certainly wasn't the kind of cop who spends his off-duty hours doing bonding numbers with his brother officers.

He said, "I mean, you know what happened, Roper. The fuck'd I say, everybody's so bent out of shape?"

He blew out a cloud of smoke that made my eyes sting and

my sinuses swell. I didn't complain. Carcinogenic or not, it was at least an improvement on his normal breath. "Getting so you can't say *anything,*" he added morosely. "So much for free fucking speech."

I looked at him through the smoke, wondering why Rita had called him a toad. He was a little on the stocky side, maybe even borderline squat, but I couldn't see that he looked particularly toadlike. Maybe she meant he was disgusting. He did seem to have that effect on a lot of people.

His current problems were an example. Lately Detective Sergeant Wiley P. Harmon had been at the center of controversy, both in the news and within the Department.

As he'd said, I knew the story, at least in general outline. Last winter, Harmon had through great persistence and excellent investigative work collared a young man who had brutally raped a college girl in her own south Tulsa apartment. The accused had been definitely identified by the victim; there were also numerous items of physical evidence placing him at the scene. The doctor who had examined the victim testified unequivocally that she had been forcibly penetrated, front and rear, and had taken color photographs to prove it.

The accused, however, was a well-heeled white yuppie type who had hired himself a famous lawyer from Texas. Counsel for the defense had fallen back on the classic rape-trial strategy: when the evidence is against the defendant, go after the victim. All through the last couple of months, the Texas lawyer had bullied, insinuated, and accused, until at last the girl had gone into hysterics on the witness stand and had to be carried out of the courtroom. Not long afterward, the jury had brought in a not-guilty verdict.

The Texas lawyer had been standing in front of the courthouse, answering questions from journalists, when Wiley Harmon, red-faced and furious, had shoved his way through the crowd of reporters. And had said, in a loud and clear voice and

28

before the cameras and microphones of local, state, and national news media:

"Listen, you sorry cocksucker, you better get on the plane back to Dallas and not come back. Because if you ever show up in this town again, I'm gonna bust you for spitting on the sidewalk and I'm gonna take you in and lock your fat ass in a cell with a bunch of the biggest, meanest nigger queers I can find and tell them to show you how it feels."

The general outcry against "bigotry in blue" (in the language of one national news show, quickly copied by all the others) had all but eclipsed the public outrage over the jury's verdict. Both the black and gay communities had held rallies and demonstrations, their leaders howling for Harmon's dismissal. Various white and, presumably, heterosexual political and religious figures had denounced his "intemperate remarks."

From Wiley Harmon's viewpoint, however, the cruelest blow had come from a visiting feminist leader who had been covering the trial for a book she was writing on the treatment of rape victims. "It makes me physically sick," she had said to a TV interviewer, "to find myself on the same side as a man like Sergeant Harmon."

"Fuck's she think she is?" Harmon said indignantly. "I mean, okay, the faggots and the spooks were pissed off, but you'd think a woman—" He reached for his beer. "If you're still allowed to call them that. All I know, they've decided they wanta be called Ovary Americans or something."

"People are sensitive nowadays, Wiley."

"Yeah, fucking tell me about it. You ask me, a lot of people out there make a regular fucking lifestyle out of getting offended. I damn near got kicked off the force, you know that? My rank's hanging by a thread right now. They even threatened to transfer me to the Hate Crimes Unit. Said it would teach me sensitivity, for God's sake."

He waved his hand, scattering cigarette ashes over the table and the front of his rumpled suit. "The fuck would I do in Hate Crimes? I wouldn't mind busting a few of those Nazi assholes, get to kick the shit out of a skinhead or two, but how's a man to turn a buck? Take a payoff to let some dickheads in sheets get away with burning a cross?"

There didn't seem to be any appropriate response, so I kept quiet. Harmon picked up his beer and tasted it. "What I call pistol beer," he said. "Drink a couple and pistol morning. Well." He ground out his cigarette. "You got something on your mind. Talk to Uncle Wiley."

I gave him Hondo Loomis's story. At the end he said, "Well, I'm a son of a bitch. So the old Flying Tiger Club's open again. Funny I never heard about it."

"You know the place?"

"Used to go there a lot, back ten, fifteen years ago? I don't know, it was when I was still in uniform. They had this waitress I was taking out after she got off. Now what was her name? Donna Fay, right." His eyes took on a dreamy look. "Total vacuum from ear to ear, but man, you shoulda seen her. Specially once she got out of that waitress outfit."

I was just as glad I hadn't had the privilege. I knew Wiley Harmon's taste in women: as fat as possible. He even subscribed to a German porno magazine entitled *Roly-Poly*.

"Yeah," he went on, "that was a pretty decent joint back then. Hated to see it go under . . . and now this guy Loomis is running it, huh? Hondo Loomis? You know, I think I caught part of his act once, back when I was on the force in St. Louis. Son of a bitch could play the shit out of a piano."

He stared off across the badly-lit room. "And now he thinks some wiseguys are leaning on him."

"Could they be?"

"I don't know. Garvin, sure, that was a real punk. Shaking

down a little old roadhouse, not even in town, that's just the kind of chickenshit game he'd try."

"And Freddie Manzano?"

"Well, Freddie's different, all right. A hell of a lot tougher than Garvin, runs his rackets a lot tighter. He was Garvin's number one boy," Harmon said, "and if you're wondering, the answer is that nobody's ever known for sure whether it was Freddie who whacked Garvin, but nobody would be a bit surprised. But if he did, it's never gonna be proved."

He grinned at me. "Hey, I'll tell you something not many people know. What do you think Freddie is? You know, what kind of name's Manzano? Guinea, some kind of spic? Colombian, maybe?"

I didn't venture a guess. Wiley Harmon laughed, a short wheezy burst of damp breath that would have stunned a buffalo. "Believe it or not, the little fucker's Jewish. The way he dresses and comes on and tries to talk, people think he's some kind of big-deal wop, but I found out, never mind how. He's from some little town in Mississippi," Harmon said, "and his family's a bunch of those Spanish Jews you find all over the South, been there since before the Civil War. Just like any other bunch of rednecks now, except they don't go in for fucking their cousins so they're a little smarter . . . anyway, that's Freddie Manzano's big secret. The closest thing this town's got to a Godfather, and he's a hebe."

Harmon drank his beer, chuckling to himself, while I thought the information over. It was interesting, in a way—I even made a mental note to try to find out more about Jewish families in the antebellum South; there might be a story there—but it didn't seem very relevant to the present situation.

"So," I said finally, "any suggestions? As to where I could start finding out whether Manzano is behind Hondo Loomis's problems?"

"The fuck," Harmon said, "why not just go ask the son of a bitch? That's what I'd do, it was me wanted to know."

"You've got a badge," I pointed out. "I don't. Not even a private one."

"Hell, no problem." He set his beer down and belched. "He won't jerk you around if I'm along."

"You'd go with me to talk to Manzano?" The idea hadn't even occurred to me.

"Why not? Of course I'll expect my usual small percentage of whatever you're getting. Could be I'll learn something useful, too."

I said, "Thanks," but he flapped his hand dismissively.

"It never hurts to remind these punks who's who," he said. "You know that Burger King over by the fairgrounds? Meet me there in the morning, say ten. We'll go pay a little social call on Freddie Manzano."

But it was almost eleven the following morning, and I was on the verge of giving up and going home, when he showed up at the Burger King parking lot. "Sorry about that," he said. "Lieutenant Birdshit was on my ass all morning and I couldn't get away."

I didn't ask for details; Wiley Harmon's stories about his troubles with Lieutenant Bradshear had a certain sameness after a time. He said, "Come on, we'll take my car. It ain't far."

A few minutes later, heading north on Yale, he said, "I made a couple phone calls, once Birdshit finally left. Freddie Manzano oughta be at this joint called Drummer's—little place he owns, uses for a legit front—going over the books. It's what he does every Friday about this time, and Freddie's a boy of real regular habits."

"Does he know we're coming?"

"Fuck, no. Little surprise visit to break the routine, he oughta thank us."

32

Drummer's was located on a side street not far from the downtown area. I'd been expecting something pretty sleazy, but this was obviously upscale country, with pricey-looking restaurants and clothing shops and even a couple of bookstores. There wasn't a neon sign in sight. "Freddie's place is over there," Harmon said, pointing. "In the basement, under that antique shop. He owns the building, too."

We crossed the street and started down the concrete steps to the club's entrance. At the bottom, underneath the discreet sign that read DRUMMER'S, Harmon paused and looked at me. "You never been here before, have you?" I shook my head. "You're gonna love it," he said cryptically, and pushed open the door.

Drummer's was a small place, half the size of the Flying Tiger Club. The chairs were all up on the tables and the lights were low. Huge ferns sprouted from wall boxes and hanging planters, making the place look like a rainforest. The walls were covered by enormous pictures of Judy Garland, Joan Crawford, Bette Davis, and Marlene Dietrich.

Wiley Harmon and I looked at each other. I said, "Down these mean streets a man must go."

"I don't know that I'd say *mean*," he said. "Maybe a little bitchy."

A slender figure materialized from behind a bank of ferns. A voice called, "Sorry, we're not open yet. Come back after two."

Harmon started to walk between the tables, heading toward an unmarked door at the rear of the main room. The slender character came quickly over to intercept him. "I'm *sorry*, we are *not* open—"

He was a nice-looking young guy, in a lightweight sort of way; he looked a little like David Bowie and I guessed he knew it. He had on sandals and white jeans and a white dress shirt and a paisley scarf. Harmon looked at him and said, "Relax. We're here to see Freddie."

The elegant eyebrows went up. "And you are . . . ?"

"No," Wiley Harmon said, "but you sure are, aren't you?" And walked past, toward the unmarked door, while I trailed along behind and the Bowie lookalike made gobbling sounds of protest.

The door was closed. Harmon didn't knock. He said to me, "Gimme a little elbow room when we go in, just in case," and grabbed the knob left-handed and yanked.

Beyond the door was an office that was a little too big for a club this size. Large metal filing cabinets lined the walls and the wooden desk in the middle of the room was covered with stacks of paper. I didn't see a computer anywhere.

Back of the desk sat a small, dark, hawk-faced man with slicked-back black hair. He was wearing, for God's sake, a gray pinstriped suit with a black shirt. I judged him to be somewhere in his late forties. As we came in the door he looked up and said, "What the fuck?"

He didn't have the place to himself. Standing beside the desk, wearing a yellow shirt and blue suspenders and a worried expression, was a chubby man with curly gray hair. Over in one corner stood a very big man in a brown suit that didn't fit him worth a damn. His right hand was moving rapidly toward the front of his jacket.

I'd seen Wiley Harmon do the move a couple of times before, but it was still something worth seeing. His hand barely appeared to move, but suddenly it held a blocky-looking automatic pistol, pointed straight at the big guy's chest. "Go ahead, asshole," he said with an evil smile. "They just issued us these fucking things. I been waiting for a chance to try mine out."

There was an extremely tense fraction of a second, while the big guy looked uncertain and I glanced around for something to get behind. But then the man behind the desk said, "Christ, Danny, he's a cop," and the big guy's hand dropped to his side and everybody relaxed. More or less.

"Shit," Danny said in a surprisingly high-pitched voice. "How'd I know?"

"You mean you didn't hear me identify myself as a police officer?" Harmon said, putting away his gun. "I can't understand that. Sure can't be the fucking acoustics in here, because I didn't have no trouble hearing your boss when he invited us to come in." He turned his yellow-toothed grin on the man at the desk. "That right, Freddie?"

The man behind the desk leaned back and returned Harmon's look. He didn't seem particularly upset. He didn't seem particularly anything. "What's your problem, Harmon? Payday don't come till next week, best I remember."

Harmon leaned against the wall and got out a cigarette. There was a NO SMOKING sign beside his head. "This ain't a collection, Freddie. Just need to get some shit straight . . . you been running shakedowns, Freddie? I thought that went out with Mitch Garvin, God rest his sorry ass."

Without looking around, Freddie Manzano made a quick gesture. The chubby gray-haired guy nodded and scuttled out of the room, looking profoundly relieved. As he brushed past he gave me a nervous little smile. "Hi," he said.

"The fuck," Manzano said when he was gone, "you been getting yours regular, Harmon. What're you on the rag about?"

He had an interesting double accent: generic Upper Midwest wiseguy on the surface, so thick it was like something out of a bad gangster movie, but unmistakable traces of Deep South underneath. I could see where Freddie Manzano might have an identity problem.

"I been getting mine," Harmon said calmly, "like always, not to notice certain business that goes on around this town. Shit that's always gone on, always gonna go on no matter what any cop does or doesn't try to do about it, because it's the way things work. So you wanta run hookers, dope, loans, I'll take it and I'll play the game. But." He pointed a thick finger at Manzano.

35

"You start leaning on the straight citizens, that's another story. If you're getting into the shakedown racket, that ain't covered by your policy."

Freddie Manzano put his elbows on the desk and clasped his hands together and leaned his chin on them. "How about," he suggested, "you tell me what the fuck this is all about."

Harmon looked at me. "Tell the man," he said. So I did.

Before I was done, Freddie Manzano was already shaking his head. "Christ," he said at the end, "is that what I'm getting rousted for? Cops busting in here, pointing pieces at my help, getting in my face, when I'm trying to balance these fucking books—all that for something you coulda settled with a phone call? I don't believe it."

He looked at Harmon. "Who the fuck is this guy? New on the force?"

"He ain't on the force at all," Harmon said. "But I'd rather you didn't give him any trouble about this. If you follow me."

"Just a friend of yours, huh?" Manzano raised an eyebrow. "Old buddy or something?"

"I'm the wind beneath his fucking wings," Harmon said. "So talk to us."

Manzano made a disgusted face. "Boy, Harmon, you must be losing it. Either that or you think I am." He looked at me. "Listen, whoever you are, this is Freddie Manzano talking. I got serious *business* around this town. I got no time to be dicking around with nickel-and-dime shakedown games, you know?"

"Garvin did," I pointed out.

"Garvin did a lot of dumb-ass stuff," Manzano said. "I know what you're talking about, understand. I was there when he started that stupid routine, trying to collect protection money from those little jackoff joints across the river. Told him then it wasn't gonna be worth the trouble." He flashed his teeth at me, very briefly. "I remember when your buddy told him to go fuck himself, too. Guy's got some stones for a one-armed piano jock.

36

Tell him, he ever wants to come work for me, I'll treat him right."

He stood up. "But tell him he wasted his time sending you here. Whoever's handing him grief, it ain't me and it ain't anybody who works for me. Fucking period."

Hondo Loomis said, "You think he's telling the truth?"

"I think so. So does, um, this friend of mine who knows him. Anyway," I said, "why would he lie about it? He can't very well shake you down if you don't know who's doing the shaking. Tell the truth, the whole scenario always did sound a little screwy to me."

A heavy sigh came through the telephone. "Man, that's a hell of a relief. You just made my day, Roper."

"You still don't know who's harassing you."

"Yeah, but whoever it is, I'll find a way to deal with them. Just as long as it's not mob types. I've had, well, some bad experiences with those cats in other towns."

He laughed suddenly. "Hey, Roper, I tell you what, why don't you come out to the club tonight? I have to give you the rest of your bread anyway. It's Friday, we got a show, you might like it. You got somebody you'd like to bring, that's cool too."

I thought of last night's broken date. "As a matter of fact, there is somebody—"

"Boss. Come on out, then, make a night of it. Everything on the house. Call it a bonus for fast work. Say," he said, "you happen to blow anything? Guitar, sax, whatever?"

"Harmonica," I said, feeling even sillier than I usually do when the subject comes up. "After a fashion."

"Well, hell," he said, "bring your axe along. Maybe you can sit in."

Rita said, "The Flying Tiger Club? Sure, I'd love to go." She hesitated. "Only—Tag, I've never been there, but I know people who have, and I have an impression it's a pretty upscale scene. Don't be offended, but are you sure you can afford this?"

Before I could answer she added, "It's only that I'd hate for you to break yourself, out of some notion of making it up to me for last night."

"No problem," I said a little smugly. "We'll be guests of the management."

Then I laid it on her, the name-drop I'd been building up to: "Personal invitation," I said, "of Hondo Loomis."

Rita said, "Who?"

Rita's apartment was on the south side of Tulsa, in one of those overpriced, pretentiously-styled buildings that have been springing up all over the area like toadstools after a wet spell. I picked her up a little after eight and we got onto Interstate 44 and headed west. The traffic was even heavier and wilder than Tulsa base standard, this being Friday night, so I held the Camaro down to a careful seventy-five or so until we crossed the river.

Rita didn't have much to say at first. But then just as we came off the I-44 bridge she said suddenly, "Hondo Loomis. Now it's coming back to me."

She turned in her seat to face me. "That night at your old place, back when you were at the *Courier* and we were sort of seeing each other off and on, remember? Back before you quit the paper to be a full-time novelist and I started making a total fool of myself with that worthless Chandler—" She tossed her head angrily, making her long black hair flare for a moment. "Anyway, that first night we went to bed together, I remember you had a record playing on the stereo. Wasn't that Hondo Loomis?"

The memory came back sharp and sweet, like tequila with lime. "Yes," I said, "that was him."

"Damn," she said, turning back to face forward. "I'm looking forward to this, Tag."

"Memory Lane, huh?"

"Memory Lane my Native American ass," she said. "That guy had the sexiest voice I ever heard. I can hardly wait."

The Flying Tiger Club's parking area was nearly full when we arrived, and I had to do a little hunting before I found a place to stick the Camaro. I got out and went around and opened Rita's door and put out my hand. Nowadays you never know whether or not to do things like that, because a lot of women get pissed off about it, but I already knew Rita's feelings on the subject. So did most of Tulsa County and surrounding areas, now; she'd gotten a good deal of notice, and considerable flak from her more militant sisters, with the opinion piece she'd written in the *Courier* last year. "No one is really liberated," she'd written, "who is still too insecure to accept simple courtesies."

She took my hand and swung her long legs out of the car. "Thanks. Whoever designed this dress didn't have your car in mind. . . ." The parking lot was lit by bright lights at the corners of the roof, and I had a good look as she went through the business of settling everything into place. She had on a close-fitting white dress of some shimmery material, with little shiny dinguses in a pattern over the upper works. The skirt was slit well up the side, showing a lot of leg when she moved. The white material set off her dark skin and black hair, as did the long dangling beaded earrings and the silver choker around her neck.

"Have I told you lately," I said, "what a hell of a fine-looking woman you are?"

"Not nearly often enough." She took my arm. "Christ, it's cold. Let's get inside before I freeze something off."

The lobby was empty except for a woman who smiled at us from behind the cash register. Through the bamboo curtain came the throb and wail of a small band. I flipped a salute to John Wayne on the wall. "Fascist asshole," Rita muttered beside me.

Beyond the bamboo curtain, the main room was almost crowded; most of the tables seemed to be full. Out on the dance floor, several couples slow-danced to a tune I didn't recognize. The group on stage consisted of guitar, sax, bass, and drums. Hondo Loomis's keyboard setup stood at one end of the stage, unoccupied.

We stopped at the bottom of the carpeted steps and an attractive young woman in a vaguely Chinese-looking red dress came up and asked if we wanted to sit at a table or the bar. I said, "My name's Roper. I think we're expected," and she smiled and nodded and said, "Oh, yes, please come this way." As we followed her between the tables she added over her shoulder, "Mr. Loomis wants you to sit at his table."

She led the way to a table near the stage, where Hondo Loomis was already getting up, grinning and sticking out his hand. "Roper, my main man. Glad you could make it." He looked admiringly at Rita while I made the introductions. "Ninekiller," he said. "I'm guessing that's Indian."

"Cherokee."

"Boy, that's something I'm really getting interested in," he said as we sat down. "Never met any Indians till I moved to Oklahoma. Well, not unless you count Wayne Newton. I want to find out more about Indian music. What little I've heard, there's some really fascinating ideas in there."

"You've probably heard powwow music," Rita told him. "Plains Indian styles. I don't know much about it myself."

"That's right, you people do that stomp dance, don't you? Is that the one where they don't use a drum and the women carry the rhythm with those turtle-shell rattles on their legs? Man, I'd like to hear some of that."

"I've got a few tapes," Rita offered.

"Hey, boss." Loomis tilted his head toward the stage. "The long-haired kid on guitar, there, he's half Comanche, but he doesn't seem to know shit about his own people's traditions. Damn shame, you ask me."

We ordered drinks and sat and listened as the band finished its set. The Comanche kid was pretty good on guitar and the white boy beside him knew what he was doing with his sax, but the young woman on bass was no more than adequate and I wondered what she was doing working for Hondo Loomis. The fat black guy on drums looked bored.

"Here we go," Loomis said as the musicians began leaving the stage. "Somebody I want you to meet."

The bass player was coming toward our table. She was a small, nicely-built black woman—"black" in the ethnic sense only; her skin was lighter than Rita's—with her hair done up in a lot of little tight braids. She wore a crotch-short red dress and high-topped black boots. "Julie," Loomis called, "look who's here."

Loomis and I got to our feet and he went through the introductions. Julie didn't look particularly whelmed. She had huge dark eyes and soft-looking, slightly petulant lips. I guessed she was around twenty-five. Sitting down, she rubbed her left shoulder. "Baby," she said to Loomis, "we got to do shorter sets or else find me a lighter axe. That old Bassman's beating me to death."

42

Loomis slipped his arm around her shoulders and gave her a little squeeze. "We'll see what we can do." The look on his face pretty much answered my earlier question about her qualifications.

She looked at me. "Do you ever write for the movies?"

I shook my head and she lost interest in me. Loomis said, "You know, I don't see why you don't write mysteries. With all your experience, and—you know."

I shrugged. "I suppose I got enough of that sort of thing while I was working for the *Courier*. I've seen enough real murder scenes and met enough real murderers, I don't think I'd ever be able to make the subject entertaining."

Actually that was only part of the truth, but the rest was too embarrassing. In fact I've never been able to understand mystery stories. The ones I've tried to read all had some scene at the end where the detective explained how he knew who did it, but I never could follow his reasoning. I read *The Big Sleep* through twice and I'll be damned if I ever figured out who pushed that guy off the dock.

The drinks came and we made inconsequential talk for a few minutes. The place continued to fill up. "I wonder whether we ought to have dancing here at all," Loomis mused. "That dance floor takes up a lot of valuable space and still it's too small." He looked at me and laughed. "Remember that scene in *A Night in Casablanca*, where Harpo keeps putting out more tables till everybody's dancing all jammed together—"

"Excuse me, Mr. Loomis." The waitress had appeared at his side. She bent down and whispered in his ear and he said, "Thanks," and got to his feet. "Roper, would you mind coming along for a minute? Seems we got a little problem in the kitchen. I might need some backup."

I followed him toward the rear of the main room. "Woman who tends bar," he said, "has this worthless ex-husband, now

43

and then he comes around making trouble. Seems like tonight's one of the now and thens."

At the back of the room a set of swinging doors led to the kitchen. A short middle-aged woman stood there wiping her hands on her white apron. She wasn't really fat, just sort of soft and shapeless, like the Pillsbury Doughboy in drag. "I'm sorry, Mr. Loomis." Her voice was ragged and there were tears on her pale puffy cheeks. "He knows better than to come here—"

"It's all right." Loomis patted her on the shoulder. "Stay out here, Doris. We'll handle it."

He pushed open the swinging doors. Angry voices filled the kitchen but Loomis said, not particularly loudly, "What's going on?" and the place fell silent.

We had walked in on a dramatic little tableau, and not a hard one to read. Most of the white-uniformed kitchen crew were backed up against sinks and counters, looking scared. A single large black woman stood beside the chef's counter, holding some unidentifiable but nasty-looking item of kitchen hardware and wearing a defiant expression.

In the middle of the room stood a tall, rangy white man with a long, horselike face. He wore a military field jacket over dingy khaki coveralls and, jammed down on his head, a mesh-back cap with a Red Man chewing tobacco logo. His eyes were wild. In one big hand he held what looked like a jack handle.

Hondo Loomis said, "Roy Dolan, what the hell do you think you're doing?" His voice wasn't aggressive; it was more the sort of voice you'd use to a little kid who gets out of line.

The big man waved the jack handle in a gesture that seemed confused rather than threatening. "I don't want no trouble." His voice was hoarse and high, with the nasal tones of the southern mountains. "I just want to see Doris, that's all."

The black woman said indignantly, "He come in through the back, big as you please, threatening everybody. You want to call the law?"

Loomis shook his head. "It's okay, Bernice. Roy's just had too much to drink. Now he's going home, aren't you, Roy?"

"Not without I see Doris first." The face was now less horse than mule; he had his bottom lip curled out in a childish expression of obstinacy. "I got to see her. I'll bust this place up if I have to."

Loomis took a step forward. "Now, Roy," he began in a soothing voice, "you don't want to act this way—"

But Roy was past the backing-off point. With a sudden wild cry, half whine and half sob, he launched himself forward, the jack handle raised over his shoulder. The black woman got in one ineffective pass with her weapon and was shouldered roughly aside. Hondo Loomis moved to block the way, but the big man moved quickly to Loomis's left and was past before Loomis could turn and use his one arm.

Which seemed to leave Taggart Roper holding the pass.

When he saw I wasn't getting out of the way, Roy swung the jack handle. I moved aside, let the jack handle whiz past, and grabbed Roy's wrist and elbow in a basic police come-along. He bent forward involuntarily and I turned him and ran him head-on into the nearest wall. There was a loud hollow thump and the jack handle fell to the floor. A couple of seconds later, so did Roy.

I picked up the jack handle and stepped back while Loomis bent over the big man. "Roy? Are you all right now, Roy?"

Roy was still conscious, which was fairly remarkable in itself. One of those tough hillbillies, damn near indestructible; there had been real power in that arm, too. If he'd been sober he'd have taken me apart.

He said thickly, "Sorry," and started to get to his feet, leaning against the wall. I hefted the jack handle, but he didn't even seem to know I was there.

"What did you have to do that for, Roy?" Loomis asked, still in that fatherly voice. "Come around here talking about busting my place up, scaring people. Did I ever do you any harm?"

Roy shook his head. There was blood on his forehead but he didn't appear to notice. "No," he admitted, "you always treated me square, Mr. Loomis. I got no fight with you."

"Then go home." Loomis turned him gently toward the rear of the kitchen and got him into loose-limbed motion. "I know it's hard to handle, Roy, but Doris doesn't want to see you any more. And you know the judge said he'd send you to jail if you bothered her again. Go home and get some rest."

He looked around at the kitchen crew. "A couple of you take him out to that truck of his. No, wait, he's liable to kill somebody if he tries to drive that thing. Ramon, you and Leroy take him home. He won't give you any more trouble."

One of the dishwashers said, "If he pukes in my car—"

"If he does, have it cleaned and send me the bill." Loomis turned to me. "Well. Shall we join, or rather rejoin, the ladies?"

"Man," Hondo Loomis said, a little while later, "you got some good moves. Where'd you learn that stuff?"

"Cop I know."

"God," Rita said. "I don't know what happened back in your kitchen, but if Tag did anything that he learned from Wiley Harmon, you'd better start worrying about the health department."

I filled her in on the basic story, without going into the violent details. At the end she shook her head. "How long has this been going on?" she asked Loomis.

"I couldn't say exactly. Since before I took over the place. I sort of inherited Doris from the previous management, and she was already separated from Roy and in the process of filing for divorce. In fact I had my lawyer help her get the restraining order."

He glanced over toward the bar, where Doris was mixing a

drink. Even at this distance her face looked swollen from crying. "Not that the damn order stopped him. Oh, he leaves her alone most of the time, but every now and then he has a few too many and comes around here trying to see her, and I have to throw him out. I could have had him arrested, but Doris always begs me not to."

"Doesn't he come after her at home?" Rita asked.

Loomis laughed. "Not since she moved in with her brother and his family, and their yard full of Rottweilers. Even Roy Dolan isn't crazy enough to go up against all those teeth."

He picked up his drink and sighed. "Poor son of a bitch. Ninety percent of the time he's as nice a guy as you'd ever want to meet. Doris says he could be the kindest man alive. But every now and then, for no reason, he'd flip out and start slapping her around. After the second time he put her in the hospital, she left him. And still he can't get it into his head that it's over. Hard to understand a man like that."

"Hard to understand a *woman* like that," Julie put in. "Put her in the hospital a second time? Man ever hit me just *one* time, even just a little slap, that'd be the end of the line. They might put *his* ass in the hospital, if I had a gun handy."

"It's not that easy for some women," Rita told her. "A woman of Doris's generation—I don't know, of course, but the chances are she was brought up to be submissive to men, to expect a certain amount of abuse. Women like that tend to feel it's their fault, somehow, when a husband beats them. You can't expect people to simply discard all the attitudes they were taught in childhood."

"Hell you can't," Julie said decisively. "Time I was fourteen, I already knew that everything anybody had ever taught me was a load of bullshit."

That stopped the conversation for a moment. I said to Loomis, "Any possibility that Roy might be the one harassing you?"

Loomis played with his glass while he considered this. "I

47

don't think so," he said finally. "For one thing, as you just saw, he's always been friendly to me. I bailed him out of jail once, at Doris's request, and you know these mountain people: do them a favor once and you've got a friend for life. Anyway," he added, "I doubt if Roy Dolan has the imagination to plan and carry out a systematic campaign like that. He might break a window or set something on fire on impulse, if he was drunk enough, but that's about his limit. And hell, I'm not even sure he knows how to write."

He glanced at his watch. "Looks like it's time to do it to it. Let's go, love."

He and Julie got up and moved toward the stage, where the other musicians were already getting ready for the set. The sax player stepped up to a floor-stand mike and said, "And now, ladies and gentlemen—Hondo Loomis!"

A spotlight came on, following Loomis as he walked across the stage and sat down at the keyboard. The applause was long and vigorous. Over at the bar some asshole barked like a dog. "Thank you almost to death," Loomis said into his mike. "Here's a little song I wrote back around the Ice Age—"

He nodded to the band, which began a four-bar intro. The right hand lashed out and began grabbing chords and Loomis leaned into the mike and sang, *Here she comes, there she goes, she's gone—"* The crowd applauded harder than ever as they realized he was doing "Mama's Getting Dirty Tonight." Rita and I looked at each other and traded grins, remembering.

He followed with "Hanged Man on My Mind" and then an arrangement of Billy Joel's "Innocent Man." Halfway through the third number, while the sax player was taking an extended solo, Loomis looked over and caught my eye and made a beckoning motion with his head.

I crossed the dance floor and climbed up onto the stage beside him. He said over his shoulder, "You bring your mouth harp?"

"Are you serious?"

"As a broken leg."

I reached into the inside pocket of my jacket and took out the big chromatic Hohner. He raised an eyebrow. "Damn, that's a pro axe. Let me hear you a little."

The sax solo ended and the Comanche kid stepped forward and started doing something fancy on guitar. I leaned close to Hondo Loomis's ear and came in on the Hohner, playing softly so nobody else could hear. After a few bars he began nodding in time with the music. "All right," he said approvingly. "Grab that second mike there and come in with me after the guitar solo."

I took the hand-held mike and cupped it in my hands with the Hohner, like Dan Aykroyd in *The Blues Brothers*, and waited. When the guitar run ended, Loomis leaned into his own mike again and began singing the last verse, playing only a skeletal chord accompaniment and leaving the foot-bass pedals alone, and I came in behind him on the harmonica, nervous and not very strong at first but then gaining a little confidence and trying a few things to fill in the pauses, keeping my eyes closed the whole time because I didn't dare look at the audience. And I even had sense enough, at the end, to stop blowing just in time to let Loomis finish off with a little piano coda.

The applause was probably no more than normal, but to me it sounded like an earthquake. Loomis grinned at me and said into the microphone, "Ladies and gentlemen, sitting in on harmonica, the famous Oklahoma novelist Taggart Roper!" and I got a round of applause of my own, even though it was odds-on there wasn't a human in the crowd who had ever heard of me.

All I could think was: Louis L'Amour, wherever you are, eat your heart out. You may have sold a duodecillion books but *I've* played with Hondo Loomis. . . .

"Stick around," Loomis said when I started to put down the mike. So I stayed for the rest of the set, which, luckily, consisted of songs I either knew or could fake. Loomis did "Loser's Blues" and "Georgia on My Mind" and then picked up the beat with the old Piano Red classic, "You Got the Right String, Baby, but the Wrong Yo-yo." From there we went into Roy Orbison's great "Candy Man"—I got in some good licks on that one—and then slowed down again with Elvis Costello's "Almost Blue" and James Taylor's "Fire and Rain."

Then Julie stepped up to the mike and began singing "Summertime" while the drummer did something soft and rhythmic with the brushes and the rest of us doodled minimally along in the background. She sang better than she played, not that that was saying much; she wasn't Carmen McRae by a long shot.

After that Loomis led a long instrumental medley of his own tunes from the old days—I wondered how many in the audience actually recognized the songs; it was mostly an under-thirty crowd—and at the end, without a break, slammed into "Get Your Kicks on Route 66." From the crowd's reaction, I guessed this was the standard closer.

He sang it all the way through, with Julie coming in singing harmony on the chorus, and then we each took a solo in turn. I'd never played the song before, but it was an easy tune to fake, and I did a lot of bluesy wails and vibrato effects to cover my fluffed changes. Loomis came back and sang the chorus once again, changing the lyric this time to *"Oklahoma City is oh, so shitty,"* and playing games with the phrasing, and we finished in a big *ta-daaaa* that was partly buried in a minor avalanche of applause. Loomis stood up and we all smiled and waved and got the hell off the stage while the applause was still happening.

Rita was waiting at the table, trying to look cool but just a little bit flushed. I'd already spotted her clapping like crazy as we came off the stage. "Now you've done it," she said to Loomis as he gave her a one-armed hug. "I won't be able to make him put the damn thing away all weekend."

"Well," Loomis said, sitting down, "he blows pretty fair harp."

"Huh," Rita said darkly. "What makes you think I'm talking about his harmonica?"

After the Flying Tiger Club closed I drove Rita back home. It was very late. The overhead lights along the freeway shone harshly against the black overcast sky.

Inside her apartment, Rita strode straight toward the bedroom without looking back to see if I was following her. Standing in the bedroom doorway, her back to me, she reached around and undid a couple of little hooks and a long zipper. The white dress fell away and she stepped out of it and picked it up and carefully hung it across the back of a chair. Underneath she wore only wispy white panties and a white garter belt that held up sheer skin-tone stockings. She walked toward the bed, still without turning around. The white garter straps stretched and unstretched across the dark skin of her hips and thighs as she moved.

"Well?" she said over her shoulder. "Are you going to stand there all night or what?"

By the time I left Rita's place it was almost six in the morning. The streets were all but deserted and only a few trucks rolled along the Interstate.

Normally, heading home from Rita's at that hour, I'd have crossed the river and then turned south on Highway 75 to Glenpool, where the old two-lane leads off eastward to Yuchi Park. But by now I was in a strange, wired-up mood, not at all sleepy and certainly in no hurry to get back to the trailer and listen to Harry snore.

So I stayed on I-44, on out toward Oakhurst and the junction with the Redfork Expressway; and, just before the first toll booth and the start of the Turnpike, I swung the Camaro left and onto Route 66. A few minutes later I was pulling into the parking lot of the Flying Tiger Club.

I don't know what I thought I was doing. The club was obviously closed and deserted, the parking lot empty of vehicles, and dark except for the all-night security lights around the building. It was too cold to get out or even to sit there in the Camaro for very long. Still I sat and stared out through the misty glass, thinking about this and that, until at last my toes started to go numb and I reached reluctantly for the key.

Just then there was a sharp tapping at the window beside me. I jumped and turned my head and saw a face looking in at me.

It wasn't much of a face. It was small and dark and heavily wrinkled, like one of those doll faces cut from an apple and allowed to dry in the sun. A hand appeared beside it and tapped again on the glass. A thin reedy voice said, "Hey, buddy."

I rolled down the window. A little old man, dressed in layers of ragged clothes, was standing beside the Camaro. I say "old"; he could have been anywhere from forty to eighty. He had a long nose and pale watery eyes and, as far as I could tell, no teeth at all. I don't imagine he weighed more than a hundred pounds.

He said very seriously, "Excuse me, buddy, but there's a man in the trash bin around back. I think he's kind of dead."

It took a bit of driving around before I could find an all-night convenience store with a telephone, and a little talking before I could convince the tired woman at the dispatcher's desk to take me seriously.

"Are you sure the person is dead, sir?" she wanted to know. "Because sometimes drunks and homeless people sleep in those dumpsters—"

"I'm sure," I said, and shuddered.

"I'll send a unit out," she said. "Please go back to the scene and wait for the officers to arrive."

I promised I would, and, after getting a big foam cup of lousy coffee to keep me warm, that was what I did. By now it was getting on toward seven, the night all but over, but the sky was as dark as ever. A fine drizzling rain had begun to fall.

There was no sign of the little ragged man when I got back to the Flying Tiger Club. No big surprise there.

I sat in the Camaro and drank my coffee and waited. The sheriff's office responded quickly enough; I was still working on the coffee when the first car pulled into the parking lot. Not long afterward—after I'd shown the body, and then my identification, to a couple of understandably suspicious young deputies—the area around the club began to fill up with official vehicles and people in official uniforms doing presumably official things. Actually it was hard to tell what most of them were doing, except standing around cursing the cold and the rain, but no doubt they had their duties.

Deputy Ellis of the Creek County Sheriff's Department was a tall, imposing man, somewhere near my age from the look of him, with high cheekbones and straight black hair suggestive of Indian blood, and shoulders that indicated he might be part buffalo too. Most of the people on the scene had donned yellow or blaze-orange rain gear—the effect was weirdly festive—but Deputy Ellis had chosen to ignore the gelid drizzle that spotted his brown uniform and beaded the brim of his hat. There was no question about his function; he could have shown up in a jockstrap and been instantly recognized as the Man in Charge.

He said, "Roper. Now I remember that name. Aren't you the writer? The one who got mixed up in that business last year, with the TV preacher and the hooker and the psycho wrestler?"

I said, "Yes," and he nodded in a satisfied way. "Used to write for the *Courier*, didn't you? Police beat?"

I confessed to that too. Standing there in that cold wind, with nothing between me and the rain but my increasingly soggy suit, I'd have confessed to anything.

He said, "Well, then, I guess you've seen nearly as many of these affairs as I have. They all look alike, don't they?"

I knew what he meant. I'd been at the scenes of murders and suicides and police shootings and allegedly accidental deaths, in all sorts of places—motels and posh apartments, trailer parks and slum houses and fine mansions, and once under a bridge where a homeless derelict had killed his best friend over a bottle of Night Train—in all kinds of weather and at all hours of the day or night; and there was indeed a depressing sameness to them all after a time. The same lights flashing, the same radios sputtering, the same little groups of people standing around talking in low voices and waiting to do whatever they were there to do. . . . The banality of violent death, I'd called it in an early piece, but the editor had cut the line out.

Only the details varied. Here, the details were the rain and the cold and the grotesque shape of the old P-40 up on the roof, lit by the security floodlights, seeming to hover over the scene like some prehistoric flying creature. The painted eyes and the great cruel shark mouth leered down sardonically at the scurrying figures below.

"Have to admit, though," Ellis remarked, "this is my first time to find one in a dumpster."

And that was the other detail, of course, the one that shoved all the others clear off the stage. From where I stood beside Deputy Ellis, in the service parking area back of the Flying Tiger Club, I couldn't see the body or even the dumpster itself for the cluster of people in the way. I didn't need to see it, though. I'd had myself one good look already tonight and that had been plenty. True, I hadn't been able to actually see the whole corpse—it was dark inside the dumpster and I didn't have a flashlight with me—but the mental picture of those sneaker-shod feet and skinny, sockless ankles sticking out of that dumpster would stay with me for a long time. That and the feel of that cold white skin when I'd touched one ankle, just for a second, to find out if he was really dead. . . .

"We're probably overreacting," Ellis added after a couple of minutes. "We still haven't got an official cause of death, let alone evidence of foul play. Chances are this is just some bum who crawled in there to sleep and never woke up. The hell's that guy from the coroner's office doing in there, anyway, playing solitaire?"

As if Ellis's words had carried, there was a stir of movement over by the dumpster. A man's head and shoulders appeared briefly above the heads of the onlookers. Hands reached up to help the man climb out of the dumpster. "Ah," Ellis said. "Now maybe we can get these men in out of the hot sun."

The group around the dumpster opened up and a short, pale-faced man in a yellow raincoat came toward us. His head was uncovered to the rain; he didn't even have any hair.

He stopped in front of Deputy Ellis and took off a pair of rimless glasses and wiped futilely at the damp lenses with even damper fingers. "We've got a white male," he said tiredly, "I'd estimate age about forty. Cause of death appears to have been an impact to the back of the head. Massive skull damage, considerable bleeding."

He put the glasses back on and squinted up at Ellis. "He was put in the dumpster a very short time after death, because there's a lot of blood in there. May even have been technically alive for a few minutes after he was put in, though not enough to move around."

Ellis was fast. "Was put?"

"He sure as hell didn't climb in there by himself, not with the back of his head caved in like that. I can't tell you yet what did the damage—struck by a blunt instrument, hit by a car, a fall on a hard surface, plenty of possibilities. Maybe we'll learn something at the autopsy."

Ellis nodded. "Okay, thanks. Go tell the boys to go ahead and start getting him out of there." To me he said, "Well, it's now officially a felony case, anyway. Homicide or accident, somebody moved a dead man and concealed him and then went off and left him. That'll do for starters."

He looked thoughtful. "Say, I don't suppose that little bum you ran into—"

I shook my head. "I doubt if he could have lifted a dead kitten, let alone a grown man."

"Hm. Well, we'll put an APB out on him anyway, maybe he saw something. Although the chances are we'll never find him. Probably scared to death of cops, like most of those people, and good at hiding from us. I don't guess I blame the poor bastards."

They were lifting the body out of the dumpster now. I wondered what they'd done about the traditional outline. The bald man was giving instructions, which everyone seemed to be ignoring, and a young cop was shooting flash pictures. The deceased appeared to be a medium-slender man, dressed in jeans and a cheap-looking nylon jacket. At this distance I couldn't see his face clearly. That was just fine with me.

Suddenly one of the cops stepped forward and bent down to peer closely at the dead man's face. "Shit fire," he said in a loud surprised voice. "It's Jimmy Wilburn!"

Somebody said, "Bullshit."

"Yeah," somebody else said, "you been up too late, Marty. Jimmy Wilburn's doing time down at McAlester. Auto theft, wasn't it?"

The first cop was shaking his head vigorously. "I don't give a fuck if he's supposed to be on Death Row for aggravated loitering. I *know* the son of a bitch, all right? I was the first one ever busted his ass, back when he was eighteen. Hell, *look* at him. I bet I'm not the only one here, ever pulled him in."

Ellis was already striding toward the arguing deputies. "Are you sure?" I heard him say.

"Sure as I am that there's a hole in my ass." The deputy gestured at the body. "If that ain't Jimmy Wilburn I'm a nig— uh, a suck-egg dog."

By now all sorts of people were converging on the spot. In a few minutes I couldn't see the body or Ellis or even the dumpster. Since matters seemed to have taken a turn that didn't involve me, I walked over to the Camaro and got in and closed the door. Nobody tried to stop me. I didn't attempt to drive away, though.

How long I sat there, freezing my ass and watching the various incomprehensible goings-on in the parking lot, I don't know. But the sky in the east was getting lighter by the time Deputy Ellis appeared beside the Camaro and tapped on the window with a big knuckle. I rolled the window down and he bent down and looked in at me. "You can go," he said. "Should have cut you loose long ago, but I swear I forgot all about you." He looked slightly embarrassed. "Something sort of unexpected came up."

I nodded and started to roll the glass back up. He laid a hand over the window's edge. "You need to come in and give us a statement," he said. "Monday if you can make it."

I nodded. "I don't know why not."

"Well, give me a call if you can't, all right?" He stepped back and gave me a salute with one finger to the brim of his hat. As I pulled out onto Route 66 I could see him walking back toward the Flying Tiger Club.

By the time I got back to Yuchi Park it was getting to be daylight, a wet gray daylight that looked even colder than the darkness. The quarter-mile gravel lane from the road to my trailer was a streak of mud, as it had been for days. At least the reddish-brown splatters hid some of the scabbier areas of the Camaro's once-white paint.

Harry went into his standard paroxysm of joy when I came in the door, but I was too tired to play with him. I poured some kibble into his bowl, made sure he had enough water—wondering sleepily why I bothered, since given any choice he preferred the contents of the toilet bowl—and went back to the bedroom and got out of my damp suit and crawled into bed and fell instantly asleep, without even the usual double-Jim nightcap.

And yet it was a poor kind of sleep, restless and filled with vague, disturbing dreams that didn't make any sense. I woke up three or four times in as many hours, fighting the covers and sweating despite the chill in the room.

A little after noon, Harry blasted me out of bed with a crescendo of hysterical barking, while a clatter near the front door told me that Harry had once again saved me from an assault by a killer mailman. I went in and took a hot shower and padded into the kitchen to get myself some breakfast or lunch or whatever the hell it was by now. There was still some coffee in the pot, well aged by now but too much to throw out. I put a cup in the microwave, stuck in a blueberry Pop-Tart to keep it company, and put on my old wool robe to go check the mail. Not that there was anybody out there to see my shortcomings, but it was too damn cold to go opening the door bare-assed, even for a couple of seconds.

Getting mail delivered to my door represented a minor triumph for me. The Postal Service had made it known that they considered it unreasonable for the mail carrier to have to come all the way to the end of that dirt road just to bring the mail to one single-occupancy trailer. They'd suggested, and then tried to decree, that I should put up a mailbox down at the main road. But Yuchi Park incorporated a few years ago, and, for reasons of zoning technicalities, the gravel lane was officially a city street, even though nobody lived on it but me and old Mr. Berryhill up at the corner.

So Mr. Postman had to make house calls, and I suppose on a muddy day like this he didn't appreciate it. But he'd brought me a generous load today, all the same; the metal mailbox was stuffed, and there was a big thick yellow envelope resting precariously in the twin hooks beneath the box.

Sitting at the table, washing blueberry Pop-Tart down with

day-old coffee, I sorted through the day's take. Despite the impressive look of it, it really didn't amount to much: people trying to sell me things—one outfit wanted to interest me in aluminum siding—and other people claiming I already owed them money. I set the most unignorable bills aside, for whatever attention I could give them once I'd deposited Loomis's checks, and threw the rest of the junk into the overflowing kitchen wastebasket.

The last envelope bore the printed logo of a major New York publishing house. I ripped it open, unfolded the enclosed one-sheet letter, and read:

> *Dear Mr. Roper:*
> *Thanks for the chance to read* Staked Plain. *I enjoyed the story, and the characters are well-drawn.*
>
> *I'm afraid, however, that I'll have to pass on this submission. We do not, as you may know, publish genre Westerns, and I feel* Staked Plain *reads too much like a category novel for our fiction list.*
>
> *Best wishes in placing this elsewhere. Have you tried the paperback-original houses?*
>
> *Regards,*
> *C. Eliot Fernwood*
> *Editor*
>
> *P.S. I'm returning your manuscript by separate package.*

Which no doubt meant . . . but no; when I examined the big manila envelope, the mailing label was from a different publisher. I knew what was inside, though, all the same; I'd known that as soon as I'd picked the damn thing up. A book-length manuscript has a feel and heft unlike anything else, and a bounced manuscript has an aura all its own—something like the "smell of death" that the gypsy woman talks about in *For Whom the Bell Tolls.*

Sure enough, the big envelope contained a typed manuscript, held together with rubber bands, with a three-quarter-size sheet of publisher's letterhead tucked in on top of the title page:

Dear Taggert,
Thanks for letting me see THE STAKED PLAINS. I liked the characters and the story is an alright read.

Trouble is, you've written a serious historical novel here, and Gamecock Press is pretty much a category outfit, except for reprints. I can't see this going anywhere as a paperback original.

Good luck, though. Why don't you try the hardback publishers? I think they'd like it alot better.

> *Ron Price*
> *Associate Editor*

I said, "Shit," and then I said, "Son of a *bitch*," and threw the half-eaten Pop-Tart against the wall. While Harry happily gobbled up the pieces, I wadded up the two letters into a single ball and tried unsuccessfully to hit the wastebasket with them. Then I cursed a little more, and gave some thought to getting into the Jim Beam, but it was too early for that and I hadn't had enough sleep; I knew I'd get stupid drunk and pass out and wake up on the couch around one in the morning with a bad head. Even so, it was a close decision, and I knew if I stayed here much longer I'd go ahead and do it.

Well, hell. I said, "Let's go get a burger, Harry."

We went out and got into the Camaro and cruised down to the Sonic and had ourselves a burger apiece. They put pickles in Harry's even though I told them not to—pickles make him fart—but he didn't seem to mind; he was done with his, and snuffling eagerly around the back seat for crumbs, before I had the paper off mine.

Later, back at the trailer, I sat down at the typewriter and tried to do some work. After all the encouraging mail I'd gotten lately, it was the least I could do.

But it was no good. I couldn't get my mind back onto swamps and Seminoles and nineteenth-century military tactics, not to-night. I couldn't stop seeing those two pathetic damn feet, sticking out of that dumpster in the rain . . . and finally I switched off the typewriter and went and got the Hohner from my jacket pocket and sat on the couch playing old songs, while Harry snored and the rain drummed on the trailer's metal shell.

Hondo Loomis called a little before dark.

"They came by the house and asked a lot of questions," he said. "Not that I knew any answers. Christ, one thing after another."

"They ask about me?"

"Sure. I told them you were a personal friend, been jamming with me and the band. Don't worry, I didn't tell them anything about our private business." He laughed. "Hey, man, you're talking to an old sixties dope veteran, dig? I was lying to cops back when you were lying to your grade-school teacher."

I hadn't really worried about Loomis's discretion, but it was still nice to get confirmation.

"Boy," he said, "that's a hell of a thing to do to a human being, shove him into a trash bin like so much garbage. Whoever he was, whatever he was doing there, nobody deserves to be treated like that. Well, unless maybe it would be Rush Lim-baugh. Which I assume it wasn't."

"From what I heard," I said, "the deputies think it was some-body named Jimmy Wilburn. Mean anything to you?"

"Not a damn thing," Loomis said. "As I told Deputy Ellis

when he dropped the name on me this morning. Well, take care of yourself, Roper. Come by the club any time."

When he had hung up I sat for a few minutes staring at various mental pictures; and then I got up and went back to the kitchen to see what there was for supper.

When Deputy Ellis had finished reading my statement he said, "You know, Roper, this is the first time I ever got one of these from a real professional writer. I think I'll have it framed."

"It's not likely that I'll ever be famous enough to justify that," I told him. "At least not at my present rate of progress."

He shook his head and held up the two-page typed statement. "Hell, I don't care about that. What I mean, I want to show this around as an example of what a written statement ought to be. Good clear descriptions, order of events laid out so there's no chance of confusion, why, you even typed the damn thing for me. Got all the facts down—"

"Such as they are."

"Yeah, okay, point taken. Nothing you saw tells us anything, except to narrow down the time frame a little. But that's not your fault, is it?" He gave me a short grin. "Wish you'd come over to Creek County and be an eyewitness next time we have a really major case—"

He laid the statement back on the desk and grimaced. "Damn, I didn't mean that the way it sounded. Any man's death is supposed to be major. Even a man like Jimmy Wilburn."

I said, "Who is this Jimmy Wilburn, anyway? Or was? I got the impression he was local."

Ellis leaned back in his chair and looked out the window. It was a little after one in the afternoon and the sun was finally shining again. It hadn't warmed up any, though.

"I suppose," Ellis said ruminatively, "you get men like Jimmy Wilburn anywhere in the country. The kind, you know, later on local people say, 'Oh, he never was a *bad* ol' boy, he just couldn't stay out of trouble.' Never finished high school, got kicked out for fighting and taking a swing at a teacher. Minor brushes with the law as a juvenile, then at eighteen—you might have heard Marty talking about it—he took his first real bust, for trying to steal a bottle from a liquor store. Judge let him off with a warning and a few weeks' time served, but he didn't learn anything from the experience."

"You knew him?"

"Knew who he was, couldn't say I *knew* him. We were about the same age, you understand. I was off doing a hitch in the marines when he left these parts. Seems he went to Oklahoma City, where they picked him up a few times on suspicion—usually armed robbery—but nothing ever stuck. Till about ten years ago."

"I overheard something about auto theft."

"Right. Funny thing, when he finally did step in the deep shit, he came back here to do it. Hot-wired a pickup truck right here in Sapulpa, got stopped by the city cops before he'd gone half a dozen blocks. He'd stolen a vehicle with no working tail-lights." Ellis gave a snort of laughter. "Later on the same night,

65

the Highway Patrol found a new Nissan abandoned on the Interstate, out of gas. Turned out it had been stolen in Oklahoma City, earlier the same evening."

"Wilburn stole both vehicles?"

"The assumption was that he'd boosted the Nissan, ditched it when it ran dry, and grabbed the first available replacement. He never admitted it, though, and there was no proof. They let him plead to stealing the pickup, plus possession and carrying a concealed weapon—he had a gun and a little coke on him when they stopped him—and off he went to McAlester."

Ellis looked disgusted. "Which was where we all thought he was, only now I find out he made parole and they let him out last week. We were supposed to be informed, but somebody dropped the ball."

"You wouldn't think he'd come back here," I remarked. "After all the trouble he'd been in, knowing the law would be watching him."

"Who can figure these people out? It's like they've got a compulsion to make all the wrong moves. And," Ellis said, "it looks like he was already up to his old tricks. This morning some boys found a 'ninety-one Oldsmobile parked behind that boarded-up steak house, down the road from your friend's club."

"Hot?"

"As the well-known two-dollar pistol. Stolen Thursday night in Norman, which was where Jimmy Wiilburn was supposed to report to his parole officer and didn't. No actual physical evidence to link the car to the deceased, but hell, he got out there on 66 somehow, and I don't imagine he walked."

"Talk about returning to the scene of the crime."

"No shit. And it was only a short distance away, over on the Turnpike, that they found that stolen Nissan ten years ago. It's like there was some kind of curse on Jimmy Wilburn," Ellis said. "He kept coming back to that area, and he kept having bad luck.

Until some time in the dark hours of Sunday morning, when his luck ran out all the way."

"Anything yet on what killed him? Or who?"

I half expected Ellis to tell me that wasn't any of my business, but he answered readily enough: "Cause of death, as the man said, was massive damage to the back of the head. After a careful examination, the county ghouls believe his head struck some hard, flat surface, rather than being hit with any sort of instrument. Might possibly have been hit by a car or truck, but it's unlikely."

"So it was an accident?"

"Not necessarily. Could be he fell from a height, could be he was pushed, could be somebody slammed him hard against a wall or something."

Ellis got up and went over to a file cabinet and opened a drawer. "Right now," he said, placing my statement in a folder, "the only scenario I can come up with, Wilburn was trying to break into the club—"

"Why?" I interrupted. "I mean, why the Flying Tiger Club in particular?"

Ellis shrugged impatiently. "Isolated location, handy to the highway, who the hell knows? Roper, I've spent my adult life dealing with the Jimmy Wilburns of the world, and there's not a whole lot of logic to their actions, all right? Anyway, my best guess is that Wilburn was trying to get up on the roof—maybe hoping to find a skylight or ventilator—and fell. A drop like that, on that asphalt parking lot, would definitely do the job."

He slammed the file drawer shut and turned back to face me. "Not that we've got any solid proof of that theory or any other, thanks to the damn rain that washed away any bloodstains or other useful evidence. We did find a couple of big screwdrivers on the ground nearby, and a pair of cutters in Wilburn's pocket, which would support the attempted-burglary idea. But that's damn little."

67

"And nothing to indicate who put him in the dumpster?"

"No, God damn it." Ellis dropped back into his chair, looking frustrated. "That's where it gets weird. If he'd been found lying on the ground, okay, accidental fall while trying to commit B and E, case closed. But," Ellis said, "somebody put him into that dumpster, and that raises all sorts of questions. Such as how he came to fall in the first place."

"You think he was pushed?"

"Christ, Roper, I don't know *what* the hell I think. Maybe he had a partner, they got into a fight up on the roof and Wilburn lost. Any way you figure it, though, homicide or accident, why put the body in a conspicuous place like that? I can see somebody trying to hide the corpse, dropping it into the river or something, because he killed Wilburn or thought he might get blamed for it. But cramming him into that dumpster and leaving his feet sticking out, so he was sure to be found? It's crazy."

"And if Wilburn had a partner," I pointed out, "why was the car still parked down the road? Why didn't the partner use it to get away?"

"Exactly. Plenty of other questions, too, like how Wilburn got up there in the first place. We didn't find a ladder." Ellis spread his palms. "So maybe my whole theory's a load of crap. Maybe Jimmy Wilburn died somewhere else, under circumstances nobody's even guessed at, and was brought there and dumped. It's a bitch, all right."

He waved a big hand in a gesture that took in the whole office. "For God's sake, Roper, this isn't the FBI or Scotland Yard. We're just a little old pissant county sheriff's office. Hauling in drunks, serving papers, that's the kind of thing we know how to do. Even then, well—"

He laughed. "There used to be this big old tree growing next to this building, and the prisoners upstairs kept using it to escape. I mean, they'd get out through a window somehow and do a Tarzan along the limbs and take off. Sheriff tried for years

68

to get the county to do something, till finally he got pissed off and went out there and cut the damn thing down himself. That's the kind of setup we've got here. Mysterious murders, fancy detective work—forget it."

He stood up again and I did the same. We shook hands and he said, "Well, thanks for your cooperation anyway. We'll call you if we need anything else."

I turned to go. As I reached the door his voice stopped me. "Oh, Roper?"

He was still standing behind the desk, looking at me with an absolutely expressionless face. Only very experienced cops and very experienced criminals can make their faces as blank as that.

"I don't suppose," he said very casually, "there's anything you haven't told me?"

I didn't reply. I only stood there and returned his look. I'd been waiting for this.

"What I mean," he said, still in that carefully conversational tone, "I don't suppose there's any chance that you got to the scene a little earlier than you say, like maybe in time to see a man climbing up onto the roof? And, being a friend of the proprietor's, you might have gone and tried to stop the burglary on your own, resulting in a scuffle and an unfortunate accident?"

I still didn't speak. He leaned forward over the desk, putting his weight on his knuckles. "Because, Roper," he said in a more natural voice, "there's no way you'd be in any serious trouble for something like that. Not if you told me right now, before this thing goes any further. Oh, technically you'd be guilty of tampering with evidence and making a false official statement, but I guarantee you nobody around here would do anything about it. Not in this county, not over Jimmy Wilburn. There's people would probably want to buy you dinner."

His eyebrows moved a little bit closer together. For such a tiny movement, the effect was pretty disturbing. "On the other hand, if we were to find out later on, after a long and costly investigation, that would be a whole different stack of pancakes."

I said, "There's someone I was with that night, after I left the club. She can verify when I left her place in Tulsa. I'd rather not bring her into this, though, unless it's absolutely necessary."

I'd already checked with Rita and gotten her permission. Still, I wasn't comfortable giving her name to the cops, and I hoped Ellis wouldn't force me.

He said slowly, "Of course, by your own admission, it was some time after you discovered the body before you called it in."

"I was looking for a phone."

"Right." He didn't say it sarcastically; he just said it. "So the time you left this, ah, person's home in Tulsa doesn't really prove anything one way or the other, does it?"

I said, "No," and stood waiting.

And after a couple of seconds he straightened up and folded his arms and nodded, once. "Okay, Roper," he said. "Figured it might be worth a try. Go write a book or something."

Heading out of Sapulpa, I meant to go back home, but then on impulse I took a left and drove up Route 66 to the Flying Tiger Club. The sky was clear now except for a few straggler clouds getting torn to shreds by the wind. A big hawk hung high above the road, balancing against the wind, looking for roadkill. He looked cold.

The big blue van was parked beside the club when I pulled in. The front door opened readily to my push. I went in and found Hondo Loomis standing in the lobby with a hammer in his hand. "Roper," he said. "Just the man I need. You any good at driving nails? I can't figure out how to do this one-handed."

I took the hammer and picked a nail from the little pile on the counter. Loomis indicated a spot at eye level on the lobby wall, next to the office door. I got the nail started without banging my thumb and he said, "Not all the way in. Got a picture I want to hang."

A framed eight-by-ten photograph lay on the counter beside the pile of nails. Loomis picked it up and hung it on the nail, fiddled with it a bit to get it straight, and stepped back and looked at it. "Look okay to you?" he asked. "I never can get these things to hang right."

It looked fine to me. It was an old, brownish photo of the Flying Tiger Club, airplane and all. The building exterior looked different, more ornate.

"Found this on a shelf in the dressing-room closet," Loomis said. "Taken in the old days, when the place was new. Thought it would dress up the lobby a little."

He tapped the glass. "Man, that first guy had it fixed up fancy. Had all this bogus Oriental crap all over the outside, must have cost a pile. I guess over the years it deteriorated until somebody stripped it all off, down to the bare concrete blocks. Last owner, cat who did all the heavy renovation, seems to have run out of money before he could get the exterior redone. Me, I thought about fixing it back to original, till I got some quotes. Couldn't see spending that much bread to make the place look like the Teahouse of the August fucking Moon."

"Just as well," I said. "Considering the vandalism problem you've been having."

"Hey, you got that right." His face had tightened up. "Look what was stuck under the door this morning."

He took a folded sheet of white paper from his hip pocket and passed it over. When I unfolded it, big hand-printed letters, in what looked like red marker, jumped up at me:

TOO BAD IT WASN'T YOU, LOOMIS MAYBE NEXT TIME

"When they called me about finding that dead guy out back," Loomis said, "I thought at first maybe he was the one, maybe it was finally over. Obviously it's not over at all."

I handed the note back. "He couldn't have been involved anyway. He was in prison up till a week ago."

"Oh?" Loomis put the note back in his hip pocket. "Looks like you know more than I do. Come on back and let's get a drink and you can tell me about it."

We walked back through the darkened club. Loomis touched a switch and a couple of lights came on over the bar. I took a stool and he went around and got a bottle of Wild Turkey and a couple of glasses. After pouring, he picked up a rag and began wiping here and there with quick annoyed motions. "Damn, Doris left a mess the other night. Can't blame her, she was upset. That fucking Roy Dolan comes around here again, I'm calling the law, I don't give a shit."

He put down the rag and reached for his glass. "Talk to me."

I told him, between sips, what Ellis had told me about the late Jimmy Wilburn. "Man," Loomis said at the end, "what a loser, huh? And he wouldn't have gotten much out of here, you know. We don't keep any real cash on the place after closing time— now if he'd bushwhacked me on my way out of here with the night's take, that would have been more like it. I guess he could have gotten my keyboard, maybe the speakers, some booze, that's about it. Lucky to fence the whole load for a couple of yards."

"Not much to die for."

"Damn straight . . . So," Loomis said, "was it an accident or did he have help? What do the cops think?"

"Deputy Ellis," I said, "thinks maybe I killed him."

"You're shitting me."

"Afraid not. Oh, I don't suppose the idea ranks very high on his list of possibilities, but he's definitely keeping it in mind. I think it's mostly that it would be such a nice simple explanation of a lot of things." I finished my drink. "Don't worry about it. I'd take that note in and show it to Ellis, though. I don't see any plausible connection between the threats and the dead guy, but it's not impossible."

Loomis frowned. "You think maybe Wilburn ran into whoever's been hassling me? Like they had some kind of fight in the dark or something?"

It sounded even more farfetched when he said it. I said, "I'd turn the note in. Cover yourself, just in case."

"Yeah." He nodded. I knew he wasn't going to do anything of the sort. For a man of his background, cops were people you talked to as rarely as possible. Not that it was a policy I could criticize.

We walked back across the dance floor and through the bamboo curtain. Loomis said, "Son of a bitch still looks crooked," and went to adjust the framed photograph again. I looked at the poster beside the doorway. John Wayne was still looking heroic beneath square-cut goggles.

Loomis turned and saw what I was looking at. "Hey," he said, "you want a poster like that? There's a whole shitload of them stored in back. I think they're originals."

I considered it. The trailer could use some decoration, but—"I better not," I said with regret. "Rita wouldn't like it. She's got a thing about John Wayne."

"What the hell? Oh, because of the way they showed Indians in his movies? Yeah, I can see that, all right." He came over beside me and tapped the poster with his fingertips. "You know, I met him once."

"The Duke?"

"Yeah. It was at this gig in Vegas. Elvis Presley introduced us." He grinned. "How's that for a double name-drop?"

Without thinking I said, "What was he like?"

"The Duke or Elvis?"

"Both, I guess."

"Well, as I say, I only met John Wayne that one time, and I never really knew Elvis all that well. Just going by impressions, though—" He ran his fingers through his silvery hair. "Basically a couple of big good-natured guys who didn't know their butts from third base. I don't think the Duke was quite as dumb as Elvis—Christ, if Elvis had been any dumber he'd have been a plant—but he didn't seem as friendly, either."

"On the other hand," I said, "the Duke never put on half a ton of blubber. Or took to wearing white jumpsuits."

"True." Loomis looked at me. "I'll tell you something, Roper. One night, watching Elvis lumbering around the stage dressed like Liberace's garage sale, I had a terrible thought: Is this what Buddy Holly would have looked like if he'd lived?"

"Christ!"

"Yeah." He reached across his chest and touched the empty sleeve. "Maybe I was lucky after all, Roper. At least I never got the chance to become a parody of myself."

When I got back home Freddie Manzano was waiting for me.

So help me Edward G. Robinson, he had a black limo. I saw the big black shape beside my trailer as soon as I turned off the main road, and I had my eyes on it all the way down the gravel drive.

I didn't recognize the exact model—my first-hand knowledge of luxury automobiles is a trifle limited—but it was an impressive collection of metal; it was, I guessed, as long as they come before they qualify for the stretch class. Even in city traffic it would have been an eye-catching object. Sitting in that weedy yard next to my battered old trailer, it was as conspicuous and incongruous as the airplane on the roof of the Flying Tiger Club.

There was a subdued but definite air of menace about the limo, too; and if the sinister look was also a little on the corny side, that didn't make it any less effective.

I parked the Camaro nearby—not too near, until I found out more about the situation—and sat for a moment looking at the black car, wondering who it belonged to and what he or she wanted with me. For some reason I didn't think of Freddie Manzano. Maybe, having eliminated him as a possible factor in Hondo Loomis's problems, I'd quit thinking about him entirely.

Even when the limo's left front door opened and a large man in a bad brown suit got out, it didn't occur to me that this was a personal visit. I just assumed that Manzano had sent his bodyguard to give me a message, or to fetch me for some reason. But then the big man walked back and opened the rear door and, finally, I realized what was going on.

Freddie Manzano got out of the limo while I dismounted from the Camaro. He had on the same pricey-looking pin-striped suit he'd worn Friday morning, or more likely another identical one. Out here in the open, he looked even smaller than he had in the office.

For some reason the same optical principle didn't affect the bodyguard. If anything he looked bigger than ever. I'd had some dealings, the preceding year, with some wrestlers and body-builders—one had tried to kill me, and damn near made it—and this guy could have matched any of them for size and build. His face showed the effects of having been hit a few times, too, and I doubted that his response had been one of Gandhian passivity. His hands were great big lumps of meat and gristle and bone, but I couldn't forget the speed and precision with which he'd reached for his gun that morning at Drummer's.

There was that, too. Big as he was, his first reaction had been to go for a gun. That *really* bothered me.

Freddie Manzano said, "Thanks, Danny," and then to me, "Roper. How you been? I was starting to wonder if you were gonna come home at all."

I said, "I hope you haven't been waiting long."

If the sarcasm bothered him he didn't let it show. "Wanted

76

to have a little conversation with you," he said. His face cracked suddenly in a white-toothed grin. "Don't sweat it, I didn't come to lean on you about the other day. This is a whole different matter. Might work out to some bucks for both of us."

He jerked a thumb toward the trailer. "Think we oughta go inside? It's colder than a witch's tit out here."

Why not? I said, "Sure," and headed toward the trailer. Manzano fell in beside me, flanked by Danny, who was watching me with expressionless eyes. I could make out a bulky object under the left armpit of the brown suit. Make out hell, I could practically read the serial number. Freddie Manzano definitely needed to send his bodyguard to a good tailor. Personnel appearance is very important in projecting a top business image.

Halfway up the little metal steps, I stopped and looked back. "I've got a dog." That was highly unnecessary; Harry's barking had been rattling the whole trailer ever since I'd arrived, and, I was fairly sure, as long as Manzano and his gorilla had been waiting for me. "Better let me go in and put him up."

But when I opened the door Harry came bursting out under full frenzied boost, ramming past me before I could grab him and charging toward our visitors, still barking. Freddie Manzano said, "Christ!" and jumped back, while I lunged after Harry and missed again.

Danny looked at the oncoming shaggy beast and his face broke into a huge delighted smile. "Awww!" he cried. "Look, boss, it's a dog!"

"The fuck you think we been listening to barking for the last hour," Manzano said irritably, "a fucking canary?"

Danny didn't reply. Dropping to one knee in the muddy yard, he spread his arms as Harry leaped up on him. "*Nice* doggy," he said happily. "Is him a dood wittle doggy?" The big arms folded and clasped in a bearlike hug, while Harry licked frantically at the battered face. "*What* a dood wittle poochy-woochy—"

Freddie Manzano and I looked at each other. "You got to understand," Manzano said, "this is news to me. This, uh, side of the big bastard's personality."

He turned his gaze back to the yard, where Danny and Harry were now rolling around together on the ground, Harry still licking and Danny still babbling baby talk. "Okay, Danny," Manzano said, "you can stay out here and play with your new friend while the fucking grownups go inside and talk business."

He followed me up the steps and into the trailer. As I shut the door he glanced out the window and shook his head. "Damn, you think you know somebody . . . you know, he ain't stupid or punchy or anything, like you might think. Maybe not what you'd call management-level smarts, but he always seemed to have pretty good sense. I've seen him handle some real tense situations, you know what I mean?"

He'd had sense enough not to tangle with Wiley Harmon, I recalled; but I didn't want to bring that business up just now. I said, "Well, some people have a thing about animals."

Manzano shook his head again. "You don't know, Roper. Some of the things Danny's been known to do to people, you'd figure his idea of playing with pets would be pulling the fucking wings off flies. Oh, well." He looked around. "Anything to drink? I got some stuff out in the limo if you're dry—"

"There's beer. And Jim Beam."

He considered. "Any mixer? Coke or anything?"

"Not unless you count water."

"Then beer's okay. I ain't much on straight bourbon, least not this early in the day."

I got a couple of beers from the refrigerator and handed him one. He said, "Thanks," and sat down on the couch. He was going to have a lot of Harry's shed hairs all over the back and ass of that natty suit when he stood up, but I didn't feel inclined to warn him. "Sit down," he said. "This is gonna take a little time to explain."

I parked myself in the ruinous armchair opposite the couch and we both sipped at our beers for a minute or so. Finally he said, "Hear you had kind of a strange experience Friday night out at your buddy's roadhouse. Found a stiff in the garbage."

I nodded. "Also," he went on, "I understand you had to go make a little statement for the shitkicker county mounties over in Sapulpa. I could get a copy if I wanted, but why don't you tell me what you told them?"

There was no reason not to, that I could think of. I gave him essentially the same story I'd given Ellis. At the end he said, "Okay. Now how about you tell me any stuff you *didn't* tell the heat."

I looked at him over my beer. "The only thing I left out," I said, "was the part that involved you."

"Which I appreciate, just on general principles, even though I know you didn't do it as a favor to me. But that's not what I meant."

"Then," I said, "why don't we start at the other end? Why don't you give me some idea what you're after, so we can both save a lot of wasted time and talk?"

He blinked slowly, like a lizard. "Okay. Cut the shit, makes sense." He looked at the coffee table in front of him, evidently searching for an unoccupied spot where he could set his beer. When he failed to find one he put the beer on the floor between his feet and leaned back. "They happen to tell you the dead guy's name?"

"Jimmy Wilburn."

"Yeah. 'Fast Jimmy,' he tried to get people to call him. Only thing fast about him was the way he went from one fuckup to another. Kind of guy gives losers a bad name."

"You knew him?"

"Come on, Roper." He looked offended. "You think I got where I am, hanging out with jackoffs like that? I never so much as laid eyes on the punk. But I knew *about* him," he said. "Hell,

79

everybody did. Guy was a fucking legend in his own time, you know?"

He reached down and picked up his beer. "I guess they also told you," he said, "where he spent the last ten years."

"Yes."

"And I guess it won't come as a big shock to you," he went on after a swallow of beer, "that I got a fair number of sources—as you paper pushers call them—inside the joint."

"I would have assumed as much."

He nodded, set his beer back down, and paused for a few seconds. I didn't speak. I figured the pause was merely for effect.

"Jimmy Wilburn was a world-record fuckup," he said at last, "but one thing you had to say for the son of a bitch, he knew how to keep his mouth shut. Which ain't too common with his kind . . . anyway, he did his time quiet, kept his head down, didn't go in for bragging and signifying."

He crossed his legs and folded his hands over one pinstriped knee. "Still, ten years is a long time and nobody's perfect. A few times, mainly when he'd managed to score some pills or prison rotgut, Wilburn was heard to make these little remarks about how he could blow everybody's mind if he told his whole story. Usually nothing more than that, but once he did tell a couple of guys that he had a lot of money stashed on the outside, waiting for him as soon as he got out. Claimed it was from a job that nobody even knew he'd pulled."

"That was all?"

"Yeah, I know, doesn't sound like much. Guys in the joint always like to tell stories like that, specially small-time punks like Jimmy Wilburn. Still," Manzano said, "the guys he told it to knew him pretty well, and they thought he sounded like he was telling the truth. And, like I say, he wasn't usually one to run his mouth—"

I got it then. "You think Wilburn came looking for his money the other night."

"Well, put it together, Roper. You're a writer, for Christ sake, you're supposed to have some imagination. Wilburn ditches a hot car over on the Turnpike, within pissing distance of the Flying Tiger Club—which incidentally would have been closed and deserted at the time—and then gets nailed stealing more wheels in the nearest town. Ten years later he gets out of the joint and the first thing he does is hot-wire a car and head for the exact same place, where he turns up cold in the trash can. You got to admit," Manzano said, "it adds up."

I thought it over. It was possible, if you were prepared to accept a few slightly weird premises, and you had to do that any time you tried to understand the world of a Jimmy Wilburn. Or a Freddie Manzano, for that matter.

I said, "If you don't mind my asking, what's your interest in all this? As you say, Jimmy Wilburn was well beneath your usual business and social level."

"The *money,* Roper." He raised a hand, palm out, as I started to speak. "Oh, sure, I know what you're thinking, and basically you're right. What looked like a fortune to Jimmy Wilburn would like as not be chump change to anybody else."

He leaned forward, his expression growing intense. "But listen to this. There was talk for a long time around Oklahoma City, in certain circles if you know what I mean, about a really major ripoff that was supposed to have gone down. Nothing specific, you understand, this was just a rumor, but it was a hell of a strong one for a while there."

"I'm guessing," I said, "this big heist, or score or takeoff or whatever they call it nowadays, happened around the time Jimmy Wilburn left Oklahoma City in somebody else's Nissan."

"You're getting it. And something else interesting," Manzano said, "there weren't any big robberies of the official kind—banks, stores, anything that got reported—anywhere around the City that whole month. Which means, if this happened at all, the victims were doing something they didn't want to discuss with the law."

"Somebody held up a drug operation?"

"Hey, it happens. Big dope deal under way, you got a lot of cash on hand and no danger of anybody calling the cops—only reason it doesn't happen more often, the dealers got so much firepower around." He made a pistol with his right hand and pointed it at me and grinned. "And don't mind using it. But there's lots of other possibilities. Hell of a lot of money floating around out there, Roper, that never gets recorded or reported. Now and then somebody decides to cut himself a piece."

I said carefully, "I'd think you'd have ways of finding out about something like that."

He looked puzzled for a second. "Oh, yeah," he said then. "You mean if somebody knocked over a big dope deal, a loan operation, something like that, a guy like me could get the story from the inside. That's another interesting thing, though," he went on. "Whatever did or didn't happen, it didn't happen to anybody who was part of any regular organization, know what I mean? Had to be somebody independent."

"Is that possible? Or was it, ten years ago?"

"Oh, sure. Nothing's sewed up very tight in this part of the country. Plenty of free-lance operations going on." He grinned again. He had small even teeth. "Although I'm working on that."

I drank some more beer and did some more thinking. "And your idea is that Jimmy Wilburn was part of the robbery, or got his hands on the money somehow? And hid the loot somewhere around the old Flying Tiger Club, and came back looking for it?"

"And got dead," Manzano pointed out, "which raises the possibility maybe he found it and now somebody else has it."

He picked up his beer and drained it. "Which in turn brings us to the man on the scene. Mr. Taggart Roper of Yuchi Park."

"I've told you all I know—"

"Maybe. All I know about you, Roper, you came around asking screwy questions about the Flying Tiger Club just before Wilburn turned up there dead, and you're supposedly the one who found him. And you're a pal of Wiley Harmon's," he added, "which ain't exactly a character reference, and when I ask around about you I hear all these interesting stories about these little jobs you been known to do for people."

Great. I said, "Christ, Manzano, look around this place. Does it look like I've come into any money lately, stolen or otherwise?"

He shrugged. "It's only been a couple days or so. If you did get that bread, you'd still be sitting on it."

He stood up and I did likewise. "Look, Roper," he said, "I don't know what the fuck went down Friday. Maybe you just happened to run into Wilburn in the dark, little scuffle, he wound up dead and you found yourself looking at more cash than you probably ever saw before. Or maybe there's more to it, maybe you knew something and you were waiting for him."

I opened my mouth but the hand came up again. "All I'm getting at," he said, "if you do have that money, or know where it is, you want to give me a call. Because there's no way in hell a guy like you can do anything with that kind of cash without some help. You start trying to spend it, you'll be ass-deep in badges before you know it. Nowadays they got all kind of ways of watching out for shit like that, you know? They claim it's to stop the drug dealers, but that's bullshit. It's just the fucking government getting on people's backs again."

Freddie Manzano, conservative political analyst? He was right about the facts, though. Between the drug cops and the tax people and all those computers, it's getting very hard to spend or bank any serious amount of cash without attracting the attention of a lot of people who want to know where you got it. Even if they can't make a charge stick, they can confiscate the whole pile—along with the car you drove to the bank, and just about everything else you own—and demand that you prove you *didn't* do anything illegal. Due process of law, I think they call it. . . . Of course, if you actually are a big-time drug dealer or racketeer, you have plenty of ways to launder the money and probably have the authorities paid off anyway.

"So if you do have Wilburn's bread," Manzano said, "or know where it is, remember that it's no good to you without some professional handling."

"Which you'll be happy to provide for a modest percentage."

"Modest my crack," he said candidly. "And don't say anything about that, either. There's plenty of guys in my position would just have you worked on till you talked, take the money, and leave you at the bottom of the river."

I said, "Well, it's all been fascinating. Unfortunately, as I keep telling people, I don't know anything beyond what I've already told you and Deputy Ellis and everyone else."

"Could be." He didn't sound either convinced or skeptical. "But you still want to keep all this in mind. In case you hear something or think of something, or your memory suddenly improves, or whatever." He moved toward the door. "Or, what the fuck, maybe your one-armed buddy goes to clean out the shithouse and finds something strange inside the rubber machine. In fact you might want to pass our little conversation on to him."

He reached into his jacket and took out a pen and a white card. "Here," he said, scribbling. "You come up with anything, call this number, they'll put you through to me."

I took the card. He said, "If you do call, be careful what you say, know what I'm saying? Fucking phone's probably got more bugs than an ant farm."

I opened the door. The sound of Harry's barking drifted in, mixed with Danny's laughter. Freddie Manzano winced. "Jesus," he said under his breath.

"Hard to get good help these days," I remarked.

"No shit," he said feelingly. "Tell me about it."

There was nobody at the Flying Tiger Club when I tried to phone, but I got Loomis's home number off the check he'd given me. I wasn't exactly amazed when Julie answered the phone. She said he'd be down in a minute. She didn't seem interested in small talk while I waited.

"Man," Loomis said when I'd given him an account of Freddie Manzano's visit, "it keeps getting stranger and stranger, doesn't it? I need to change the name of the club to the Twilight Zone."

"Think there's any possibility there could be anything to it?" I asked. "About stolen money hidden somewhere around the club, I mean."

"I don't see how. Like I told you, the last owner gave the place a hell of a working over. I don't think there's any part of the building that didn't get some attention."

"The plane too?"

"Yeah. At least the paint looked fresh when I took over, and it weathers fast up there in the sun and wind. No, I can't see how anything could be stashed on the place without somebody finding it by now."

He laughed. "Of course maybe somebody did find it. Maybe there's some carpenter or painter or air-conditioning repairman out there, got himself a new house and everything, nobody ever knew."

"What about the owner? The one who had the work done?"

"Christ, that poor son of a bitch didn't have a pot to piss in or a window to dump it out of, time I bought him out. God knows he'd have liked to find some cash lying around." Loomis sighed. "I know how he felt. Damn, I could stand to get my hands on a big bundle right now. But I can't believe there's anything like that at the Flying Tiger Club."

Wiley Harmon's reaction was even more negative. "Bullshit," he said flatly. "I never knew this Jimmy Wilburn, but I know his kind. Punks like that don't take down big-stakes dope dealers. Maybe he had a few hundred from some half-assed stickup, buried in a jar somewhere across the river, and he built it up in his own mind to a real pile. More likely the whole story's a crock."

We were sitting in his car in a nearly empty parking lot just off the Broken Arrow Expressway. I'd had to give Harmon his cut of the Loomis money, and he had a fixed and inviolate rule against taking payoffs at the Copper Bottom, where he suspected Internal Affairs of having eyes.

"What you don't know," he went on, "this is fucking classic Freddie Manzano. See, the little bastard's got a permanent wild hair up his ass about treasure, hidden loot, anything like that.

Tell him a story about a lost gold mine, show him an old map, he starts to sweat and breathe hard. Don't ask me why. Maybe he saw a pirate movie when he was a kid."

Harmon laughed. "He dropped a bundle last year, in fact, although I wouldn't recommend saying anything to him about it. This old hillbilly—claimed to be an Indian, but if he was I'm Jesse Jackson—sold Freddie a story about some gold that Belle Starr and Cole Younger were supposed to have buried back in the hills in Adair County. Had this old sheet of paper with writing in Cherokee, claimed it gave the location. Turned out later to be the clerk's minutes from an Indian Baptist church meeting. Word is that Freddie's still got a standing dead-or-alive reward offer on the old turd, but of course he's vanished back into the woods forever."

"Manzano seemed pretty sure of his information this time."

"He's always sure," Harmon said, "and he's always full of shit. What I bet happened, some geek got out of the pen, needed some walking money and knew about Freddie's weakness." He dug me in the ribs with an elbow. "Made up a bullshit story and sold it, sounds like you got a professional colleague around here somewhere. Better get back to work before the competition overtakes you."

"If he got any money for his story," I said, "he already did."

I started to get out of the car. Harmon said, "Hey, Roper. Did you whack that Wilburn guy?"

I started to call him a son of a bitch, but his face was reasonably straight; I realized then that he wasn't kidding. So I called him a son of a bitch anyway.

"No fucking offense," he said mildly. "I just wondered. I mean, it's not like I give a shit. You of all people ought to know that."

I still didn't know how seriously to take Freddie Manzano's rather bizarre tale, or the various theories that had surfaced in the wake of Jimmy Wilburn's fatal homecoming, except that I seemed to be the only person who didn't suspect me of killing him. Getting back to work, however, was the best idea I'd heard lately; and, next day, that was what I did. As soon as Harry came back in from his morning business, I made a fresh pot of coffee and sat down at the typewriter and dived back into the Work in Progress.

And stayed there, running submerged and barely coming up for air, for a good many days. The block had disappeared, at least for the time being; the words ran out my fingertips and through the keys and onto the paper as readily as the coffee and Jim Beam ran through my hard-working kidneys. There were days when I only left the desk to eat and take care of other basic physical needs, or to let Harry take care of his. Writers are like gamblers: nobody dares to break a hot streak.

Not that it was easy; God, it was anything but that. . . . The Second Seminole War, as very few people know, was the longest single continuous war in U.S. history. Look it up; it went on longer than Nam, let alone any of the others, and it soaked up so many troops that Congress on two occasions had to authorize the enlargement of the standing army just to keep up. The Seminoles had no reserves to call on, being fully committed from the word go, but they managed to fight the U.S. Army and Marine Corps to a bloody standstill—and were never really defeated in combat; their top leaders were grabbed while under flags of truce, and the others eventually said fuck it and moved to Oklahoma, where their descendants tend to be regarded by the other tribes with a certain special respect. And of course there were others who never left or surrendered at all, whose great-great-grandchildren are still very much in business on their home turf.

All of which made a splendid setting for the kind of story I was writing, very colorful and exciting and all that; but it also added up to a hell of a lot of research work. It wasn't all sitting at the keyboard watching the phrases and paragraphs form up on the paper. A great deal of the time was spent with my face stuck in various books, some of them old and yellowed and hard to read, or down on the floor examining spread-out maps of Florida, which Harry kept using to take naps on. At least that was all he took.

Still, I slogged onward through my paper Everglades, and gradually the pages began to pile up in the plastic tray beside the typewriter. (Am I the only one, or has anybody else noticed that it's gotten damn near impossible to find a solid 8½-by-11 cardboard box?) And nobody came looking for me, or telephoned—except Rita on Tuesday night, and she hung up instantly when I explained the situation—or otherwise tried to talk with me about the late Jimmy Wilburn or anything else.

The first real interruption came on Friday; and even that wouldn't have amounted to much if I hadn't let it get to me.

That day the mail carrier brought a big heavy brown envelope, the kind with the shredded-paper padding that makes a dribbling gray mess when you tear it open. At first I thought it must be another returned manuscript, but it was too light for that; and then I recognized the logo on the mailing label and knew what had to be inside. I said, "Hot damn," or something to that effect, and headed for the kitchen to get a knife.

A couple of years back, I'd written a novel about a family of ex-Confederates living in Mexico in the late 1800s. *Ceremonies of the Horsemen,* I'd called it, from a Bob Dylan line; it was quite a bit more complex than anything I'd done before, and I was pretty proud of it.

My high opinion of the book, it turned out, wasn't shared by the publishing world. Editor after editor had sent it back—not to mention the two who'd failed to return the manuscript or even my phone calls.

I'd been just about ready to give up on *Ceremonies of the Horsemen* when I'd gotten a call from an editor who'd bounced the manuscript some months before. He'd admired the story, he said, but his boss had refused to let him buy it. Now he was with a different house, and in the market for quality material. Did I still have . . . ?

I did. Some weeks later, we'd signed a contract. The editor had been most complimentary and encouraging. I wasn't to worry; even though this was to be a paperback original, everybody at Putney Books recognized *Ceremonies* as genuine literature, and it would be packaged and marketed as such. He was sorry the advance money wasn't better, but hey, things were tight these days.

That had been not quite a year ago. I'd been pretty excited at the time, but that had faded as I'd gone back to work on *Staked Plain* and gotten involved in other affairs. Now, standing at the table prying at staples with a steak knife, I felt a little of the original rush come back.

The last staple came free and I gave the package a shake. A folded sheet of white paper fell out onto the table. I laid the envelope aside, picked up the paper and unfolded it, and read:

Tag—
Well, your book is finally here. You should get your author's copies in a few days. Meanwhile, here's a couple of advance copies for you.

I think the cover turned out pretty well. Sorry about the title change. I wasn't entirely happy with it myself, but I was overruled in committee. They felt your title just didn't have enough mass-market appeal.

Hope we can work together again soon—

Nate

I believe I said, "Oh, shit." But maybe I only thought it.

When I shook the envelope again a couple of paperback

books fell onto the Formica. I picked one up and studied the front cover, feeling a growing hollow sensation in my stomach.

The jacket bore a garishly-colored depiction of a bodybuilder in a cowboy outfit out of Buffalo Bill's Wild West Show. He had a long drooping Custer mustache and sideburns. One hand clutched a large revolver of unidentifiable make. The other clutched a girl who was wearing the shredded remains of a Mexican-style dress. Actually for all practical purposes she was naked; the shreds covered less area than a standard bra-and-panties set. In the background a buzzard perched on a phallic cactus.

Much of the cover, however, was occupied by the title:

STEEL SPURS

I said, "Oh, shit. *Oh*, shit."

Above the title, smaller lettering declared:

Ride Fast--Fight Hard--Die Free
Six-Gun Action Below the Border

And down at the bottom, a quarter-inch or so below the cowpunk's B&D boots and almost touching the Mexican girl's bare ass:

An Explosive New Western by
TAGGART ROPER

I don't remember what I said immediately after that. It probably wouldn't bear repeating.

Rita came over, a little after dark, to see if I needed anything. She let herself in and found me sitting at the table drinking Jim

Beam with a beer chaser. "Tag?" she said worriedly, and came to stand beside me. "What's happened, Tag? You look—"

She paused, seeing the book lying on the table. I'd already destroyed the other copy in various ways. "What's this?" she said, picking it up, and then a moment later, very softly and sadly, "Oh, Tag. Oh, Tag, I'm so sorry."

"You work your ass off." It wasn't easy for me to speak; even after all the liquid intake, my throat was still trying to close up. "You work your ass off learning to write, and then you work it off again for better than a year writing and rewriting until you've got something you're satisfied with, even proud of. Later on you work your ass off all over again, fighting off the nitwit editor who wants to change everything because he doesn't understand the story, and the fucking copyeditor who learned English as a second language—" I shook my head. "Christ, that's three times I worked my ass off. Overusing a not very original image. Well, what do you expect from a damn hack paperback-Western writer?"

Rita put her arm around my shoulders. "Don't, Tag. Please."

"But you do it all," I went on, "because you really care about what you do, you really believe in this thing you've created, and you want it to be as good as you can make it because it's going to have your name on it . . . and then," I picked up the book and held it out at arm's length, "then, they do *this* to you."

I threw the book in the general direction of the living room. It hit the wall and fell down behind the couch. Harry looked up to make sure I hadn't been throwing it at him, sighed, and went back to sleep. He never was very supportive in these situations.

Rita was stroking my hair with one hand. "Oh, Tag," she said once more. She seemed to be crying. Well, there were a few tears on my own face. True, they were probably about fifty percent alcohol by that time, but they were there.

"I don't understand," she said after a minute. "Why did they do it?"

"Damn if I know." I took another pull at the Jim and chased it down with a swallow of beer. By now my stomach hardly noticed. "I think," I said, "maybe they don't know how not to. They publish so much drivel for people who move their lips when they read a stop sign, I think after a while that's all they know."

I waved the beer bottle, knocking over a couple of empties. "What gets my ass more than anything, though, I *trusted* that son of a bitch. Bought every word of that bullshit he handed out, wide-eyed and stupid as some secretary believing her boss when he tells her he's about to get a divorce. I mean, it's not like I was a virgin, Rita. Two published books behind me, I should have known better than to believe one of those assholes if he told me shit smelled bad. . . ."

"So you're angry at yourself too?"

"Yeah." I leaned back against her arm. Another empty rolled off the table and clattered to the floor. No wonder, the way the room was starting to tilt. "Or maybe I'm just pissed off at life."

"Come on," she said, starting to tug at me. "Let's go to bed."

I got to my feet and looked at her. "Hell, Rita, I hate to say this but I'm not sure I'd be much good right now—"

"Oh, for God's sake. I mean *bed*. You're right on the verge of falling down and passing out, and I don't want to have to carry you in there. Come on."

"Okay." I didn't feel I was all that drunk, but no gentleman refuses a lady who wants to take him into the bedroom. I collared the Jim Beam bottle, for supplies along the trek, and let her lead me down the hallway. Passing the bathroom door, I felt a sudden urgent need, and she had to wait in the hall while I took care of it.

"I've had it with this shit," I said over my shoulder. "The bounced manuscripts and the chickenshit reviews and the end-less fucking lying and never any money . . . I bet Freddie Manzano would give me a job."

"You go to work for Freddie Manzano," she said, taking my arm as I emerged from the bathroom, "and you and I are extremely ancient history. Let's go."

I stood in the middle of the bedroom while she yanked the tangled sheets into a semblance of order. "You know," I told her, gesturing dramatically with the Jim Beam bottle, "there are people around this area who think I killed a man last Friday night. At least one of them thinks I killed him over a fortune in stolen drug money. Boy, what a cackle."

She guided me over to the bed and I fell back on my ass. "I tell you what," I said, while she bent to take off my pants, "I wish I did know where that money was. I wouldn't have to write another word, wouldn't have to take any more shit. By God, I think I *would* kill somebody for that."

Rita pulled my pants off and hung them over the bedroom's single chair. "But you didn't kill anybody," she said gently, unbuttoning my shirt, "and you don't have the money and you're not going to. So you've got to sleep it off and get up tomorrow and go back to work on the new book. Sit up."

"What for?"

"So I can get this shirt off you. My God, when did you change—"

"No," I said with some difficulty, "why do I have to go back to work on the damn book?"

"Because," she said, "that's what you do."

" 'To be is to do,' " I quoted, while she pulled the covers over me. "Think Nietzsche said that. Or was it Kierkegaard? No, he said 'To do is to be.' "

"Good night, Tag."

"And then there was Frank Sinatra," I went on, "who said 'Do be do be do.' "

"Good *night*," she said firmly, and turned off the light.

* * *

94

She was gone when I got up next day, but the trailer had been tidied up somewhat and there was fresh coffee in the pot. A note on the table read:

Tag—
I made you a chicken stew. It's in the refrigerator. For God's sake start eating better if you're going to drink.
   If you need or want me for any reason at all, call me. I'll be at home.

Love (needless to say)
Rita

The stew was excellent; I had two bowls, despite the unsettled feeling in my stomach and the throbbing in my skull. I had a couple of ibuprofens for dessert and chased them with too much black coffee and went in and took a very long, very hot shower.

And then, after one more cup of coffee, I sat down at the damn typewriter and returned to my marines and my Seminoles. After all, Rita was right; this was what I did. If only for lack of alternatives. . . .

I stayed on the job till late that night, and I got a fair amount done. All the same, something had changed; the energy that had driven me through the week, and the feeling-hot confidence, wouldn't quite come back. I was still rolling, but I seemed to be stuck in bottom gear.

And every time I let my attention wander, I saw those words: STEEL SPURS.

So there was a certain feeling of relief on Sunday afternoon when Hondo Loomis called and wanted to know if I could come out to the club. He sounded upset.

I told him I was on my way. A few minutes later I was.

* * *

Loomis was standing in front of the club, beside the entrance, when I arrived. "Look," he said, but the command was unnecessary. I was already looking. Anybody would have.

Not that the object hanging in the middle of the front door was so remarkable in itself. It was just a smallish plastic doll, male variety, a little over a foot tall; I think it may have been Ken or another of Barbie's boyfriends. The only unusual things about it were the big nail through the chest that pinned it to the door, and the fact that the left arm had been pulled off.

I said, "Jesus Christ!" and Loomis nodded grimly and reached up with his hammer and yanked the nail out, letting the doll fall to the ground. He gave it a hard kick and it skittered across the asphalt and disappeared beneath his parked blue van.

"Came by here around noon," he said, "wanted to do a little work on that foot bass, it still doesn't sound right. Found that thing on the door."

He opened the door and I followed him inside. The office door was open and he went in and laid his hammer on the desk. Without turning around he said, "Roper, I can't take much more of this shit. It's starting to get to me. When I first saw that fucking doll if I'd had some pills I'd have taken them. First time I've had the urge in a long time. I've got to put a stop to this."

"What are you going to do?"

"Hire me a security guard. It'll be a hell of an expense, but I don't see any other way."

He turned to face me. "Which gets us to why I called you. Could I hire you to spend a few nights here, keep an eye on the place, till I can get somebody? I'll pay anything reasonable." His mouth pulled into an attempted smile. "Hell, I don't expect you to do it for the kind of minimum-ass wages those security guards get."

I opened my mouth to tell him I couldn't do it. The words were all lined up and ready to go: hard at work on the new novel, most of my best work done at night, no guard experience

96

anyway since the army, be glad to recommend a couple of good agencies . . . but then there floated across my inner vision the embossed-foil words STEEL SPURS.

"What the hell," I said. "Why not?"

"Good," he said.

It was getting dark by the time I returned to the Flying Tiger Club. Nothing was moving on Route 66 but over on the Turnpike the late-Sunday-afternoon traffic was heavy, the drivers beginning to turn on their lights as they rolled homeward from Grandma's or wherever they'd been. The outside lights were already on around the club. The old P-40 on the roof grinned knowingly down at me, as if we shared some dirty secret, as I drove in.

I started to park in front, next to Hondo Loomis's big blue van, but then I thought about it and drove around and parked in back of the club. There was no point in presenting an irresistible temptation to any passing sociopaths—I didn't really think anybody would steal a ratty-looking old car like mine, but vandalism seemed highly possible—and there was also the risk of attracting the interest of cruising county cops, who might get curious about a car parked in front of a closed night club. I didn't need slashed tires and I wasn't eager to spend any more time talking to men with badges.

I locked the Camaro and went back around the building, swinging the little nylon bag into which I'd packed a few possibly useful items for the night. The dumpster, I noticed, had been replaced with a new one, this one painted yellow. I seemed to remember that the old one had been green, though I'd only seen it in bad light. I wondered what had happened to the old one. Impounded as evidence? That didn't seem likely, but then everything about this business was unlikely. Maybe it was in use somewhere else, with other people throwing trash into Jimmy Wilburn's next-to-last resting place, unaware of what it had recently contained.

Hondo Loomis met me at the front door. "I really appreciate this, Roper," he said as I entered. "Most nights, I wouldn't need anybody here till closing time, but we're closed on Sundays. Guess you're going to have a long night. Sorry if this cuts into your writing time."

I raised the nylon bag. "It's okay. I've got a couple of books in here, and a notebook. There's some background research I needed to do anyway."

"Well, hell, feel free. Do whatever you like to pass the time. I just want to have somebody here."

He took me on a short tour of the premises, showing me where the light switches were and which keys fit what. "Help yourself to anything you can find in the kitchen," he said. "Won't be much tonight, but there ought to be plenty of sandwich material, and there's soft drinks on tap at the bar. Get yourself a real drink or two, for that matter, if you feel like it."

He showed me a little room behind the stage, furnished with a single bed and a couple of chairs and a dressing table with a big mirror. "Now and then we get some visiting entertainer who doesn't want to bother with a motel. You get to feeling tired, go ahead and crash. I don't expect you to prowl around here all night."

I followed him back out to the front door, where he handed me a heavy ring of keys. "Listen," he said, "you got a gun? I mean on you?"

I shook my head. The only pistol I'd owned in recent years—unless you counted an occasional loaner from Wiley Harmon—had vanished into a Tulsa pawnshop months ago. I still had the old pump shotgun my father had left me, but that was back at the trailer.

"Well," Loomis said, "you want one? I got one, if you do. Brought it along in case."

I hesitated. I've got nothing against guns—in fact I've always found them interesting, and I've done a fair amount of shooting—but they do sometimes introduce nasty complications into a situation. Still, given the various recent goings-on around this place, it might not be a bad idea to have something more authoritative than my bare hands. I said, "Sure," and he said, "Be right back," and went out the door.

He was back in a few minutes, holding a smallish shiny pistol. He said, "This thing any good? I don't know doodly about them."

I took the piece and looked it over in some surprise. Loomis had himself an authentic classic here: a nickel-plated Colt hammerless pocket automatic, the flat sleek-looking job that you see in all the old gangster movies. It was an extremely popular weapon for years, being light and handy and reliable, but Colt quit making them a long time ago. This one was probably older than I was, though it seemed to be clean and well-cared-for.

I assumed at first it was a .32, since that was by far the most popular caliber for that make, but when I checked the markings on the slide it turned out to be a .380: considerably more effective, though still not much of a personstopper. I popped the clip, which was full, and locked the slide back and checked the chamber, which was empty. The brass cartridge cases had gone a little dull, but they weren't green yet, which meant they were probably all right. I held the piece up to the light and tried to look down the bore, but all I was able to determine was that the barrel wasn't blocked. Well, it didn't matter; I couldn't imagine myself using this thing in any situation in which pinpoint accuracy would be crucial.

Loomis said, "A guy who played horn for me in Chicago left that little bastard as security when I bailed him out of jail, and he never came back. You can keep the damn thing if you want it. What would I do with it?" He raised his one hand. "Takes two hands to load and unload it. I guess I could work something out, but chances are I'd shoot myself in the nuts. Anyway, guns make me nervous."

"Thanks."

"Consider it a little something extra for coming over on short notice." Loomis moved toward the door again. "If you do shoot anybody, try not to get blood on the carpet. Costs like a son of a bitch to have it cleaned."

When he was gone I locked the door and headed back toward the rear of the building, dropping the pistol into my hip pocket for the time being. I didn't think I'd be getting any blood on the carpet or anywhere else. Not if I could help it, and usually you can.

Oklahoma's laws on self-defense and lethal force are, like most Oklahoma statutes, worded so vaguely that nobody is really sure what they mean. In practice they tend to mean whatever a prosecutor can convince a judge and jury they mean, modified by such things as the relative social positions of shooter and shootee. I've seen a man walk free after gunning down a teenage kid for trying to break into his car, and another one in the next county go to prison for shooting a man who had attacked him with a knife in his own house. There was no telling what might happen if I plugged a breaker-and-enterer in a night club that wasn't even my property, and I wasn't interested in finding out.

I checked the lock on the kitchen entrance, went back to the little dressing room, laid the Colt on the dressing table, and got out the books. As Loomis had said, it was likely to be a long night.

Actually it wasn't all that bad. I'd never done anything quite like this before, and I'd expected—perhaps with memories of guard duty at Fort Leonard Wood, more years ago than I cared to add up—that the time would pass with excruciating slowness. But it wasn't like that at all. In fact I found myself rather enjoying it.

I checked the doors frequently, and now and then I went outside and had a look around. It was damn cold out there but it was the only way to do the job; the Flying Tiger Club possessed no windows.

The rest of the time, I sat in the little dressing room and read about Seminoles and soldiers and runaway slaves—which last group constituted the main reason for the whole war; politically powerful Southern landowners wanted to put a stop to the Seminoles' custom of giving asylum to valuable farm livestock, human variety, that had been so ungrateful as to run away. . . . I took a lot of notes, drew a couple of crude maps to give myself a clearer picture of the situation, and found out I was going to have to rewrite a certain key passage. All in all, I think I got as much work done as I would have back at the trailer. Not a bad way to spend a night, especially considering that I was getting paid. Maybe I should look into this as a regular line of work.

The night had gone on a long time, though, and I was starting to get a little tired, when I finally had company.

I was back in the kitchen, constructing myself a sandwich. Loomis had understated the supply situation; there was a wide variety of sandwich-making materials in the big refrigerator, and soft rolls, still reasonably fresh, in the bread tray. In a short time I had manufactured a sandwich of, in my own immodest opinion, artistically magnificent and gastronomically heroic proportions.

I left the sandwich on the counter, went into the bar and got myself a bottle of imported beer—it was going to be damn tough to go back to the stuff I drank and ate at home; I wondered if Loomis would let me simply move in here—and stood for a moment trying to decide whether to have my snack here or take it back to the dressing room. For some reason I happened to glance up at the clock above the kitchen door. Three and a quarter hours after midnight. Maybe the beer wasn't such a good idea; maybe I ought to have a cup of coffee instead. The big coffee machine had been emptied and scoured clean, but there should be some way—

That was when I heard the sound from outside. It was just barely a sound at all, by the time it got through the heavy rear door, and if I hadn't been standing where I was I don't think I'd have heard it at all. As it was, it took a few seconds before my conscious mind registered and identified it.

Somebody had just driven a car into the parking lot and stopped near the rear of the building. As I stood there listening, there was the unmistakable clunk of a car door closing.

I set the open bottle of beer carefully but quickly on the counter, started toward the back door, and stopped. Opening doors in the night, when you don't know who or what may be out there, isn't a business to be approached casually. For starters, a flanking movement seemed appropriate.

I went back through the swinging doors and across the dance floor and the stage, moving fast and not worrying about noise— nobody outside was going to hear anything I did in there—and ducked into the little dressing room long enough to grab the Colt and the big flashlight I'd brought from home. Remembering, I paused to jack back the slide to arm the pistol, set the safety, and took off for the front door.

It was bitter cold. A stiff wind from the west tried to take the door away from me as I stepped outside and eased the door shut. The sky was clear and the stars looked distant and frozen. The parking area in front of the club was deserted.

When I went cautiously around the corner of the building, though, the first thing I saw was a car that hadn't been there before. It was a short-coupled, stocky-looking vehicle, one of Detroit's efforts to build a Japanese compact; I can't keep track of the damn things any more. It looked gray, but I couldn't be sure, because nearly everything looked gray in that treacherous light.

I took a couple of seconds to memorize the license number, which was clearly visible from where I stood, and then I went on toward the rear of the club.

A man was standing next to my Camaro, looking it over. He was holding a little notebook in one hand, folding it, and clicking the thumb button of a ballpoint pen with the other. I guessed he'd been writing down the Camaro's license number. A Hondo Loomis lyric floated through my mind: *I got your number, you got mine. . . .*

I said, "Hi."

I said it in a normal voice, but it was loud enough. Not that he jumped or screamed or anything like that. In fact his reaction was impressive. He stopped moving for just a fraction of a second; and then, very fast and all at once, he turned to face me, his left foot shot sideways in a big flatfooted step, and his right hand started to move toward his body. The left hand continued to hang on to the little notebook, but I never saw him get rid of the pen.

As he turned toward me I switched on the flashlight. I could see him fine without it; what I wanted was to blind him before his right hand got hold of whatever it was reaching for.

The beam caught him square in the face. It was a good bright beam; I thanked myself for putting in fresh batteries. His face contorted as the light hit his eyes, and his right hand paused in its movement. In that microsecond of hesitation I poked the shiny Colt forward, where the light would pick it up. Still in that conversational tone, I said, "Don't."

He saw the gun and where it was pointed, and his right hand stopped moving altogether. It was obvious, from his face and his stance, that a large part of him still wanted to go for it, and if I hadn't blinded him with the flashlight I think he would have. But after a moment—a very long moment in subjective time, at least for me and I suspect for him too—his hand dropped slowly back to his side.

He said, "Who the fuck are you?"

I studied my visitor for a minute before responding. He was a middle-aged white man, on the tall side—I estimated an even six feet—and rather lean of build. He wore a dark suit with a white shirt and a skinny tie. The light wasn't good enough to show any details.

He had a flattish face with a snub nose. Below the nose sprouted a dark mustache. There seemed to be some hair around his ears, but on top he was entirely bald. His scalp glowed slightly where the flashlight beam hit it. He had bushy dark eyebrows that were pulled together in a combination squint and scowl. All in all, he wasn't exactly your basic handsome devil.

I said finally, "That's my line, I think. Along with something about what the fuck are you doing here?"

His mouth curled in a kind of sneer. "Two hands, so it's not Loomis . . . Roper, right? White Camaro, sure. You're the one who found Wilburn." He put a heavily sarcastic intonation on "found." "What do you think you're doing, Roper?"

He had a high, raspy, unpleasant voice, like Pat Buchanan trying to do Eastwood. There was no recognizable national or regional accent.

I said, "At the moment, I'm pointing a gun at you."

"Is that right?" He stared at me, though the light must have been painful. "A real gun? Loaded and all that?"

I swung the .380 through a few degrees of lateral arc, thumbed the safety, and fired. For a relatively small weapon, it made quite a loud bang. The little 95-grain jacketed pill whacked into the wall of the Flying Tiger Club, dug a small divot out of the concrete, and zinged off into the darkness. I put the piece back on the bald man. "I don't have a lot of rounds to waste," I said, "so the next one will be aimed at you. I'll probably hit you, too. At least I managed to hit the last couple of men I shot at."

He didn't look terribly impressed. He hadn't flinched or jumped when the Colt went off, either. He said, "You don't know what you're doing, do you? I wondered, when your name came up. You don't have any idea what you've gotten yourself into."

He jerked his head in the direction of the club. "A nobody wound up dead here. He'd taken something that didn't belong to him. It belonged to some people he shouldn't have fucked with," he said. "They still want it back. Anybody who has it now would be making a serious mistake to try to keep it. Or do anything with it except return it."

He paused, seeming to expect an answer. I said, "Why do people like you always talk around corners? Wouldn't it be more efficient to simply come out and say whatever you're trying to tell me?"

His mouth made that scornful twitch again. "All right, Roper, you want it straight, here it is: Don't fuck around, because you don't know who you're fucking with."

He dropped the little notebook into an outside jacket pocket, moving carefully so I wouldn't mistake the movement for anything else. "We'll be talking soon, Roper," he said. "In fact you and I are going to have a long serious conversation. Not here, though, and not now."

I said, "Take your wallet out and toss it on the ground in front of you. Then that gun under your jacket, and do it very slowly and don't try any moves."

He cocked his head to one side like a bird. "No," he said after a second. "Fuck you."

He turned and began walking away, toward the compact car. I raised the .380. "Hold it," I said, and then more loudly, "God damn it, I'm not bluffing."

"Sure you are." He didn't even turn his head to look back at me. "You're not going to shoot. If I'm wrong, go ahead and prove it."

I started to fire one past his ear, but then I lowered the Colt, realizing it wouldn't do any good. Unless I had this guy read totally wrong, he'd just keep on walking. Whoever and whatever he was, he didn't scare worth a damn.

And he was right; I wasn't going to shoot him, not now. For one thing, there was an excellent chance I'd wind up doing hard time at McAlester; and for another, I wasn't ready to do anything until I found out who he was and what was going on.

"What I thought," he said contemptuously, and opened his car door and got in, while I stood there feeling the blood prickling the skin of my face. There are very few things that can make you feel as big a fool as running a bluff with a gun and having it called. "Be seeing you," he added as he closed the door.

I watched as he backed up and turned around and drove slowly and deliberately out of the parking lot. His taillights disappeared over the hill, headed up Route 66 toward the Turnpike interchange.

After a minute I walked back toward the club. It was too cold to hang around outside, and I didn't seem to be doing any good out here anyway.

So I went back inside and ate my damn sandwich.

Freddie Manzano said, "Jesus, Roper, you got any idea what time it is?"

"Eight-thirty," I said, "last time I looked."

"I mean, I just got out of *bed,* for Christ sake. Half the time I'm not even up this early. Maybe you're one of those early risers but some of us need our sleep."

I hadn't had any sleep all night, but I didn't think he would be interested in my problems. I said, "If this guy was working for you, I want to know about it. I'd just as soon avoid situations where I'm pointing guns at your people, okay? And if he doesn't work for you, I thought you'd want to know about him."

A sigh came through the telephone. "No, hell, you're right. Anybody else is sniffing around this business, I want to know. You can quit worrying about that first part, though. He's not anybody who works for me. I didn't send anybody out there last night, and my people all know better than to go fucking around on their own. Let me have that description again."

I did. At the end Manzano said, "Well, that doesn't sound like anybody I know in this area. Or anywhere else, far as that goes."

"He gave the impression of being connected to somebody or something pretty big."

"Shit, don't they all? Every punk on the street tries to let on he's hooked up."

"Whoever he does or doesn't work for," I said, "this guy is no street punk."

"Maybe. I'll see what I can find out. And thanks for calling," he added. "Even if you did do it in the middle of the fucking night."

Wiley Harmon said, "There's not much I can do with a description like that, Roper. Ask around, maybe, see if it rings any bells for anybody. Doesn't ring any for me." He snorted. "Hate to admit it, but if Freddie Manzano doesn't know who he is, chances are nobody around here does."

"What about the license number?"

"Sure, I'll run it down. Don't get your hopes up, though. It's liable to be a rented car. If this guy's a pro it's almost certain."

"He's a pro, all right. At least he's got pro reactions and pro moves." I hesitated. "Wiley—there's a possibility he's some kind of government agent. Or has been, at some time."

"No shit?"

"He's had the training, anyway. You know the old FBI draw, with the quick step to the left? He was going into it when I hit him with the light."

There was a brief silence over the phone while Harmon digested this. "That would be FBI, all right," he said, "or maybe Treasury. Or a federal marshal, I don't know much about their training. The drug cowboys in DEA use a different style. Actually I think that draw you're talking about went out years ago, in all the agencies."

"What about CIA?"

"Could be, for all I know. Could even be one of the military spook outfits. Or Secret Service, provided you're actually the President in disguise. Come to think of it, I never saw the two of you together."

Harmon's voice shifted to a lower register. "But listen, Roper, you better understand something right now: if this turns out to be government business, if there's any federal angle at all, I'm gone. You got me?"

"I understand."

"You better. I don't dick around with those guys and if you're smart neither will you. I'm telling you," Harmon said seriously, "they got no fucking sense of humor at all."

Hondo Loomis said, "Nah, I don't know anybody who looks like that. In fact the only bald guy I know these days is black and lives in St. Louis. And he didn't say what he wanted?"

"Only some B-movie-menace stuff about Wilburn taking something that wasn't his, and the people who owned it wanting it back. And some pretty crude threats to the effect that anybody who had it better give it back."

"Son of a bitch. I assume he meant that money Wilburn was supposed to have ripped off. I never took that story seriously."

"Neither did I. I'm not sure I do yet," I said, "but obviously this guy does. Which isn't absolute proof the money exists, or ever did, because I'm not at all sure he isn't crazy."

"Huh. Well, look," Loomis said, "under the circumstances, if you don't want to watch the place tonight, I can sure as hell understand. No need for you to get yourself—"

"Oh, I'll be there," I said. "This is getting too interesting to miss."

* * *

By the time I finished doing my calling and talking, it was after ten and closing in on eleven, which meant I'd been awake for—Christ, I'd gotten up just about this time Sunday. Twenty-four hours with my eyes open; I could do with a stretch in bed, especially since I had to be at the Flying Tiger Club around one in the morning.

But there were things that needed to be done, and, as my father had been fond of observing, most things aren't much good at doing themselves. I got up and picked up my keys off the coffee table and headed for the door, saying various words under my breath.

Halfway there, I stopped, considering this and that; and then, feeling numerous kinds of silly, I went back to the bedroom and got the little .380 Colt from the bedside stand. Much as I hated to admit it, the bald man had gotten to me, and that crack about having a long conversation kept replaying in my mind.

Since nothing on the agenda called for suit and tie, I was wearing jeans and cheap running shoes and a GI camo field jacket over a flannel work shirt. I tried dropping the .380 into a jacket pocket, but the barrel was too long and the butt stuck out. A hip pocket would have worked, but then I couldn't have gotten at the gun while sitting in the car. Finally I shoved the .380 down my pants on the left side, butt forward for a cross draw, and hoped to God the safety catch worked properly; it would be just like me to contrive to shoot myself in the ass.

When I went back through the living room Harry was whining and barking beside the door, thrashing his tail violently and crouching down with his head between his paws to show me how adorable he was. I said, "I'll be back, Harry," but that wasn't nearly good enough; he gave me a look of such heart-rending pathos that only a man with a heart of stone could have resisted the urge to kick him.

I said, "Oh, hell, *all* right, but you'll have to ride in the back seat. Rita's still bitching about the black hairs on her white cocktail dress."

Harry rushed out the door as soon as I opened it and, while I got the Camaro's door unlocked, he ran a couple of laps around the yard and pissed on the trailer's tires to show his joy. I snapped my fingers and he jumped in, planted his ass in the passenger's seat, and ignored several shouted commands and threats before he finally surrendered and clambered back into the rear seat, where he collapsed, shuddering happily, and closed his eyes. I didn't care how many hairs he shed back there; I didn't know any pygmies and the back seat of a Camaro isn't big enough for any other sort of human.

I went by the drive-in branch of my bank and deposited Hondo Loomis's checks—I dislike using the drive-in window, but I wasn't going inside with a gun in my belt—and drove on across the river to Broken Arrow, where the proprietor of a gun shop was pleased to sell me a box of hollow-point ammunition that would, he assured me, turn the little .380 into a considerably more effective weapon at close range. Somewhat shaken by the price—Winchester seemed to have confused the damn things with the Lone Ranger's silver bullets; I wondered if it might not be cheaper simply to pay any assailants to go away—I stowed the cartridges in the glove compartment and drove on.

It was a few minutes after leaving the gun shop that I thought I saw a familiar-looking gray compact car in the mirror. It was some distance back, though, and there were cars between us, and anyway little blocky gray cars are as common as dead skunks on the roads around Tulsa. No doubt I was being paranoid, I decided; and if I wasn't, if the Mysterious Stranger wanted to tail me on my little errands, I couldn't see that it did me any harm. He was sure as hell wasting his time this morning.

At a Wal-Mart I purchased a basic Polaroid camera with a built-in flash. Next time I got a chance, I was going to immortalize the bald man on film, in the hope that a picture might help find out who he was. I even remembered to buy film for it. But then, halfway home, I had a disturbing thought. I pulled over and got the camera out of its box and checked and sure enough, like all toys, it needed batteries. There was a small convenience store on the next corner; I pulled in, parked the Camaro in the service area around back to keep Harry from barking at the other customers, and went in and bought the required double-A's.

When I came back out there was no one around and Harry was lying quietly in the back seat, apparently asleep. But just as I closed the door and started to put the key in the switch, there was a muffled roar and a screech of brakes and a light-gray compact car came sliding to a stop behind the Camaro, cutting me off. Before I could react, a fast-moving human figure jumped out of the compact, dashed across the intervening space, and wrenched open the Camaro's right door. And then there he was, sitting next to me in my own car, giving me that sneering little grin. "Hello, Roper," he said.

Actually I wasn't paying all that close attention to his facial expression, or to his words either. I was looking at the big blue revolver in his right hand. It was a short-barreled, heavy-framed, brutal-looking piece, some kind of Magnum I guessed. It was looking back at me and it gave the impression it didn't like me, even though we'd just met.

"I told you we were going to have a long talk," the bald man said. "Now we're going to go somewhere good and private, and we're going to—"

Harry woke up in the back seat, sat up, and licked the back of the bald man's head.

It was only a friendly lick, maybe a little sloppy but nothing to get excited about. It must have come as a real shock to the bald man, though, because he jumped convulsively and said, "Jesus!" His eyes went wide and he turned halfway around in the seat, looking back at Harry, who immediately tried to lick his face.

The muzzle of the big revolver was a good forty-five degrees off target. That was as good as my luck was likely to get today.

I grabbed the revolver with my left hand, shoving it back and upwards, anywhere that didn't point at a part of me. The bald man reacted instantly and with amazing strength, and we did a weird little arm-wrestling number for a minute there, the revolver waving all over the place and both of us grunting and straining, while Harry barked excited encouragement and tried to lick everything that came within reach.

I think I would have lost the wrestling match if it had gone on any longer—there was real power in those wiry arms, and it was obvious that he'd had some serious training in this sort of thing—but I was only fighting a delaying action with my left hand, while my right got what it was groping for. Then everything went freeze-frame still as the bald man stared, slightly cross-eyed, at the muzzle of the .380, which was almost touching the bridge of his nose.

I said, "Let go," and when he didn't, "I'll do it this time, you know."

I hoped he believed me. I didn't want to shoot the son of a bitch, but I'd do it before I'd let him have that cannon back. There was no reason to worry about consequences this time; forcing his way into my car with a gun, in a town that was having a rash of carjackings, made him legal game if I cared to bag him.

And he must have realized that I wasn't bluffing this time, because after a second his grip loosened and his hand fell back and I had the revolver in my left hand. I did a clumsy little juggling act until I had it turned around, grip in my palm and my finger inside the trigger guard. Without lowering the .380, I pointed the revolver at him too. The two-gun bit wasn't credible even when Roy Rogers did it, but at this range I couldn't miss a man-sized target.

He slumped back in the seat, leaning against the right door. "Okay, you son of a bitch," he said, "what now?"

I said, "Hang on just a minute . . . HARRY, SHUT THE FUCK UP!"

I had to do quite a bit of yelling at Harry, who had gotten really manic from all the excitement, before he finally shut up and stretched out on the back seat, whuffling softly to himself. When he was quiet I sat back and had a good unhurried look at my new acquaintance.

He was even less pretty in good light. The mustache was unevenly trimmed and had a couple of thin spots that gave it a slightly mangy look. The line of his lip was a little crooked; he'd been born with a harelip, I suspected, and there had been a corrective operation but the results hadn't been perfect, so he'd grown a mustache to cover it. The effect was that of a permanent slight sneer.

It was the eyes that held my attention, though. They weren't particularly unusual eyes in themselves; but somewhere in their muddy brown depths was a flickering something that I couldn't put a name to. It was as if a small animal were trapped inside his head and peering out through his eyes.

I said, "Well, you said something last night about wanting to have a long conversation with me. This seems as good a time as any."

He blinked rapidly a couple of times. His pale face turned a bit paler. I knew in a second he was going to tell me to go to hell, or words to that effect.

"Or," I went on before he could speak, "I can put a three-eighty slug through your head, stick this wheelgun back in your hand, and go call the cops. I figure I'm going to have to either talk with you or kill you some time soon, and either way, I'd just as soon get it over with."

He blinked a few more times and then he nodded, once, an abrupt stiff bob of his shiny head. "All right," he said. "Maybe it's better if you do understand the situation. You have to remember, though, that there are things I can't tell you under any circumstances."

He had an odd way of talking; his voice was an absolutely flat monotone, almost like one of those electronically-generated computer voices, and his sentences came out in quick choppy bursts. His eyes stared straight at my face all the time he was speaking, but his own face never changed expressions; even his lips barely moved.

"My name is Shaw," he went on. "I represent a certain branch of the United States government. If you'll let me get my wallet—"

"Keep your hands still." I had no doubt that he had all sorts of impressive identification, but there was no way I could check its validity. And I didn't want him reaching into any pockets; I wouldn't have been at all surprised to learn that he had a backup gun on him somewhere. "What branch would that be?" I asked, though I thought I knew what the answer was going to be.

"That's one of the things I can't tell you," he said, winning me my bet with myself. "Even if I did, it would mean nothing to you. Or to any other ordinary citizen."

Oh, boy.

"Jimmy Wilburn," he went on, "as you probably know by now, was a penny-ante punk who specialized in auto theft and an occasional low-grade holdup. Ten years ago, he got his big break. A couple of Oklahoma City stickup artists needed a getaway driver in a hurry. They had a plan to knock over a big drug deal that was going down that night, and their wheelman had suddenly lost his nerve and dropped out of the job. Jimmy Wilburn wasn't much, but at least he was a good driver, and had a reputation for keeping his mouth shut.

"They pulled it off, all right, did a hell of a professional job in fact. Unfortunately for them, Jimmy Wilburn had finally worked up the balls to take the big step. At some point that night, while they were distracted, he shot them both and took off with the money."

He paused. "You understand," he added in a slightly less intense voice, "some of this is speculation and extrapolation. Nobody knows exactly what went down that night. But the two holdup artists were never seen again, alive or dead, and Jimmy Wilburn did leave the Oklahoma City area that night in the car he had stolen for the getaway."

"And ran out of gas on the Turnpike, not far from his old stomping grounds," I said, "and stashed the money somewhere in a boarded-up night club, expecting to be back in a little while to pick it up. Instead he got busted in Sapulpa and went away on various chickenshit charges, off to scenic McAlester, where he was on occasion heard to brag that he had a lot of money waiting for him on the outside."

Shaw—if that was really his name, which I doubted most severely—was looking really paranoid now. "You know all that?" His voice was even higher and scratchier than before. "Just how much do you know, anyway, Roper? Maybe I figured you wrong—"

"No, no." I made a soothing gesture with my left hand. Well, as soothing as a gesture can get when it involves a loaded pistol. "I really don't know much of anything. Just some rumor and speculation, you know, in local criminal circles."

"Hm." He calmed down a little, but the suspicion was still in his eyes. "Well, you've got the general outline of the story. There are only a couple of details that need to be added at this point."

He held up his left hand, two fingers extended like Winston Churchill, and counted off with the other hand. "One: Jimmy Wilburn and his partners were way out of their league that night, farther than they ever knew. What they hit was no routine dope deal. Somehow—and don't ask me how they found out about it in the first place, because nobody has ever been able to answer that—those third-rate Okie dirtballs had stumbled across something so big they couldn't have understood it in a million years."

"You're talking about some kind of secret federal business?"

He shook his head sharply. "That's another matter I can't talk about. Enough to say that it was part of a larger operation, with far-reaching national security implications."

He said the last words with almost natural ease. When a man uses a grotesque phrase that smoothly, it usually means he's had a lot of practice saying it. I wondered how often Shaw had used those fancy words, and how many nasty pieces of business they'd been applied to.

"The other point," he went on, touching his other fingertip, "is that the holdup men got away with some serious money. We're not talking nickels and dimes here."

He paused. Since he seemed to be waiting for me to feed him the setup line, I said, "Okay, how much?"

"Half a million dollars," Shaw said, still in that flat toneless voice. "Packed, if you're curious, in an aluminum suitcase, though of course the thieves may have repackaged it."

If he'd been trying to impress me, he'd finally succeeded. Half a million? Even allowing for possible exaggeration—and with Shaw that was almost automatic—this wasn't funny any more. I managed to keep from saying, "Holy shit!", but it wasn't easy.

"I've always wondered," Shaw added, "whether Wilburn ever knew how much money he was carrying. It's possible he never paused long enough to count it."

"No wonder he behaved himself in prison," I said, thinking out loud. "I'm not sure I wouldn't do ten years myself, for that kind of money . . . and finally he got his chance to come back for it."

"Yes." Shaw's lips pulled back for a second in what seemed to be his version of a smile. "Much good it did him."

"And now you're looking for the missing cash. What went wrong? Did you accidentally kill him before you could make him tell you where he hid it? Was he up on the roof trying to hide from you?"

"What?" Shaw's head jerked back. "Jesus Christ, Roper, I didn't wax the little bastard. I wasn't even in this part of the country when it happened. Not that it's any of your business, but I wasn't even in the *country.*"

"Then who did?"

"Actually, I had you figured for it," he said frankly. "Maybe you ran into him right after he recovered his stash, you got in a fight and you won, or he fell over his own feet and hit his head—anyway there you were with the loot. I guess not, though. I read people pretty well, Roper, and anybody could see you weren't taking any of this shit seriously until I mentioned that half a million. Anyway, why would you still be hanging around that club at night if you had the money? And you've got a gun and you're pretty handy with it, so if you wanted to grease him you wouldn't do it with a brick or whatever."

Too bad I couldn't have him go talk to Deputy Ellis. Not to mention Freddie Manzano and Wiley Harmon.

"That doesn't put you in the clear, though," he continued, "not in my book it doesn't. You've been acting pretty damn funny, Roper. What's a hack writer doing packing a gun, for one thing? Or prowling around a closed-up roadhouse in the middle of the night? I think you know something, Roper. Or think you do."

I started to tell him about the business that had brought me to the Flying Tiger Club in the first place, the threats and the vandalism. But he wouldn't have believed a word of it.

"You better not get in my way, Roper," he said. "If you've got some idea of going after that half million yourself, you better forget it. Even if you find it before I do, it won't do you any good. The way you're going to be watched, you won't be able to put a dime in a pay toilet without me knowing about it."

I sat for a minute in silence, looking at him. There were plenty of questions I wanted to ask him, but I knew he wouldn't give me any answers. Or, if he did, I wouldn't know whether or not to believe them. I didn't even know how much of what he'd already told me was the truth. If any of it.

"This is way over your head, Roper." Shaw pointed a finger at me. "I'm telling you one last time, don't fuck around."

And that, I decided, was where I came in. "Okay," I said, "out."

He blinked. "What?"

"Get out of the car." I jerked the .380 slightly for emphasis. "Go do your Secret Agent Man routine somewhere else. I'm going to go home and get some sleep."

Shaw put his hand on the door handle. "My gun," he said.

I hefted the massive revolver in my left hand. "My gun now," I pointed out. "We fight. You lose. Heap damn tough titty."

He was absolutely livid now, clear up to the top of his head. "That weapon is government property—"

"And I'm Arsenio Hall. But if it is, what the hell, I'm a taxpayer. The way they bust my ass on that self-employment tax, I must have paid for a couple of cases of these by now. Get out of the damn car."

He still wanted to object. I said, "Okay, Shaw, tell you what. You go get in your car and move it out of my way, and I'll lay your gun here on the ground. You can pick it up as soon as I'm gone."

He didn't like it, but he must have realized it was the best offer he was going to get. He got out, slammed the Camaro's door unnecessarily hard, and stalked back to the gray compact. A few seconds later, with a violent spinning and squealing of tires, the gray car backed away, leaving my exit route open.

I started the Camaro and backed out toward the street. As I passed, the gray car's left front door swung open and Shaw stuck his head and shoulders out. I could just barely hear him yelling, "My gun! What about my gun?"

I rolled down my window. "I lied," I called cheerfully. And drove away and left him there. I thought he might try to follow me, but he didn't.

I didn't keep Shaw's gun, though he probably thought I did. I got rid of it that night on my way to the Flying Tiger Club.

I hated to ditch the damn thing; it was as impressive a piece of equipment, on its own terms, as I'd ever had my hands on. A Colt King Cobra in .357 Magnum, with a two-and-a-half-inch barrel, it had been fitted with custom grips and sights and somebody had done some highly expert work on the trigger pull, as well as dehorning the hammer so the spur wouldn't catch on clothing. Not a cheap gun by any means; Shaw had reason to be pissed off about losing it. . . . It could even have been called beautiful, especially now that it wasn't pointed at me any more.

The cylinder held half a dozen cartridges that obviously hadn't come from any factory. I studied the big hollow-point bullets, remembered the scene in the Camaro's front seat, and shuddered. It was odds-on that there was a hell of a powder charge behind those slugs, too. Which, with that short barrel, would create a muzzle blast that would stun a walrus, but the poor bastard who got shot wouldn't be complaining about the noise.

I wouldn't have minded owning something like that, but keeping it was far too risky; for all I knew, Shaw had already killed somebody with it on the other side of town. I lobbed it off the old bridge at Jenks and drove on across the hills to Route 66.

I missed a turn in the dark, though—the area west of Jenks is undergoing all sorts of residential development, most of it numbingly tacky, and it's easy to get confused even in the daytime—and it took me a little while to get straightened out. By the time I got to the Flying Tiger Club, the parking lot was almost empty, and when I went inside, the waitresses were gently shooing the few remaining customers toward the bamboo-curtained door.

Hondo Loomis was sitting at the bar, talking with Julie, who had on a white-lace jumpsuit and a pouty expression. "Be right with you, Roper," he called, and to Doris, "Give the man a drink if he wants one."

He went back to his conversation—or argument, I was pretty sure—with Julie, and I sat down at the bar. Doris smiled at me. "What'll you have, Mr. Roper?"

"Jim Beam on the rocks. No, wait, I better just have a Coke. I was up all last night and I only got a few hours of sleep this afternoon."

She brought me a Coke in a tall glass. "Here you are, Mr. Roper." She had a nice voice, high and almost musical; I wondered if she could sing. She was looking a lot better than she had the last time I'd seen her, though there were still traces of red at the borders of her eyes, and dark shadows beneath.

"I wanted to thank you for helping out the other night," she told me. "I'm sorry you had to get mixed up in things."

"It's all right."

"No it's not," she said with unexpected force. "There's nothing all right about it. Nothing all right about anything to do with Roy Dolan. Believe me, Mr. Roper, I know."

She moved away, wiping at the bar with a white rag, evidently not expecting or wanting a reply. I sat and sipped my Coke and after a few minutes Hondo Loomis appeared at my elbow. "Sorry about that," he said. "Little communications problem . . . how's my man?"

I finished the Coke and glanced around. There was nobody near enough to hear anything we said; Doris was down at the far end of the bar by now, the waitresses and the last couple of customers were over by the door, and Julie was striding across the dance floor, looking slightly pissed off. All the same, I said, "I think we better go in the office to talk."

"If you've got something private on your mind," he suggested, "that dressing room would be better. Got all kind of traffic in the lobby right now, right past the office door, and that door's about as soundproof as a Kleenex box."

We crossed the dance floor and the stage to the little dressing room. I closed the door and Loomis sat down in one of the chairs. He picked up one of the books I'd left there the previous night. *"History of the Seminole Wars,* huh? Damn, you read all of this heavy old son of a bitch?" He laid the book carefully on the bed. "So what's happening now? Somebody see a UFO land in the parking lot?"

"Something nearly as strange. Come to think of it, there was kind of an outer-space quality about this guy—"

I told him about the encounter with Shaw. "I should have called you as soon as I got home," I added at the end. "But hell,

124

I was really exhausted. Besides, I wouldn't put it past the wiggy bastard to have a tap on my phone."

"You wouldn't have reached me anyway. I was off driving Julie around while she spent a whole bunch of money. Well." He leaned back and stroked his chin with his fingertips. "Half a million bananas. As we used to say, oh, wow."

"There's no telling whether that part's true or not," I said. "Or any of the rest of it, as far as that goes. As sources go, I'd say Shaw is about as unreliable as they come."

"Yeah, but Christ, think of it. What if there really *is* half a million stashed around this place somewhere?" His eyes had taken on a dreamy, wistful look. "You realize what we could do with that kind of bread, Loomis? I don't know much about your situation, but at least you wouldn't have to do these screwy little jobs for people like me any more. Maybe you could take some time, write something you really want to write. Or say fuck it and drop the whole writing game, if you felt like it. I know that's what I'd do, man. No more being a damn freak show: Hondo Loomis, the one-armed piano player, in the tent right next to the bearded lady and the guy who can stick his elbow in his ear."

We sat in silence for a minute or two, seeing private visions. Finally I said, "Freddie Manzano was right, though. We'd never get away with trying to spend that money ourselves."

Loomis moved his shoulders impatiently. "So we cut a deal with Manzano to launder it. Hell, I'm willing to let him have his piece, if that's what it takes. Any reasonable percentage of that kind of money, we can both go sit on our asses and watch the grass grow till it's time to draw Social Security."

"If Shaw was telling the truth, there'll be some government types watching for that money to surface. Manzano may not be able to cope with them. The IRS or the drug people, sure, but if we're up against somebody like the CIA—"

"Do you believe it?"

125

"Not really." I'd given the question a lot of thought; it was one reason I hadn't gotten much sleep in the afternoon. "Even if the rest of the tale is true, it's hard to believe Shaw is part of any official mission to recover a bundle of cash that went astray ten years ago. For one thing, those guys almost never work alone. He'd have a partner, especially on a case involving a lot of cash. And for another, half a million looks like a fortune to you or me, or Shaw maybe, but it's petty cash to those people in Washington. They blow that much in a few months on paper clips."

Loomis was looking around him. "Well, like I said before, I can't think of any way it could be on the premises without turning up when they remodeled the place. You suppose it's somewhere else, only there's something here that tells you where it is? Like those stories where there's this rock or tree or something that points the way to the buried treasure?"

"You sure you don't know Freddie Manzano?"

"Okay, okay. It's just that the thought of all that bread is making me silly. Oh, well." He heaved himself up out of the chair. "I have to go now and finish making peace with Julie. You're not the only one who nearly got killed today."

I walked with him through the now-empty club. As he started through the bamboo curtain he paused, turning to look back at me. "What about our other mysterious midnight visitor? You know, the asshole with the notes and the spray paint and the one-armed dolly? Wouldn't it be the shits if *he* found the loot, some night when he was screwing around here? Man, I couldn't stand the thought."

"If he comes around tonight I'll ask him."

"Yeah, you do that. Christ," Loomis said, turning to go, "I knew I should have stayed in Chicago."

But nobody came around that night. I checked outside again and again, even went out and sat in the Camaro a couple of times until the cold drove me back inside, but nobody showed up. There wasn't even much traffic along Route 66. Toward morning I went back and stretched out on the narrow bed and got a couple of hours of sleep, feeling a little guilty but too tired to stay awake any longer.

As soon as it began to grow light outside I gathered my things up and went out to the Camaro. I didn't get in and drive off, though, not right away. Tired or not, there was something I was going to do. I'd been thinking about it all night.

I had a fairly good selection of tools in a metal box in the trunk of the Camaro. I picked out the ones that seemed potentially useful, stowed them here and there about my person, and went back inside the club.

The storeroom next to the kitchen contained, among other items, an adjustable aluminum ladder. It was dented and heavily spotted with old paint, but the locking mechanism was solid. I carried it out through the service entrance, ran it out to maximum length, and propped it up against the outside wall. A moment later I was on the roof of the Flying Tiger Club.

An old detective I used to know once told me: "Never dismiss the obvious just because it's obvious."

Close up, the old P-40 was considerably less impressive than from the ground. The paint was chipped and peeling, and faded by the sun. I was pretty sure this wasn't the original military paint anyway, which would have been a dull matte finish; this looked like plain old glossy automotive paint, laid on with an amateurishly-handled spray gun, though somebody had done a reasonably clean job on the shark-mouth markings.

The wheels, which would have been invisible from the ground, had been removed, and the landing-gear legs were welded to the ends of steel beams that rose out of the tar-and-gravel roof. Somebody had built this place from the ground up with the airplane in mind.

I walked around the old airplane, looking. Empty openings

127

gaped in the leading edges of the wings where machine guns had once protruded. I climbed up onto the port wing root and looked into the cockpit. The panes of the canopy were almost opaque with dust and age and I couldn't see much. With a certain amount of tugging and grunting, I slid the canopy back on its sliding tracks. The view inside was unpromising. The plane had been stripped of everything of value—instruments, radio equipment, gunsight—leaving it literally a shell of its former self. Even the control column was gone.

I clambered into the cockpit and eased myself down in the seat, feeling like a kid playing udd'n-udd'n in Daddy's car. My ass slid down till I couldn't see over the nose; the seat had been designed for a man sitting on a parachute pack. I groped around here and there in the cockpit, shone my light into various recesses, and found nothing.

The cockpit was a close, oppressive place, even with the canopy open. My mind ran a few movies of what it might be like in there with the plane on fire, or out of control. The guys who had flown these things into combat had definitely not lacked for testosterone.

For an hour or so I went over that airplane like a jealous wife checking her husband's suit for blond hairs. It was a tedious business. I hadn't realized how many hatches and panels and compartments the damn thing incorporated.

There was a big access panel on the port side of the fuselage, to the rear of the cockpit, that looked promising; it came open easily and revealed cavernous spaces inside. From the look of the interior, this had been the compartment housing the radio— at least various connecting wires and cables still dangled about—and, forward of that, the batteries. You could even see back into the tail section. The opening was big enough to get my head and shoulders in and I swung the flashlight in all directions, even above my head, but there was no suitcase or anything else, except a deserted bird's nest back by the tail-wheel doors.

Many of the hatches and panels were secured by strange-looking fasteners that had obviously required special tools. I didn't see how Jimmy Wilburn could have gotten them open—or why he would have bothered, under the circumstances—but I made do with various crude implements and I looked, logic being one thing and compulsion another.

It was damn cold up on the roof. The wind was out of the northwest again, raw and bitter, and not warmed at all by the distant November sun. The aluminum structure of the P-40 made a powerful heat sink; it was like handling dry ice, and I hadn't brought any gloves. I cursed, paused frequently to beat my hands together to restore a minimum of circulation, and kept at it.

And, of course, didn't find a damn thing.

The last place I looked—the big compartment in the port wing that had housed machine guns and ammunition—was as empty as all the others. I put the access panel back in place, secured it after a fashion with the fasteners I'd mangled, and slid back down to the roof, feeling a strong urge to kick the airplane. But of course if anybody needed kicking it was me.

I gathered up my tools, climbed back down to the ground, put the ladder back in the storeroom, and locked up. The P-40 grinned down at me as I pulled out onto Route 66.

The telephone went off just as I was sinking into a profound and blissful sleep. I fought my way up to the surface of consciousness and padded bare-assed into the living room and picked it up and grunted at it.

A high, grating, flat voice said, "Did you have fun up on the roof, Roper?"

I said, "Shaw?" and then I said some things about his mental condition, his appearance, and his putative relationship with his mother. He didn't react with any sort of overt anger. He only made the strange rattling sound that he used for a laugh.

"For God's sake, Roper, grow up," he said. "I checked that fucking old airplane out, rivet by rivet, back last week. What did you think you were doing? You looked like a damn fool up there."

I accused him of some other perversions. He ignored that too.

"Quit trying to be cute, Roper," he went on, still in that demented monotone. "You're not worth a shit at this. You're in as far over your head as Jimmy Wilburn was. Keep it up and you'll be as dead, too."

The line went dead before I could reply. Well, I didn't have anything very original to say, anyway.

The first thing I did when I woke up that afternoon was to call Wiley Harmon. It was close to the end of the working day and I wasn't sure I'd catch him at the station, but he was still at his desk.

When I tried to give him the serial number I'd gotten from Shaw's gun, he chopped me off between digits. "I don't wanta hear it," he said very decisively. "I can't help you. With anything."

I said, "What the hell, Wiley, was it something I said?"

"Look." His voice was unnaturally low, and he spoke faster than usual. "I shouldn't even be talking to you right now, okay? I ran your car tag number down and like I thought, it's a rental, and the name the guy gave is undoubtedly a phony. That's all you get. You already got too much."

The slug dropped. "You tried to do some checking and ran into a wall."

"Ran into a wall my ass, stepped into a minefield is more like it. Jesus, Roper, like I wasn't in enough shit around here, now I got Birdshit hauling me in on the carpet and prackly threatening me with the firing squad. I don't know who or what you're fucking around with this time, Roper, but from here on out you'll do the fucking without me."

So the word had come down from Somewhere Up Above: Lay off a certain bald guy with an attitude. Nobody asks questions about him, nobody even sees him. Interesting. I said, "I understand."

"I hope to fuck you do," Harmon said feelingly. "As long as this shit's going on—whatever it is, and *don't* try to tell me—I don't want you calling me here, I don't want any meetings at the Copper Bottom or anywhere else, I don't even wanta know who you are. Sorry, Roper, but I got certain ground rules. And I already warned you about this one."

He hung up without giving me a chance to reply. I stood looking at the humming phone for a couple of minutes, and then I called Rita. She wasn't home from work yet, but her answering machine was very gracious when I asked it to tell her to call me.

Rita's brother Tommy Ninekiller was an artist, supposed to be one of the best of the younger Indian painters. My qualifications to judge art are microscopic, but his work always looked damn good to me, lots of raw strong colors and powerful images and none of the half-assed clichés that have become the curse of modern Indian art.

"This is fun," he said. "Okay . . . how's this?"

I studied the charcoal sketch for a minute. "His chin's more, I don't know, sort of pointy and jutting."

"Right," he said, and went to work with an art gum eraser. "If at first, et cetera. Don't worry, we'll get this guy yet."

We were sitting in the living room of his apartment, not far from the Tulsa University campus, where he was some kind of teaching assistant. The walls of the small room were covered with oil paintings, watercolors, and line drawings, as well as a few carved masks. One of the masks incorporated a wooden hand, the index finger extended and fitted into one nostril. The attached wooden sign read AUTHENTIC CHEROKEE BOOGER MASK. Tommy was also something of a humorist, in his own highly idiosyncratic way.

He held up the sketch. "Better?"

"Yeah, but I think his ears are smaller than that. Now I think back, he's got really little ears. Of course maybe the bald head makes them look smaller—"

"Gotcha." He bent back over the big spiral sketchpad. He was a good-looking young guy, darker than Rita, with the classic long lean face and no-ass build of the mountain Cherokee. His long black hair was done up in a single braid that hung down between his shoulder blades. As best I recalled, he was around twenty-five.

"Here we are." He showed me the sketch again. "Starting to look like your man?"

Starting hell, the likeness was amazing. I didn't think I'd given Tommy all that much to go on, yet the drawing was Shaw, right down to the crooked lip and the weird eyes. I couldn't have done better with a camera.

"It's him," I said. "Damn, Tommy, that's good."

"I don't know what the big deal is," Tommy said, straight-faced. "All you white guys look alike anyway."

Rita wandered over from where she'd been studying a painting. "Good God," she said, looking over Tommy's shoulder. "Does he look that creepy in real life?"

"I'm not sure this guy has a real life," I told her. "And 'creepy' doesn't even begin to cover the subject. Can you use this?"

"All I can do is try. But it'll be a lot better than a description alone. And I think a black-and-white drawing will actually fax clearer than a photograph. You always lose the details in the gray areas of a photo."

"If you're going to stick that in a fax machine, I'd better spray on a little fixative," Tommy suggested. "That charcoal's going to smudge if you look at it with more than one eyeball at a time."

He tore the sketch carefully from the pad and went into the next room. Rita said, "I'll get my coat."

Left alone in the living room, I looked at the paintings. There was one by the door that caught my eye. Hell, it would have caught anybody's eye.

On a tablecloth-sized sheet of black velvet—I sneaked a feel to make sure, and that was what it was, all right—a skinny Indian on horseback posed against a garish, unnaturally-colored sunset. His arms were outstretched, his face turned skyward, in an attitude of prayer. He wore only a breechcloth and moccasins, a bone-hairpipe breastplate, and a large feather war bonnet. The classic roadside-stand wall-hanger, Indian kitsch division; every tourist trap west of the Arkansas line sells them by the truckload.

Tommy Ninekiller, however, had given this one the face of Elvis Presley.

In the car, a little while later, Rita said, "I still don't know what's going on, but I'm glad you had something for Tommy to do. He's been a little down lately."

"Having trouble selling his work?"

"Among other things. And last week in Tahlequah a white cop stopped him and gave him a hard time, for no apparent reason but that Tommy was an Indian walking down the sidewalk after dark and therefore obviously up to no good."

"I thought Tahlequah was one of the better towns, that way."

"It is. Plenty of towns around Oklahoma, there'd have been four or five of them and they'd have beaten him senseless and then arrested him for public intoxication and resisting arrest. Somehow I don't think that makes Tommy feel any better . . . and of course you know how he is about things like that. He'll brood for a month and then paint something so angry no gallery will let him show it."

She turned in her seat to face me. "Tommy's not the only one who's gone strange on me. What's happening to you, Tag? Have you looked at yourself lately?"

"Did I forget to shave?"

"Don't try to turn this into a joke, God damn it. You look as if you haven't slept in weeks."

"It's starting to feel that way," I admitted. "I've been, you know, busy."

"Oh, sure," she said sarcastically. "Taggart Roper, overworked businessman." She reached out suddenly and popped open the glove compartment. The little light bulb inside had burned out years ago, but the light from the overhead street lamps winked prettily off the nickel finish of the old .380 Colt. "What's this," Rita said, "your pager or your car phone?"

I'd put the gun there because I didn't want Rita to catch me carrying it, but sometimes you couldn't get a thing past her. I said weakly, "I've been picking up some extra money as a night watchman—"

"Of course. That's why you've been glancing in the mirror every couple of seconds." She slammed the glove compartment shut with vicious force. "I don't know what makes me angrier, Tag—that you've gotten mixed up in something crazy again, or that you take me for such an idiot."

"I'm sorry," I said, for want of a less half-assed response. "I ought to be free of the whole thing in a few more days."

"I hope so." She touched the sketch on her lap. "That's the only reason I'm helping you with this, you know. I keep telling myself you might be able to get this mysterious business over with sooner if I get you the information you want. Or you might learn something you can use to protect yourself. But, God, Tag, I'm worried about you."

I braked for a red light. Waiting for it to change, I glanced at my watch. "I've got quite a few hours before I have to be, um, anywhere. I don't suppose we could . . . ?"

Rita bowed her head and pressed a forefinger to the bridge of her nose. "Why not?" she murmured. "It's the only time I know where you are and what you're doing."

You and me both, I thought. But I didn't say it.

Privately, I thought Rita was exaggerating a bit. I mean, me, acting strangely?

But then that night, prowling around the deserted night club, I found myself looking for more than intruders. I was standing beside the storeroom door, staring intently at a wholly undistinguished metal ventilation-duct grill high up on the wall, when I realized what I was doing. And realized, too, that I'd been doing it for hours, ever since Loomis went home and left me alone: studying the most ordinary objects, the most mundane features of the building's layout, with obsessive fascination. What was underneath the stage, and how easy was it to get at? Was the lobby counter secured to the floor, or could it be moved? Wasn't that dividing wall a little thicker than it ought to be?

Worst of all, even after I knew what I was doing, I kept on doing it. The kitchen, the bar area, the storeroom—everywhere I went, there was something that looked as if it might just possibly conceal an aluminum suitcase full of large-denomination bills. . . . I even went in and had a look around the rest-rooms. Both of them.

I'd heard about people acting like this. It was even a stock bit in Western-fiction tradition: the prospector who gets crazy and then murderous over a vein of gold that he never finds, till at last he turns into a mumbling, wild-eyed recluse who shoots at strangers. But I'd never imagined it could happen to me.

When I looked in the mirror in the Ladies', my eyes stared back at me with the gleam of incipient paranoia. I looked like Bogie in *The Treasure of the Sierra Madre*. That was my second reaction; my first was, "I wonder if there's a space behind that mirror?"

Shaken, I went back to the bar and poured myself a shot of the first whisky that came handy. Not a good idea, I knew, when I hadn't had a decent night's sleep in several days; but I couldn't see how it would make me any more twisted than I already seemed to be.

It wasn't the money itself, I told myself, or even the things it would buy. I'd never been all that interested in wealth, or expensive possessions, or the rich-and-famous lifestyle—if I had been, I'd have been a world-record damn fool to become a professional writer. As long as I had a warm dry place to live, and enough to eat and drink—okay, maybe a little more than enough to drink—and a few simple essentials, I was easy to please.

What had me hypnotized, I decided, was the notion Hondo Loomis had put in my head the other night: the freedom that kind of money could give me. Even a small share of half a million dollars, say two hundred grand, would let me go to Mexico and live like the Duke of Earl for years, while I finally wrote a *real* novel, taking my time and doing it right on every page; and when I was done, I wouldn't have to take the first chickenshit offer that came along, either. I could hold out until

I found a first-class publisher, an editor who understood what I was doing and didn't jack around with my style—

That was getting too far ahead, though. Mostly my imagination kept returning to an image of a big white house on a hillside above Mazatlán or Puerto Vallarta or Guadalajara or somewhere, with a broad sunny balcony where I could sit and write, and a silent, moderately worshipful Aztec woman with melonlike knockers to keep my glass full of tequila and prepare incredible dishes each night for the table of El Señor Escritor. (Yes yes *yes;* probably sexist, arguably racist, indubitably infantile—look, we've already established that this wasn't a high point in the mental life of Taggart Roper.) Maybe I'd have a view of the beach, too. I wasn't altogether sure they had a beach in Guadalajara—or hills above Puerto Vallarta, for that matter—but the details could be worked out later.

Or I could stay where I was, living pretty much the way I was already living, and tell the publishing world to kiss my glutei maximi; or I might go back to school, get a Ph.D., and start writing straight history for the university presses. Or, with a proper cash cushion behind me, see if Rita cared to revise the terms of our relationship.

For a time, at least, I could do whatever the hell I wanted to. That, I reflected, was a prize worthy of a certain amount of craziness; that was a dream to fuse the brain cells of stronger men than me. I finished the whisky, set the glass on the bar for Doris to wash, and went outside to let the cold air clear my head.

A little after four o'clock, a car pulled up outside. Out front, this time, which was why I heard it; I was standing in the lobby, examining the old photograph of the original Flying Tiger Club, hoping for inspiration. Something about the picture was bothering me; I had the feeling that I was missing something, but my tired brain wasn't coming through.

When I heard the car stop in front of the building, I forgot about the picture and headed for the back. I already had the .380 in my belt and the flashlight in my hand, but I stopped by the dressing room and picked up the quick-print camera I'd bought the other day. Tommy Ninekiller's artwork was fine, but I still wanted a photo of Shaw if I could get it.

I don't know why I assumed this was Shaw. It wasn't. As soon as I came around the corner of the building, I saw that tonight's visitor hadn't come in any airport-rental compact. This was a glossy black Grand Am, clean and shiny as Freddie Manzano's limo. A low soft throbbing came from the idling engine. It even sounded new.

The kid standing in front of the Flying Tiger Club couldn't have been many years above legal driving age, though he was taller than me and nearly as wide across the shoulders. It was hard to judge his build exactly because he wore a thick padded jacket that bulked out his upper body like the Michelin man. He had short blond hair and he seemed to be wearing glasses. I couldn't see his face clearly; he was looking the other way.

He didn't hear me coming. The purr of the idling Grand Am, and the hissing of the spray can in his hand, made sure of that. He was obviously focussed on his work, anyway, halfway through the first word of his new graffito, putting the final vertical to the M in LOOMIS. At least I assumed he was writing LOOMIS, to be followed by some insulting or threatening message. For all I knew he could be planning to print LOOMING TERROR or something of the sort. He'd found a solution to the problem of the flat-black walls; he was using aluminum spray paint, which would show up pretty well if he laid it on heavily enough.

I came up behind him and took his picture.

For such a cheap-looking device, the camera had one hell of an impressive flash. The kid jumped a couple of feet straight up, the spray can swung through a brief wild arc—wiping out most

139

of his work—and I blinked back the yellow spots and was ready when he turned to face me.

The second flash went off right in his eyes. He yelled, "Hey!" and put his hands up to cover his face. While he was fighting temporary blindness, I stepped quickly around to the rear of the Grand Am and took a photo of the license plate. The little camera kept whining and spitting out color prints and I kept grabbing them and shoving them into my field-jacket pockets. The kid had gotten unstuck at last and now here he came, galloping across the parking lot toward me, yelling, "Hey!" again, along with a number of not very creative expletives.

I got a head-on shot, like the charging-rhino pictures in the outdoor magazines, and then he was on top of me, flailing away with both hands. He had the reach on me, and the energy of youth, but he didn't have a clue what he was doing; he couldn't even seem to decide whether he was trying to demolish the camera, the photos, or me. I stiff-armed him hard with my left hand and he stumbled back and stood there blinking for a moment. He had a round, soft-looking face and not much of a chin. The reflection off the glasses hid his eyes. I decided he was even younger than I'd thought.

He said, "Gimme that camera, you son of a bitch. Who the fuck are you, anyway? Gimme those fucking pictures."

I raised my right hand, letting the camera dangle from its little wrist strap, and pointed a finger at him. "Come at me like that again," I said, "and you get hurt. Trust me on this."

He hesitated, but then his feet started to move again. I said, *"Don't!"* but he was already coming, swinging a wild fist at my face and grabbing at the camera with his other hand. I moved my head back a couple of inches, watched his fist whiz by, and punched him in the stomach with my left.

The down jacket absorbed a little of the impact, but that was okay; he wouldn't have a bruise to show anybody. Most of the blow went all the way home. I could feel it clear to my shoulder.

The breath rushed out of him in a quick *whoof!* His face went white, his mouth made a little round pucker, and his hands went to his midriff. He went backpedaling across the lot, doubled over, until his ass came up against the fender of the Grand Am. He didn't speak or make any sound. That was hardly surprising.

I watched in silence while he stood there fighting for air. I thought for a while he was going to puke, but he didn't. Finally he straightened up, after a fashion, and glared at me. He tried to say something, but it came out a wordless croak.

"Get out of here," I told him, before he could get his speech machinery working again. "It's over."

He turned and began working his way along the side of the Grand Am, leaning on the car for support. Getting the door open was a bit of a job for him, but he managed. A few minutes later I was watching his taillights disappear in the general direction of West Tulsa. The sound of the Grand Am's engine drifted back to me. The kid was trying to do some macho things with the gear changes, but he kept blowing it.

I took the last print from the camera and walked back toward the club. At least one of the current crop of mysteries seemed to be on the way to a solution, but right now I was too tired to give a very big piece of a damn.

When Wiley Harmon answered his phone I said, "Wiley—" and he hung up on me.

I dialed again. This time I managed to say, "Wiley, listen—" before he slammed the receiver down.

The third time I didn't get to speak at all. He picked up the phone and said, "This is a fucking recording. You have not reached the party you have just reached. Get the fuck out of my life." And hung up.

The fourth time the phone rang for a long time. Finally there was that click again and Harmon said, "Roper. Roper, what the fuck are you doing to me?" His voice was soft and plaintive; I'd never heard him sound like that before. "I mean, what the fuck did I ever do to you, you're trying to ruin my life now?"

"Wiley—"

"I mean," he went on, "I told you not to call me. Didn't I?"

"You said not to call you at the station," I pointed out. "I'm calling you at home."

"You son of a bitch." He didn't get much energy into saying it. "You know damn well what I meant."

"Relax, Wiley. This isn't about . . . that matter you didn't want to discuss with me. This is an entirely different affair."

"You sure?" His voice was more suspicious than angry, now. "You swear?"

"I swear. I just need a license number run down. Nothing else."

There was a long silence in the receiver. Finally Harmon let out a big gusty sigh. "Okay, but it's gonna be double the usual price."

"Fair enough."

"Gimme, then."

I read the Grand Am's number off the color print in my hand. It was a nice clear picture, showing the car and even a corner of the club in the background. Most of last night's photos, in fact, had turned out much better than I'd expected.

"And you guarantee," Harmon said, "this doesn't hook up in any way to you-know-fucking-what? What's this, some angle on that business you were working on out at the Flying Tiger Club?"

"Yes. I think I've solved—"

"I don't wanta hear it," he said. "Whatever it is, I don't wanta hear anything to do with that place. You ask me, there's a curse on the fucker."

"I wouldn't be surprised."

"I'll get back to you on the license number in a few hours," he said. "I may not be able to get on it right away. Depends on what's going down when I get to the station. Assuming," he said, "that I still work there. Way things are going, I never know."

*   *   *

It was almost noon when he called back. I sat up on the couch, where I'd been grabbing a little low-quality sleep, and rubbed my eyes, while Harmon said, "The car's a black Grand Am, ninety-three model, right?"

I mumbled agreement. "Wake the fuck up, now," Harmon said, "because I'm not gonna give you this a second time. You ready?"

"Just a second." I fumbled through the mess on the coffee table and found a working Bic and a scrap of paper. "Go."

"The car is registered to a Fallon Lerner. Lives in Oakhurst." He gave me the street and the number. "No flags on the car or the owner," he added. "Both clean all the way, on the record. If that's any help."

"It might be." I didn't see how, offhand, but the various trades I'd followed had all taught me that you can't have too much information. "Thanks, Wiley."

"Yeah. Now that's got to be *it*, you understand? No more," he said. "Don't even think about me until you're clear of this shit you're wading in. If you ever are."

Fallon Lerner was in the phone book, but when I tried to call nobody answered. I tried again an hour later with the same lack of results, and then went through the same routine at two in the afternoon. Phone in a woman's name, nobody home on a week-day, teenage boy driving around at four in the morning in an expensive new car; I was starting to assemble a pretty clear picture of the situation.

If I was right, Fallon Lerner wouldn't be home for some time.

The kid might be coming home from school soon—assuming he'd bothered to go at all; I had a feeling this wasn't something anybody could count on. Reform school might be coming up on his horizon, I thought sourly, depending on what I found out today and what Hondo Loomis wanted to do.

I set the alarm for four-thirty and stretched out on the couch and tried to make up some of my sleep deficit. I didn't do very well, though; my usual sleep schedule had gotten so scrambled that all I could manage was a restless, on-and-off doze. Rita was right: if I didn't get it together pretty soon, I was going to get as weird as Shaw.

I was already awake when the alarm went off. Nobody answered Fallon Lerner's phone this time, either, but I decided the hell with it; by the time I drove over to Oakhurst, she ought to be at home or on her way. If she didn't show up, I wouldn't have wasted the drive; I could go by the Flying Tiger Club, which wasn't far away, and pick up the things I'd left in the dressing room.

Harry wanted to go along. I told him to forget it.

Oakhurst is a small community, almost wholly residential, bunched up between West Tulsa and the Creek County line, just north of where Route 66 hooks up with the Turner Turnpike. I didn't know my way around the streets—as far as I could recall I'd never been there before, except driving past on the highway—and it took a little exploring to find the address Wiley Harmon had given me.

The street was a short, semicircular loop, guarded by the arrows of one-way signs and several blue neighborhood-watch emblems. The houses were all fairly new-looking, all about the same size—medium Cleaver—and mostly faced with yellow or red brick. The basic Midwestern-suburban street; I'd seen its kind all over the heartland, during the summer I'd spent selling encyclopedias before the draft caught up with me.

The Lerner house was one of the yellow-brick subspecies. It sat almost at the apex of the semicircle, on a very slight rise of ground. The two-car garage was open, but the only car in sight, a blue Mercury, was sitting halfway up the driveway. I parked the Camaro on the street and got out and went up to the front door, trying to look respectable and, if at all possible, a little imposing. I had on my good suit for the occasion, but I had a feeling it wasn't enough.

The woman who answered the door, though, was in no position to judge the way I was dressed. Strictly speaking, she wasn't dressed at all; the long loose turquoise-blue robe did cover everything, but it had obviously been thrown on in haste, and it gaped in enough places to make it clear that she wasn't wearing much underneath.

She was a short, fair-skinned redhead, with a round childish face that reminded me strongly of the boy's. I put her somewhere in her late thirties; she might have hit forty by now, but if so she was doing better with it than I had. She could have been called pretty, or attractive, depending on your taste. She wore large fashion-frame glasses, through which she stared suspiciously at me.

"I'm not interested in buying anything," she said before I could speak. "Or taking out any more insurance, or answering questions for a survey, or being born again. If that son of a bitch Lerner sent you, you can talk to my lawyer, and if you're from the cable TV company, I already told them twice over the phone that I sent that check last week."

I started to reply, but she was still rolling. "If you're from charity, I give at work, and if you're a pervert, my son will be home any time, try the house across the street, she's a nymphomaniac anyway. Now I just got in from work, I've got a date for the evening and I'd like to clean up and get dressed. Good*bye*."

The door slammed.

This was getting to be one of those days. I knocked again. After a minute her face appeared in the little diamond-shaped window in the upper center of the door. Her lips framed what looked like "Fuck off!" Something with two syllables, anyway.

I took one of the color photos of Sonny Boy and held it up to the glass. It was easily the best of last night's batch; it showed his face, mouth open in surprise, and the paint can in his hand,

and even the sprayed letters on the wall of the club. I'd selected it in advance, expecting something like this.

Fallon Lerner's eyes went wide behind the glass. The doorknob rattled and turned and the door flew open. That wasn't the only thing open; she'd forgotten to hang on to the robe. I got a flash of white panties and a big pale breast before she remembered and yanked everything shut.

When she spoke, though, her voice wasn't so much panicky as resigned. "All right," she said, "what's Dennis done now?"

"This is your son, then?"

"Yes, God help me." She stepped back and gestured. "You'd better come inside."

I walked into the living room, while she did something with a fabric belt to hold the robe together. The place was nicely furnished—at least the furniture had cost somebody a good bit of change, though it wasn't much to my taste—but it was pretty messy, with newspapers lying around and various items of clothing draped over the furniture. The ashtray on the coffee table was almost full of lipstick-marked butts.

Fallon Lerner said, "Just a second," and disappeared into an adjoining room. I thought she was going to get dressed, but when she came back she still wore the turquoise-blue robe. She was holding a pack of cigarettes in one hand and a lighter in the other. "Christ," she said, sticking a skinny filter-tip in her mouth, "it's one damn thing after another with that kid . . . okay, what's the story?"

I showed her the rest of the pictures and gave her a quick summary of the background: the harassment of Hondo Loomis, the vandalism and the threats. Before I was done she was nodding. "Oh, yes," she said at the end. "Oh, yes, that sounds like Dennis. That's him all the way."

I said, "Do you know of any reason he might have had? Did he have some kind of grudge against Mr. Loomis?"

She waved her cigarette in a tired gesture. "You don't know

Dennis. He wouldn't need a grudge. He just—" She looked off to one side, as if remembering something. "Actually, I think he did have some sort of run-in with Loomis, a month or so ago. Dennis and some friends of his were parking their cars in front of the night club and generally hanging around, and Loomis told them to clear off or he'd call the cops. Or something like that. I didn't get the story very clear."

She put the cigarette between her big soft lips and puffed briefly. "But it's not like Dennis set out to get even or anything. His mind doesn't work like that. Maybe the business in October was what made him pick on Loomis's place, but chances are he'd have done it anyway. It's a handy target, and with that airplane on the roof, it's the kind of thing to get Dennis's attention."

"But why would he do it at all?"

"Because that's the way he is. I can't give you a better answer." She ground her cigarette out in the ashtray and began fiddling nervously with the pack. "Don't get me wrong, he's not crazy or anything like that. At least I keep telling myself...." She shook her head. "He just, pardon the expression, he gets a wild hair up his ass now and then. Like this girl he followed around, a couple of years ago, till her parents finally sent her off to boarding school. He'd have gotten arrested for that one, if he hadn't been a juvenile."

She looked at the pack, made a resigned face, and got out another smoke. "What the hell can I do?" she said. "His father dumped me ten years ago for a little bimbo from Kansas City. I got a hell of a settlement out of the son of a bitch, and he does send the money when he's supposed to, and buys Dennis anything I can't—he paid for that Grand Am—but it's not the same as having a man around to keep a boy in line."

She paused to set fire to her cigarette. "I work all day," she resumed, "running a real-estate operation that I put together from the ground up. Okay, I go out at night sometimes." She gave me a look that was part suggestive and part defensive.

"What the hell, sometimes I spend the night somewhere else. I've got a right to some kind of life of my own, for God's sake. I didn't hang it all up just because I let that son of a bitch get me pregnant."

"What's a mother to do?"

"Don't get sarcastic. You've got no idea what it's like." She put a hand on her hip and looked up at me. "The question is, what are *you* going to do? What's Loomis want? Of course I'll pay for any damage the kid did, within reason—"

"I don't think that's it. I'll have to talk with him, but I don't think Mr. Loomis cares all that much about the costs." I held up the little collection of photos. "I think what he wants is some sort of assurance that this is going to stop."

"It will," she said, too quickly. "I'll guarantee that."

"Oh?" I hoisted one eyebrow like Leonard Nimoy. "From what you've already told me, I wonder if you can guarantee anything where Dennis is concerned." I was into the part now, face stern, voice down in the lower registers, righteous as a Vice lieutenant shaking down a madam. "You admit you can't control him—"

"Hey, I do the best anyone could do." She blew smoke out the side of her mouth without taking her eyes off my face. Lauren Bacall did it better. "I'd like to see anybody do any better."

"The state of Oklahoma may take a shot at it. If I drive down to Sapulpa and show these pictures to the people in the sheriff's office."

She took a step backward. "Oh, you wouldn't do that." Her face and voice registered genuine shock; obviously the idea hadn't occurred to her. "He's only sixteen, just a child—"

When my father was sixteen he was working from dawn to dark in a Kansas wheat field. When my grandfather was sixteen he picked up a rifle and helped make dogmeat of the Dalton gang on the streets of Coffeyville. My bunch in Vietnam had a guide who was all of fifteen; he saved my life twice and he was worth half a dozen men in a fire fight. Fallon Lerner, however, wouldn't be interested in hearing any of this. Or much of anything else, I suspected, that didn't fit in with what she wanted to hear.

I said, "An isolated act of vandalism, that's one thing. An extended campaign of this sort—and according to you, he's got a history of compulsive antisocial behavior—might make a court wonder if Dennis doesn't have major problems. And then there's your own, well, lifestyle—"

"Oh, Jesus." She closed her eyes. "This is just the kind of thing that bastard Lerner would love to use against me."

She opened her eyes and looked at me again. Her expression had changed, not very subtly. "I'd do nearly anything," she said slowly, making sure I understood each word, "to keep this from going any farther. Anything." She shifted her body pointedly. It was quite a body, though it didn't need to put on any more pounds. "You understand what I'm saying?"

Well, it was a more attractive offer than anything I'd had from Shaw or Freddie Manzano. I was too strung out from fatigue and nerves, though, to be even normally tempted.

I put the pictures in my jacket pocket. "I'll have to talk with Mr. Loomis," I told her, speaking very formally. "Really, it's going to be his decision."

"Tell him to come see me," she said as I started out the door. "Tell him we can talk about this. Okay?"

I went out and got into the Camaro. When I drove away she was still standing in the doorway, staring after me, smoking her cigarette. I looked to see if the robe had come open again, but it hadn't.

Hondo Loomis said, "She really said it, huh? Offered to get down and do the dirty if it would get Dennis the Menace off? Man, that's what I call mother love."

I'd found nobody at the club, so I'd called Loomis at home from a convenience-store pay phone. Standing there in the deepening dusk, I realized suddenly that I'd used the same phone to call the sheriff's office about Wilburn's body.

I said, "What do you want me to do? Go down to Sapulpa in the morning and give the pictures and the story to Ellis or somebody? Or give you the photos and let you do it, or what?"

"Maybe I ought to go pay Mama a visit. Sounds like it might be good for a little fun and games." He chuckled. "Oh, hell, Roper, I don't know. I hate to turn anybody in to the law, especially a kid. Even if he is a punk like you say."

He paused. I waited.

"I tell you what," he said finally. "Go back and tell the woman I'll give her one chance to put a stop to this shit. If she can make him quit bothering me, we'll forget the whole thing. One more beef with the little bastard, though—I don't give a shit what it is, I don't even want him driving by and giving me the finger—and that's all. They better both hope nobody else comes around here playing games, too, because the next time I find any crap painted on my wall, or anything like that, I'm having him picked up by the fuzz. And we all know how painful that can be."

"I don't know if she'll deliver. She's decided she can't control him, and she seems to think that excuses her from trying."

"Yeah, well, give her a shot at it, what the hell. I don't need all that hassle anyway, courts and statements and lawyers. See if you can make her do something. Maybe she can send the little prick away to military school. That's what the world needs," he said, "another psycho in a uniform."

It was only about half a mile from the pay phone to the street where Fallon Lerner lived. The last of the light was gone, though, by the time I got there. My headlights picked up a car pulling out of the driveway and for a moment I thought I'd missed her. But then I remembered that her Mercury had been blue, and this car looked gray—

I said, "Son of a bitch," and started to gun the Camaro, to follow Shaw and corner him somewhere and have it out with him. But the only possible end to that would be a shootout—I had no doubt whatever that he had another gun by now—and I wasn't ready for that yet. Instead I parked the Camaro and went up the walk toward the Lerner house. The Mercury was still sitting in the driveway. I couldn't see the Grand Am anywhere.

I knocked several times, pretty hard, before the door finally opened. Fallon Lerner stared up at me with no sign of recognition. "What?" she said indistinctly, and then, "Oh. Oh, Jesus, it's you."

I couldn't speak at all for a moment. I should have been ready for it, but I wasn't.

Fallon Lerner had been roughed up. Not badly, from what I could see; she hadn't been given even a taste of the real treatment. The glasses were gone, and a reddened swelling beneath one eye would be an ugly bruise tomorrow morning. The robe was ripped at one shoulder and the skin beneath bore a few scratches and abrasions. She was holding one hand against her belly, as if it hurt. That was all, in terms of visible physical damage. Plenty of people do that much in the course of minor domestic quarrels, or even rough sex.

There are, however, other kinds of damage. The shock and fear in Fallon Lerner's eyes was a wicked thing to see; "terrorized" is an overused word, but that was what had happened here. This wasn't simple deer-in-the-headlights panic. Something had come into her world and shaken her loose from the whole fast-lane reality she'd constructed for herself. There hadn't been room in that reality for a man like Shaw, who was ready to do absolutely anything to her, including killing her, if he found it necessary. And wouldn't *care*. . . .

She said, "You son of a bitch." She recognized me now, all right. "You dirty fucking son of a bitch."

The robe fell open again. The white panties were still in place, undamaged as far as I could see. That fitted in with my picture of Shaw; I didn't think he had much interest in sex, even as a weapon.

"Get out of here." Her voice was starting to get louder and shriller; she was on the edge of screaming hysterics. "Get out of here, you son of a bitch—"

I was already moving. Any minute, somebody on the block might decide to call the police—if they hadn't already; I didn't know how much noise Shaw might have made, or caused her to make—and God knew what Fallon Lerner would tell them. And there I was with a gun in my belt, not to mention a cop in the next county suspecting me of homicide.

"You stay away from me," she called as I hurried down the walk. "All of you bastards, just stay away from me. Just leave me alone."

And now at last there was nothing to stop me from turning in and getting a long, long night's sleep. Nothing but the image of Fallon Lerner's frightened, battered face, which I saw every time I closed my eyes; and around midnight, after a sufficient dosage of Jim Beam, I managed to make her go away. . . .

I must have been even tireder than I'd realized. It was going on noon when I finally awakened; I'd slept clear around the clock. I hadn't done anything like that in years.

Fuzz-mouthed, disoriented, and more than a little embarrassed, I stumbled into the matchbox-sized bathroom and stood under the shower until I began to feel at least minimally alert. I should have felt wonderfully rested, and physically I suppose I did, but my brain was turning over slower than it had before I went to sleep. Maybe it had gotten stuck in the sleep mode;

maybe my consciousness had developed a taste for being shut down. Considering the things I'd been subjecting it to while awake, you could hardly blame it.

Harry was scratching and whining frantically at the door; poor bastard, he must be about ready to explode by now. I let him out, taking a blast of winter air on my exposed skin, and went back to get dressed.

While I was pulling on my jeans the phone rang.

I ran into the living room, holding up my unbuttoned jeans with one hand, and picked up the phone. Rita's voice said, "Tag?"

And right then, like that, it hit me, something I'd totally missed the previous evening. I said instantly and very fast, "I'll call you back. Stay by the phone, it's going to be a few minutes."

I set the phone down and dashed back to the bedroom and finished dressing, after a fashion; I didn't even bother with socks or a shirt, sticking my bare feet into my Wal-Mart running shoes and zipping the old field jacket over my naked chest. Speed was far more important right now than sartorial correctness. I ran out to the Camaro, stopped, ran back inside and got my keys and a handful of change, and went back out to the car, cursing steadily. Harry was just finishing up. I let him get in the car; it was quicker than dragging him back into the trailer.

It was only a short drive to the neighborhood supermarket, where they had a row of pay phones out front. At the time, though, it felt like a hundred miles; and every slow-moving moron in Oklahoma seemed to have chosen this time to pull out in front of me and sit blinking for a left turn. I pulled into the supermarket parking lot, stopped in the NO PARKING area next to the phones, and leaped out of the car, digging in my pockets for change. A couple of minutes later Rita's phone at the *Courier* office began to ring.

When she picked it up I said, "Sorry I had to hang up on you, but I didn't know what you were about to say. Listen, don't call me at the trailer until I tell you otherwise, okay?"

"What do I do when—" She stopped. The extensions at the *Courier* office were far from secure, and the staff eavesdropped on each other with the enthusiasm of a bunch of old women in a housing project. "When I have something for you," she finished.

"When you do, okay, call me, but don't actually tell me anything over the phone. What we'll do—" I thought for a moment. "All right, when you've got something, call me at the trailer and ask for Bob."

"Bob? Any particular reason for Bob?"

"No, no. Any name as long as it isn't mine. I'll tell you you've got the wrong number. Then I'll go somewhere and call you back from a public phone."

There was a silence while she thought this over. It wasn't a very long silence; Rita had been a working journalist for a number of years, been involved in a few fairly tricky investigations, and she knew the score.

"You think your phone is bugged," she said at last.

"I practically know it. For reasons I better not discuss on this line."

"Oh, Tag," she said softly. "What am I going to do with you?"

"Also," I said, "don't open your door to anybody you don't know."

"You're starting to scare me."

"That," I told her, "is precisely the idea."

After I finished talking with Rita, I went into the supermarket and bought a twelve-pack of Michelob. Coming back out, I stopped in amazement. A large black limo was parked behind the Camaro, and Freddie Manzano was looking out a rolled-down rear window, waving to me. "Hey, Roper," he called.

I let him wait while I stowed the beer in the Camaro's trunk.

"What are you doing around here, Freddie?" I asked when I finally went over to the limo. "Comparison shopping?"

"Happens I was on my way to see you. Then I saw what looked like your short parked here, I thought hey, save a little driving. Besides, I figured this way I wouldn't have to watch a certain person make a fucking fool of himself again." He glanced toward the driver's seat. "If you know what I mean."

"The hell." Danny's voice came back from the front seat, sounding slightly aggrieved. "So I like dogs. What's wrong with that?"

"I like pussy, too," Manzano told him. "I don't recall I ever went in for rolling around on the ground in broad daylight talking baby talk to one, fronta God and everybody." He looked back at me. "Of course then I find out you got the fucking dog with you, but at least he's locked in the car. Maybe I oughta lock Danny in too."

"Did you have something in mind?" I asked. "I don't imagine you drove all the way to Yuchi Park to pay me a social call."

"Right." His face grew serious. "Understand you been hanging out at the Flying Tiger Club lately."

"Loomis had some more trouble," I said, "the sort of thing I told you about that day at Drummer's. I spent a few nights at the place, trying to catch whoever was doing it."

"Did you?"

I nodded. "Local punk," I said, shrugging dismissively, making a no-big-deal face. "Teenage stuff."

"What I figured all along. So tell me," he said, "you been thinking about the story I told you? About Wilburn and the money, and all? You see anything, hear anything, might be an angle on that?"

"Not really." That wasn't going to satisfy him; I fed him a little meaningless truth. "I went up on the roof and checked that old airplane. Thought that might have been what Wilburn was doing, trying to get up on the roof, when he fell or got pushed. I didn't find anything."

He made a scornful face. "Jesus fucking Christ, Roper, I coulda told you not to waste your time. I had a couple guys check that thing out, back before I even came to talk to you."

Loomis was missing a bet, I thought; he should have been charging admission to his roof. It seemed to have become the most popular spot in eastern Oklahoma. He could sell postcards.

"Something else," Manzano said. "I been hearing word there's a new guy in town, weird son of a bitch, been asking a lot of questions. Kind of seems like he's after Wilburn's stash, too. Or he's on something to do with it." He was watching my face carefully now. "Would that maybe be the same dude you called me about, a while back? The one you ran into that night out back of the Flying Tiger Club?"

I nodded. Manzano said, "Seen him since?"

"A couple of times." I shrugged again. "He didn't make much sense. Pulled a gun on me and I had to take it away from him."

Freddie Manzano's eyes widened slightly. "No shit?" He sounded genuinely impressed.

I should have kept that to myself, I reflected. There were many excellent reasons why it might be good to have Freddie Manzano think of me as a harmless coward. Should have resisted the temptation to get a rise out of him, but it was too late now. I said, "He got careless."

"Sounds like it." Manzano grinned. "Nice going, Roper. Well, anyway, they say this asshole—what's his name?"

"Shaw, he says. If you believe that you'll believe anything."

"Right. They say he's been coming on like he's some kind of a Fed, you know? Maybe not a government cop, maybe more like a spy, a spook. You know anything about that?"

I shook my head. "I don't know anything at all about him. Except the sort of thing you've already heard from other people."

"Like that he's ugly as shit and maybe a nutcase too? Yeah, that's what everybody says. Okay, Roper." Manzano lifted two fingers in a salutelike gesture of farewell. "You find out anything about this dipshit, I'd be real grateful for a call, you know what I'm saying? Or if you pick up on anything at all, sounds like there might be federal heat working on this business. I like to know things like that."

The window slid silently back up. The interview was ended. I turned and walked back to the Camaro, where Harry was barking wildly, hoping his friend would come play with him.

Driving back home, I thought again about what had happened to Fallon Lerner, and why it had happened. Why the hell, I wondered, hadn't I simply gone ahead and beaten her up myself? Indirectly, I'd been responsible for the visit from Shaw.

I couldn't understand why it had taken me so long to see the obvious explanation: Shaw had been listening when I'd asked Wiley Harmon to check that license number, and had heard me telling Harmon that it had to do with that business at the Flying Tiger Club. I'd even said something about having it solved.

And he'd listened, later, when Harmon had called back with the name and address—or, for all I knew, he'd checked that out on his own; I didn't know what sources and contacts he might have—and that had been that. You couldn't even fault his logic; based on what he'd heard, it would have been entirely reasonable to conclude that Fallon Lerner held some sort of key to the location of the money, maybe even had the money itself.

I wondered what the poor woman had said or done to convince him otherwise. There was no doubt he'd been convinced; if he'd harbored any doubts in the matter, she would have been hurt much, much worse. Or he'd have taken her with him, someplace where he could work on her systematically. . . . I wasn't ass enough to think that my own timely arrival had scared him off; he'd have killed me and considered it a bonus.

Back at the trailer, I looked at my phone for a few minutes, wondering whether I ought to take it apart and look for circuitry that shouldn't be there. But I wouldn't have known a bug if I'd seen one, and I didn't even know if the device was in the phone itself or hooked up to a line somewhere. My knowledge of such matters was very close to zero, but I did know that the technology had developed to the point that it was almost impossible to locate a professional bug, except with special electronic equipment and a trained sweeper.

The hell with him. I'd just go on treating the phone as bugged, and watch what I talked about and who I talked to. It was about time I started doing that anyway.

The rest of Thursday afternoon passed quietly enough. Nobody came around and the phone didn't ring. A little before sundown I took Harry out for a burger and, coming back along the main road in the evening traffic, I thought a dark-colored car might be following me. But I couldn't be sure in the fading light, and by the time I got home it didn't seem to be back there any more. Getting crazier by the day, I thought as I pulled into my yard. Next come the UFO visits and the messages from God.

I tried to do a little writing in the evening, but I couldn't concentrate, and I'd left my main reference books and my notes back at the Flying Tiger Club anyway. I switched off the typewriter and went over and stretched out on the couch and watched television for a few hours. There wasn't much worth watching—the usual brain-dead situation comedies, the usual celebrity-fucker interviews, the entirely too damn usual crypto-fascist cop shows—but I found a pretty good British mystery program on PBS and watched that with real enjoyment, even though I never understood how the hell that French detective figured out who killed that guy. Diana Rigg came on at the end with a few words; I remembered how I used to have the hots for her when she was on "The Avengers."

And I even managed to get to sleep without an unreasonable amount of ethanol assistance; and the dreams weren't too frequent, or too bad. I'd had worse, anyway. . . .

Friday was another quiet day. The only visitor I had was the mail carrier, who brought me another couple of parcels. One contained the returned manuscript of *Staked Plain* from C. Eliot Fernwood at Piper Books, who had sent it back fourth class. The pages were creased and ragged and a coffee stain had soaked through the first few chapters. The other package held another copy of the same manuscript, this one bounced by Factor House, with a little printed form note stating that they no longer accepted "unagented" manuscripts. I put the lunched manuscript in the trash, stuck the other underneath my desk— where there was quite a growing pile by now—and sat for a little while contemplating the vision of that house in Mexico. Maybe instead of writing I'd use the place as headquarters to train a force of terrorists, and send them north to assassinate editors and dynamite publishing houses.

Besides the packages, the mail included a card from the veterinarian notifying me that Harry was due for his shots. That, at least, was something I could handle. Since I didn't seem to be doing anything else, I took him out to the Camaro and drove over to Broken Arrow to the vet's office. There I spent a hellish half-hour or so—Harry believing unshakably that the vet was a torturer whose mission in life was to maim innocent dogs, and that elderly ladies bring their female toy poodles to the vet's for purposes of fornication—before the receptionist handed me a fresh tag and certificate.

"If we had to do this more than once a year," I told Harry as we rolled away, "I'd turn you into a Kiowa stew."

Rather than go straight home, I headed north and got onto I-44, crossing the river and picking up Route 66 just beyond Oakhurst. I had it in mind to go by the Flying Tiger Club and pick up the stuff I'd left there. But when I got to the club there was nobody around, and I'd already given Hondo Loomis back his keys.

Well, now I had an excuse for not doing any work for another night or two. I pulled back onto 66 and drove back the way I'd just come. It was a bit longer this way, but I'd been making that drive a lot of times lately between my place and the Flying Tiger Club, and I was getting a little tired of looking at the same scenes.

I was heading back across the river when I noticed the dark-green car, and I was almost to my exit before I was sure it was on my tail. I played a few standard games—sudden deceleration, abrupt lane changes, the usual routine—but they wouldn't play. It was a "they," all right; I did get them close enough, just for a second, to see that there were two men in the car.

My exit was coming up fast, but I didn't want to turn down Memorial Drive now; I wanted to stay on the slab, where there was room for serious driving if it came to that. I kept going east on I-44 and then south down the Broken Arrow Expressway, picking up speed, snaking through traffic, not really trying to shake them but seeing how bad they wanted to stick with me. They stuck; whoever was driving that dark-green job had done this a few times before.

Well, all right; time to get better acquainted. We were almost out of Tulsa, going to be in Broken Arrow in a few minutes if we kept going. Up ahead was an off-ramp I remembered, the kind that makes a big circular loop and forces you to slow down almost to bicycle speed before you reach the intersecting street below the overpass. I slid over into the right lane, not trying to be slick now, wanting them to follow me; and sure enough, when I looked back, there they came, around and down the banked ramp after me. They were trying to stay back there, but there was no way to be anything but obvious on that narrow curl of concrete.

There didn't seem to be anything coming behind them. Good

enough. Just before I got to the bottom, I hit the brakes. The Camaro slid to a stop, blocking the ramp. I set the parking brake and got out, while the green car came to a stop twenty feet or so back up the ramp.

The afternoon sun was reflecting off the windshield and I couldn't see the people inside as I approached. I kept my hands in sight and walked with a casual ambling gait, trying for a zero-threat look, and trying not to think about what sort of ordnance might be pointed at me already.

I walked up beside the green car and bent down and peered in. The driver looked at me with a completely expressionless face. He was a middle-aged man with a long nose and a slightly receding hairline. Shades hid his eyes. I couldn't tell much about the man beside him except that he seemed short and stocky and a good deal younger than the driver, and he had a little dark goatee but no mustache.

I'd never seen either of them before.

I grinned at the driver. "Hey," I shouted through the rolled-up glass. "Do you know how to get to Oral Roberts University from here?"

The driver stared at me for a moment and then slowly shook his head. The other guy didn't respond at all.

There was a big truck coming off the expressway above us, starting down the ramp with its brakes hissing and its engine blaring under deceleration. I said, "Well, thanks anyway, y'all," and trotted back to the Camaro and got out of there. By the time I got back onto Memorial Drive, the green car was long gone.

And what the hell, I wondered, was *that* all about? Just when you think you've at least got all the players sorted out. . . .

The phone started ringing as I came in the door of the trailer. I grabbed it up and Rita's voice said, "Hello, is this Mr. Max Brand?"

"Sorry," I said, "you must have dialed the wrong number."

Harry was delighted that I was going out again, but the delight vanished as soon as I dragged him into the trailer and locked the door. The supermarket parking lot was crowded with late-afternoon shoppers when I arrived. I found a vacant parking slot, walked an unreasonable distance in the cold wind, and fed change to the same phone I'd used the day before. I didn't know whether Rita would still be at work at this hour, but when I dialed the *Courier*'s number and punched in her extension she picked up the phone right away.

"I've got the information you wanted," she said. "Do you want to come over tonight, or do you want me to come there?"

"I'll be there," I told her.

"Give me that ratty field jacket," Rita said. "Hm, it's wet. Has it started raining again?"

"No, I just ran into a tall dog." I looked around the apartment. "Where—"

"Oh, no. First we have a decent meal, with a little conversation about the sort of topics normal people discuss in the evenings. Then we'll get to the dirt." She hoisted my damp field jacket. "I'll just go hang this up . . . no arguments, God damn it. I've been working on this meal for two hours and you're going to sit down and eat it like a sane man—I know that's a reach for you, but do your best—and you'd better figure on telling me how good I look, too."

She did look good, now I stopped to notice. She had on a close-fitting black dress, short at the bottom and low at the top;

on a lot of women it would have looked maybe a little bimbo-esque, but Rita had the long legs and neck and straight back to keep everything classy. She wore little silver earrings, a single strand of silver beads, and a copper bracelet that almost matched her dark skin. She even had on hose and heels.

"Nice dress," I offered. "What there is of it."

"You mean I never wore it for you before? This is my Betty Boop dress. I'll be right back." She disappeared through the bedroom door, lugging the field jacket. The view from behind was if anything even better. She didn't look a bit like Betty Boop, though.

Dinner was something more or less Oriental. At least it looked Oriental to me, with long wiggly noodles and various little bits of crisp unidentifiable vegetable matter, and slivers of white meat that Rita said was turkey. "Speaking of which," she said, "you realize next Thursday's Thanksgiving?"

Christ, where had the year gone? To say nothing of my life . . . I said, "You want to get together and have dinner? Or are you going home for the holiday?"

She made a face. "It's not *our* holiday, is it? Those Indians up in New England fed a bunch of starving white people, and the *yonegs* showed their gratitude by starting a war and massacring every Indian they could get a shot at. Not exactly an occasion some of us care to commemorate."

I remembered one of Tommy's drawings: a mixed group of Indians and turkeys shoving a white man in Pilgrim dress into a huge oven. The title had been, "How We Should Have Done It."

"But," she went on, "the family usually gets together anyway. My father says we're celebrating having survived five hundred years of this crap. I don't know. At any rate, I'll be out of town."

So Harry and I would spend Thanksgiving alone again. That wasn't as bad as it might have been. As long as Shaw and these other people were running around the area, I was glad enough of anything that got Rita out of town. I wished I could get her to leave right now, but I knew better than to try.

"Here," she said, "try a little of this sauce. I'm telling you, Roper, sometimes I truly amaze myself. I say this humbly."

After dinner we went into the living room and sat down together on the couch. "All right," she said. "Here's what you wanted. At least I hope it's what you wanted, because it's all I could get. Or rather all my friend in Washington could get."

She reached down and took a yellow legal pad from the little shelf beneath the coffee table. "All this came over the phone, you understand. If you need to see any sort of detailed breakdown, dates and places and names and so on, I can ask, but you'll have to wait quite a bit longer. And I don't know how much we'll be able to get."

"All I want," I said, "is the basic story on Shaw, or whatever his real name is. I'm trying to find out who and what I'm up against, not write an investigative report."

"That's what I thought. So what I've got here is a lot of notes, and I'd better read them to you. If you try to read my scribbling and figure out my private abbreviations, you'll go blind and crazy."

"Fine with me." I leaned back on the couch and put my hands behind my head. "Incidentally, how good is this source of yours? How reliable, I mean?"

She tapped briefly on the legal pad with her fingertips, looking thoughtful. "It's hard to explain, if you never worked politics and public affairs. He's what they call an 'insider'—he knows people, and he knows which people know what, and how to get access to what they know."

I'd had quite a lot of dealings with people like that, in my cop-reporter days and afterward. Wiley Harmon and his colleagues referred to them as "snitches." I had to admit that words like "insider" and "confidential source" sounded classier.

"Specifically," she went on, "his field, his angle as you'd say, is the intelligence-and-security community. I know he worked for NSA for a long time when he was younger, and I think he did a hitch in military intelligence. Anyway, he has connections that an enemy agent would kill for. Literally, I imagine."

"Sounds like an interesting guy." I didn't ask her how she'd happened to know this mysterious character, or why he was willing to give her that kind of information. You never ask a journalist such questions, no matter how close you are.

"As to how reliable he is," she said, "you can take anything he says to the bank—because if he doesn't know something, he doesn't try to fake it. Or pass off guesses and rumor as fact."

"Good enough. Let's hear it."

She looked down at the legal pad on her lap. "To begin with, your man's name is Sanford Gilette—"

"Gilette? Like the razor blades?"

"Yes."

"Well, I'll be damned." I tried to fit the name to the face I knew. It was no go; I'd thought of the bastard as Shaw for too long. "Go on calling him Shaw, for now at least. I'm probably going to get confused enough as it is."

"All right. Well, Gilette—Shaw, sorry—was a CIA cowboy, starting back in Johnson's time. Seems to have done all right, rose slowly but steadily in the Company ranks, but then during the Nixon years he took to hanging out in very bad company."

"Liddy?"

"Among others. At least Shaw knew him. Don't get the wrong idea, Shaw wasn't mixed up in Watergate or anything like that—he never got that high in the order of things—but when the big scandal broke, he had a history of dubious associations, and that was enough to torpedo his career."

She flipped a long yellow page over and studied the next one. "Now it gets pretty murky. He stayed on in the CIA for a number of years, working domestic and Latin American affairs, getting passed over for promotions and generally ignored. Then—this was during Carter's administration—Shaw did something they couldn't ignore."

"Which was?"

"That's what nobody knows, or is willing to talk about. My source couldn't find out a thing, except that it had to do with something that happened in some Central American country—which wouldn't have gotten any public notice at the time; this was at the height of the Iran hostage affair—and, at the end, Shaw wasn't working for the CIA any longer."

"Son of a bitch."

"I have no doubt the term has often come up," she said drily, "in connection with Mr. Gilette a.k.a. Shaw. Anyway, he seems to have dropped out of sight, more or less, for several years. Vague rumors had him working as a mercenary in Latin America, or involved with international arms deals, or even in the drug trade, but my source wouldn't guarantee any of it."

"Hm. And now he turns up in the Tulsa area."

"No, no, wait. You're getting ahead of the story. This is all background, Tag, we're just about to hit the good stuff."

She leaned back and looked at me. "I don't know how much you know about how things work in Washington, Tag. I don't know that much myself, to tell the truth, I only lived there a little over a year and I never had any dealings with the intelligence-and-security crowd . . . but I'm sure you know that there's a way things are supposed to work, and then there's the way they actually work."

"Hit me again with that one."

"I mean," she said, "there are all these official bureaus and agencies, run by people who get their pictures in the paper when the President appoints them, and they all have things they're supposed to do, and they may even do them after a fashion. Or think they do.

"But then, back in the shadows, there are any number of

strange little groups that hardly anyone ever hears about. Some have vaguely-worded official titles—committees on this, councils on that—and some degree of legal status. Others don't even exist at all, on the record. At least not until they get caught at something particularly rancid, or become useful tools to embarrass an administration."

"Like Liddy and the Plumbers? Or that hustle Oliver North was running? Whatever happened to him, anyway? I lost track."

"I believe the Colonel's wrist is still tender where the judge slapped it. But yes, you've got the idea."

"And Shaw turned up in one of these outfits?"

"Evidently. Interesting that you bring up North and the Contra affair," Rita said, "because it appears that Shaw got involved in a similar operation. At least it had to do with clandestine funding and arming of rightist military groups in Latin America, though there was no known Middle East connection."

She consulted her notes again. "Now there have been, over the years, persistent rumors about the involvement of secret U.S. agencies in the drug trade—"

"Rumors my ass," I said. "I picked up a few things in Nam besides jungle rot. It was common knowledge that the Company was up to its hair roots in the opium racket over in Laos."

Rita was nodding. "Nowadays it's Latin America and cocaine, but the same stories keep surfacing. When there's no legal way to bankroll a secret operation or a private war, the logical alternative—logical to a certain type of mind—is to turn to illegal sources. And where large amounts of illegal cash are concerned, you can't beat drugs."

All the little red and green lights were starting to light up inside my head. It was like Christmas in there. "Damn," I said, "I'm beginning to see it."

"No doubt." She tossed her legal pad onto the coffee table.

"And I have a feeling we're getting into an area where you know more than I do."

"Maybe. Listen, this illegal operation with the Latino dope guys and the secret outfit that didn't exist. Would it have been going on about ten years ago?"

"It would have been in full swing." She was giving me her no-more-bullshit look. "And now are you going to tell me what's going on, for once? This time I think I've earned it."

"I still don't understand everything," I said, "but the main parts of the picture are starting to come into focus. Remember that night when I took you to the Flying Tiger Club? After I left here, I drove back by the place—"

I told her the whole story, or as much of it as seemed relevant; if I'd tried to fill in all the details I'd have been talking all night. I told her about the short frustrated life of Jimmy Wilburn, and the goings-on that had followed his demise, and the story Shaw had told me.

"I didn't really believe it," I said, "but now it all adds up. There was some kind of deal going down between the dopers and the spooks, and then at a critical moment a couple of local hardcases took the whole thing down and rode off into the sunset with half a mill that, I'd guess, didn't exist for official purposes either."

Rita was checking her notes again. "Around that time," she said, "Shaw was said to be somewhere in the Midwest, in charge of unspecified and highly secret operations." She frowned. "Why would a transaction like that take place in Oklahoma City, of all places? You'd think they'd do it in one of the bigger cities, or else somewhere along the border—"

"Nothing strange about that part. Dope and dope money are like domestic airline flights. They take strange and indirect routes, and you have to be on the inside to understand the reasons."

I got up and began to walk aimlessly around the room, too

excited to keep still. "That's it," I said. "Shaw was top soldier on the scene for this semi-mythical organization. He was supposed to see that everything went down as planned. Only it didn't." I swung around to face her. "They canned him, didn't they? He fucked up and they dumped him."

"That's what I've got here. No details, just that—yes, it was almost exactly ten years ago—Shaw suddenly found himself unemployed again." She looked at the last page of her notes. "The whole project came to an end a couple of years later, anyway, because of changes in the political picture in the countries involved. There is some question whether the organization still exists."

"How can you disband something that wasn't there to begin with?"

"Exactly. But Shaw definitely doesn't work for them, and hasn't worked for any government agency, official or otherwise, since his disgrace a decade ago. He's considered unstable."

"For once, some people in Washington know what they're talking about. What's he do, then? Run the ugly dealership in the District of Columbia?"

"Again, nothing's certain. Free-lances at this and that, it would seem."

"Christ, another odd-jobs man? Maybe we need a union."

I paced the floor some more. "That's why the son of a bitch is so hot to recover that money. It's not just the money itself, though I guess by now he needs it. It's some kind of vindication thing. They blamed him for losing it, now he's going to be the one to find it when nobody else could. I bet he's been waiting all this time for Jimmy Wilburn to get out," I said. "Had somebody paid off to let him know the day Wilburn walked. Only by the time he got to Oklahoma, Wilburn was already dead. No wonder he's acting so wild."

I shook my head. "And that's what he meant about Wilburn taking money from people he shouldn't have been fucking with.

Hell, I thought he was talking about some bunch of dopers—"

"For God's sake," Rita said suddenly. "You're after the money. You're trying to find that half-million yourself. I just realized it."

She came up off the couch in one fast smooth motion and stood facing me. "Tag Roper, have you completely lost your mind? I've known you to do some loony things, but this is worse than everything else put together." She put her hands on her hips. "You've got a nerve calling Shaw crazy. You're as bad as he is."

I held up my hands. "Wait, wait. Okay, I admit it, I've done some thinking about all that money. Hell, a man in my situation can't help thinking about what he could do with that kind of cash—"

"What he could do," Rita said furiously, "is wind up in the river with a lot of bullet holes in him. Or stuffed into a dumpster with his head smashed in. My *God*, Tag."

"But it doesn't matter," I went on. "Believe me, that money isn't anywhere on the premises of the Flying Tiger Club. Or if it is, it's somewhere you couldn't get at without demolishing the whole building. Hondo Loomis was right. There's just no way it's there. Somebody already found it, or it never was there to begin with. I mean, nobody really knows that Wilburn hid it there. That's only a theory."

She stepped closer. "Tag Roper, are you feeding me a line of bullshit?"

"Look," I said, "if I thought there was any serious chance of getting my hands on half a million bucks in unrecorded cash, I wouldn't have spent the last couple of days diddling around with the dog and sitting on my ass watching TV. Or behind that damn typewriter, either. I'd have been out looking for loot. In, no doubt, all the wrong places, but I'd have been giving it my best shot. And Shaw wouldn't have been enough to stop me, and—with all due etcetera—neither, my love, would you."

I gestured at the legal pad lying on the coffee table. "But as it is, the only reason I'm still looking into this business is that I've got people hanging around who think I know more than I do. Not just Shaw, you know, there's Freddie Manzano—who is ten times as scary as Shaw, believe me—and maybe others I don't even know about." I paused, remembering the two men in the green car. I hadn't mentioned them to Rita.

"Besides," I continued, "various people—including one good cop and one bad one—keep suggesting that *I* might have killed Jimmy Wilburn. I'm not really worried about that, but it's not the sort of thing you like to have floating around. I wouldn't mind a chance to clear that up."

Rita's eyes weren't quite so angry now, but the heat was still there. In ancient times, they say, the Cherokee women just about ran the tribe, and the men were afraid to cross them. I believe it.

"All right," she said. "All right, do whatever you have to do. Or think you have to do. Only be careful."

She laughed suddenly. "Listen to me," she said in a different voice. "Of course you're not going to be *careful.* If you were careful I wouldn't have you in my apartment right now. Careful people are boring, damn it. I'm not careful myself. If I were, I wouldn't let you within a mile of me."

She reached around behind her and did something with both hands. The black dress opened down the back and she let it slide forward and down over her arms and body, catching it before it touched the floor and stepping out of it with a dancer's grace.

"Usually," she said, "we spend the time after dinner drinking and screwing. Which one would you like to get started on first?"

I didn't answer for a second. "Slack-jawed" is, I believe, the term.

Rita wasn't wearing anything at all under that little black Betty Boop dress. The black sheer stockings ended high up on her thighs, in a scalloped line of fancy black lace, but there was no garter belt. In fact I couldn't see what was holding them up. I was certainly glad something was, though. From there on up was just Rita.

"What the hell," I said finally, "I'm trying to cut back on the drinking anyway. . . ."

As I've said, I could never write mystery stories of the classic or I Suppose You're Wondering Why I've Called You All Together school, because my mind isn't worth a damn at deductive analysis. And I think you either have it or you don't. Rita was a hell of an investigative journalist because she could look at a lot of seemingly unrelated facts and see patterns; I envied her that.

Or maybe I have the gift and don't know it. Maybe some part of my subconscious works on problems while the rest of me is sleeping, like those sleepwalkers you hear about who perform feats of balance they never could duplicate when awake. Because I'll go along for days, hopelessly baffled, and then suddenly see the answer as clearly as if I'd known it all my life.

A psychologist I met at a party told me that writers tend to have intuitive rather than analytical minds. That sounded so good that I told Rita about it.

I remember her reaction. "Bullshit," she said. "It's just that sometimes it takes you forever to see the obvious."

Saturday I went back to the Flying Tiger Club to collect my things. This time I called Hondo Loomis at home first, to make sure somebody would be there.

"Sure, man," he said. "Come by between two and four this afternoon. Going to be working on some arrangements."

Which was what was happening when I came through the bamboo curtain into the club's main room. Loomis was seated at the keyboard, the other musicians were standing around the stage, and Julie was holding some sheet music and looking uptight.

"No, no," Loomis was saying. "This is torch stuff, baby, you gotta reach down in the old gut and belt it out. Like Tracy Nelson."

"Who?" Julie said, in a tone that indicated she didn't care.

"All right, k.d. lang, then. You got to sing your face off on this kind of—oh, hey, Roper. Go on and get your stuff, man, if you want, don't worry about us. We're nearly done anyway."

There was something I needed to do first, and I went into the men's and did it. The face in the mirror didn't look crazy any more, but it didn't look smart either. Through the door I could hear the band cranking into "An Arm and a Leg." Julie definitely wasn't in the Tracy Nelson class. Of course almost nobody is, but she didn't even have the idea; she was strictly a front-of-the-mouth singer and it was never going to come from any deeper place. Too bad, I thought, she looked as if she'd be so much better than she was.

When I went back to the dressing room they were still on that song, going into the second chorus, and Julie still didn't have a clue and didn't seem particularly to care. As I closed the

177

dressing-room door behind me the music suddenly trailed to a ragged stop and Hondo Loomis said, "Wait, wait. This ain't working at all."

I gathered up my belongings: the camera and the remaining box of film, the flashlight, the notebook and the reference books—well, technically the books weren't my belongings, they were just sort of on indefinite loan from the Tulsa library—and various oddments and endments that I hadn't even remembered bringing over here. Everything went back into the nylon bag, and I started for the door. But I stopped to have a last look around, in case I'd missed anything, and while I was standing there the door opened and Julie came in.

She had on her pouty look, but she said, "Hi, Roper," and her voice was friendly enough. "You clearing out?" she asked.

I nodded. "There shouldn't be any more trouble," I told her. "If there is, Hondo has the photographs and the information. He can take it from there."

"He won't do shit," Julie said scornfully. "Old man doesn't know his ass from a hole in the ground about taking care of business. Pays the help too much, never docks that fool Doris when she misses work, lets every drunk in three counties run up a tab. Wonder he's not closer to broke than he is."

She went over and sat down on the bed. She was wearing a red one-piece outfit—I don't think it was a jumpsuit, but I don't know what you'd call it; it was damn tight anyway—and shiny cowboy boots. She crossed her legs and looked around. "This where you been staying? Damn, I wouldn't keep a dog in here."

"I've stayed longer in worse."

"Shit, so have I, so what? I worked worse jobs than this, too, showed my titties six nights a week, four shows a night, to a bunch of horny losers. That don't mean I'm ready to quit, say, 'Oh, this is good enough for a little nigger girl from north Tulsa, thank you Jesus,' just because I got it a little bit better." She curled a soft full lip. "That's the kind of thinking got old stupid

Doris where she is, working her fat white ass off for a worthless redneck and getting shit back for it."

"I thought Doris was divorced from Roy Dolan."

"Who the fuck's talking about him? I mean that damn brother of hers that she lives with. Takes most of her pay every week, uses her for a free babysitter and housekeeper while his wife lays around and bitches. I heard her telling Hondo about it. But that's what I meant," Julie said. "She thinks at least she's not getting beat up, so it's better than it was, so it's good enough. Man, I don't think that way."

She made a little gesture that somehow took in the entire Flying Tiger Club, everyone in or associated with it, and possibly the Greater Tulsa area as well. "I don't aim to spend my life singing in a nothing roadhouse outside a nowhere town, taking a bunch of shit off a crippled-up old has-been who can't do me any good."

"Material girl?"

"Hey, don't knock it. I like that Madonna, man, she knows what she wants and she goes for it." Julie leaned back slightly and looked me over in a speculative sort of way. "Is there really half a million dollars hid around this place?"

Hondo had been talking. I didn't see that it mattered; the story seemed to have become as popular a subject for discussion as the Kennedy assassination. I said, "Some people think so. I've got my doubts."

"Bullshit. You been looking for it. That's what you been doing here all night, every night. I knew that was a damn lie about you watching the place for Hondo. You think I don't know much, but I know a man who writes books don't hire out for a night watchman."

She got up off the bed and came toward me. "You found it?"

"No."

"Huh." She could have given Ellis and Shaw lessons in skeptical intonation. "Somebody had that kind of money could go a

179

long way from here. Wouldn't be no need to cut old Hondo in on it, either."

She stepped in close. She was wearing some sort of musky perfume. Quite a bit of it, in fact, or so it seemed in that small room. Suddenly she pushed herself against me, full length.

"I could be awful good to a man with that kind of money," she said in a very soft voice. She bent her knees and slid downward a little way and then back up, sort of slithering against me. "You got no idea how good I can be. You find that money, baby, give me a call and I'll show you."

She slipped past me and was gone. I stood there for a few minutes waiting for the shock to subside—all right, I was waiting for something else to subside too—and left the dressing room. On the stage, the musicians were putting their instruments away. Loomis was doing something to a speaker. Out of the corner of my eye I saw Julie vanishing into the ladies' room.

In the lobby John Wayne stared heroically at me from the cockpit of his movie-studio P-40. I nodded to him—we were old all-night buddies by now—and went out the front door. Standing beside the Camaro, tossing the nylon bag into the trunk, I looked back at the club and then out across Route 66, seeing a kind of movie in my mind. Somewhere over there along the Turnpike, one night ten years ago, Jimmy Wilburn had climbed out of a hot car that had suddenly gone very cold. I wondered how he'd let himself run out of gas. Trying to make Tulsa before gassing up, maybe; there weren't many service stops along that stretch of the Turnpike. Or maybe it had just been his lifelong ineptitude catching up with him again.

His first priority would have been to get off the Interstate, where at any moment a state trooper might stop to check out a man on foot. In my mind I saw a thin, shabbily-dressed figure, clutching an aluminum suitcase, scuttling down the embankment and across the brush-grown strip that separated the Turnpike from Route 66. He'd have climbed the fence, a clumsy business with one hand hanging on to that suitcase, and hustled up the slope to the old highway. For some reason, in my mental picture, it was raining. Maybe I was thinking of the night he'd returned, after I'd found him.

And he'd known he had to get more wheels, fast; but he hadn't dared carry the money with him to steal a car. He'd looked around and seen the boarded-up night club with the old airplane on the roof, and he'd gone running across the road, telling himself he only needed a place to leave the money for an hour or so, but knowing he'd better hide it well, just in case. . . .

Or maybe it hadn't been like that at all. I shook my head and looked up at the P-40 again. "You son of a bitch," I said to the grinning shark face, "I wish you could talk—"

I stopped, looked a second longer, and said, "Huh."

I went back inside, leaving the Camaro's trunk open, and stood for a minute or two in the lobby, checking something that had suddenly begun to bother me. Then I went back out and got the quick-print camera from the nylon bag and started taking pictures. The musicians were coming out of the club, carrying cased instruments and talking among themselves. They looked at me but none of them spoke to me. I noticed Julie getting into a car with the sax player.

The camera ran dry and I got out the other pack of film and used it up too, walking around the club and shooting at various angles. I wanted to get back up on the roof but it would have been a big pain in the ass dragging that ladder out again. Loomis's van had a heavy-duty rack on the roof and a little chromed metal ladder up the back, so I climbed on top of the van and used that as a vantage point to shoot the last couple of frames. By the time I was finished the musicians had all departed.

I clambered down off the van roof and walked back to the Camaro and put the camera back in the bag, stuffing the color prints into my field-jacket pocket. Another possibly useful idea occurred to me; I went back into the club and found Hondo Loomis in the office, examining some official-looking forms.

"Could I borrow this picture?" I said from the office doorway.

He looked up, startled. "What picture?"

"This old photograph on the wall here. The one of the original Flying Tiger Club. I'll have it back soon—"

"Hell, that don't matter, man. Take it, for God's sake." He gave me a quizzical look. "Don't suppose you want to tell me what you want with it."

"It's only an idea I had. Probably nothing to it."

"Yeah? Well, if it's anything that leads you to that half a mill, don't forget your Uncle Hondo."

He leaned back in his chair. "Had a visitor yesterday," he said, a little too casually. "Your friend Shaw came by my place."

"Jesus Christ!"

"No, I'd say more like a member of the opposing team. Man, that is one strange dude." Loomis shook his head. "And I've been around some weird mothers in my life, you know."

"What did he want?"

"Shit, what do you think? He wanted to know if I had any kind of an angle on that suitcase full of bread. Made a lot of noises about what would happen to my ass if I didn't come across. Waved a gun around some, showed me some bogus-looking ID. You probably know his act well enough to fill in the details."

"What finally happened?"

"Oh, I managed to persuade him I didn't know shit. Told him, look, as long as I been the owner of the joint, if I was gonna find anything like that I'd have found it by now, and if I had I wouldn't be in hock up to my nuts at the bank. Seemed like he bought the logic. Man," Loomis said, "I don't know what that cat's on but I'd like to be his supplier."

"You think he's on something?" The idea hadn't occurred to me, but it should have.

"I couldn't say what," Loomis said, "but he's on some kind of shit and has been for a while. Believe me, Roper, I know these things. By God, I ought to."

"Be careful, if he shows up again," I said. "He's ready to do anything to anybody to find that money."

"Well, I'm starting to feel the same way myself. I never been the greedy type, but I need some slack, man." He ran his hand over his face. "You remember Pat Sky? He might have been a little before your time. Kid from Georgia, one of those sixties folksingers, pretty good if you liked that stuff. He wrote this song," Loomis said, "said the blues was a ten-dollar woman and a five-dollar man."

Loomis looked depressed. I wished I could think of something encouraging to say. The trouble was, I knew something about one of his problems, maybe more than he realized I knew.

"I tell you, Roper," he said meditatively, "I wish sometimes I could just shut it all down and walk away."

"Close the club?"

"Not just the club, man, the whole scene. Playing one-hand riffs for a bunch of yuppie phonies and nostalgia freaks who can't get a life. Keeping up the big smile and the line of bullshit and holding back from killing the assholes who try to clap in time with the music or send up requests for something by Barry Manilow. Running around after a bimbo half my age, kissing her tight little ass and making the band carry the no-talent bitch when I should have kicked her off the stage long ago, all the time knowing damn well she's gonna take off as soon as she thinks she's got a better offer. . . . Oh, man, I'm so fucking *tired*."

He waved his hand. "Take the picture, Roper, take anything you want. Go find the money. Then we'll both take a long break."

Outside it had started to rain again.

*   *   *

"You want the Red Baron," Rita said that night. "Who else?"

We were sitting on the couch in her apartment, having an after-dinner glass of wine. We were both naked, having gotten off on a tangent again. It had been decided that I would spend another night at her place. I thought this would be safer for her. Not, of course, that I harbored any less noble motives.

"The Red Baron," I mused. "Christ, I'd forgotten about him. Is he still working for the *Courier?*"

"Would anybody else put up with him?" Rita said, reaching for the wine. "Sure, he's still around. I even know where he lives."

I might have forgotten the Red Baron, but he hadn't forgotten me. "Tag Roper, you old hack," he said fondly, wrapping my hand in long chemical-stained fingers. "How long's it been?" He looked past me. "Rita didn't come with you? When she phoned I got the impression she'd be coming along."

"She was going to. Then she got a phone call—" I hesitated. But hell, this was the Red Baron. "Her brother Tommy. You know him."

"Sure, sure." He put a hand to his face and scratched at his bristling, none-too-clean beard. "He in one of his moods?"

"Rita had the feeling he might be. She went over to make sure he was all right, maybe stay with him if necessary."

"Damn, that's too bad. I like Tommy. Rita too." He leered at me through thick rimless glasses. "So you two finally got back together. You lucky bastard, she never would go out with me. And she keeps looking better and better, and all you look is older and meaner."

The Red Baron, for his part, looked much as he had the last time I'd seen him, which had been many years ago. He still wore his hair down to his shoulders and his whiskers out to wherever they wanted to grow. His big round face was lined and rough-looking, but it had been that way as far back as I could recall, even though we were about the same age. He wore ratty jeans and a khaki work shirt. It was the sort of ensemble he'd always worn for all occasions, from north-Tulsa multiple shootings to interviews with presidential candidates.

He got away with looking like a refugee from a Grateful Dead concert, even at the notoriously staid and proper *Courier,* because he was one of the best photographers in the Midwest, maybe in the country. He'd received a number of awards and, rumor had it, come very close to a Pulitzer nomination on one occasion.

"You want a beer?" He headed back toward the kitchen, plowing and stumbling through accumulated layers of assorted living-room litter. "Never saw you when you didn't," he added over his shoulder.

While he was in the kitchen I had a look around the living room. There were a few items from the Red Baron's trade—a folded tripod leaning in a corner, a gadget bag hanging from a nail, a few photo magazines—but mostly the decor was about airplanes. The walls were almost covered with big photos and drawings and paintings of airplanes, mainly old ones. Shelves held rows of aviation books and tiny, incredibly detailed model airplanes. There was even an old wooden two-bladed propeller hanging above the door on pegs.

That was the other thing about the Red Baron. That was the reason for the nickname—although God knows he needed one; his real name was a virtually unpronounceable Czech handle that consisted almost entirely of consonants. The Red Baron was a stone aircraft freak.

Oddly, he didn't fly. Looking at the thick glasses, you could see why he hadn't become a pilot; but the Red Baron didn't even like to fly as a commercial passenger, though he'd happily spend the day hanging around an airport watching planes land and take off. Well, I once knew a firearms collector, owner of a gun collection that could have equipped a Third World army, who never ever dirtied his gleaming prizes by actually firing them. He claimed it would have detracted from their market value, but I had the impression he simply didn't like loud noises. For all I knew, the Red Baron was afraid of heights.

"Here you go," he said, coming back with a sixteen-ounce can in each hand. "Miller time. Rita said you needed to ask me something."

I took the framed photo from under my arm and held it out. He set the beers down on his coffee table, on top of a stack of aviation magazines, and took the photo and looked at it. "Oh, sure," he said instantly, "the old Flying Tiger Club. I've got a few pictures I took of the place, years ago. Thought about going out there when I heard it was open again, but I don't think I'd care for some of the assholes who hang out there. Now what's this?"

I gave him the little stack of color snapshots and asked my question. He didn't even have to look at all the shots. "Right you are," he said, flipping through the first two or three. "No question about it."

He went over to the bookshelf and came back carrying a big thin book, about the size of one of Dr. Seuss's larger-format works. There was a color painting of a P-38 on the cover. The title read *U.S. Army Air Force Fighters, 1940–45, Volume I.*

"Look here," he said, sitting down on the couch and opening the book. "I'll show you how we know—"

I pushed aside a couple of empty pizza boxes and sat down

beside him. He'd already found the pages he was looking for. "See for yourself." He held the old framed photograph of the Flying Tiger Club next to a full-page line drawing of a P-40. "What you've got in this old black-and-white—nice work, by the way, I'd like to know who did it—is a Curtiss P-40C. Or possibly a B, but I doubt it. Which would actually be the correct model for the Flying Tiger bit, since that was the one the original Tigers flew, though I wonder if the builder knew that."

He laid the photo aside and turned the page. "Now check this out." He spread the little color snapshots, fanning them out like a hand of cards, on a printed page opposite another aircraft drawing. "This is a P-40N. See how this air scoop under the engine is a lot bigger, looks like Dudley Doright's chin, right? And the upper part of the nose is different, too, because the old C model had a pair of fifty-caliber machine guns in the nose, while the later marks had all their armament in the wings."

"I went over that thing pretty carefully the other day," I said. "I don't think there was any place in the nose to mount guns."

"Exactly. And that's not all. Look back here, how the cockpit canopy extends farther back, like a greenhouse. Better visibility for the pilot."

He tapped the drawing. "This was the late-model P-40, and the original Flying Tigers were history before the first one ever came off the line. In fact the P-40 was obsolete by then, but Curtiss had the contacts and the contracts and they kept on cranking them out. Most of the N models were used for training, I think. Not many of them ever saw combat. This paint scheme is completely incorrect." He looked disapprovingly at the color photos. "I hate it when people don't bother to get things right. Like on 'Black Sheep Squadron' where they had at least three different models of F-4U Corsair—"

"Right." I picked up my beer with one hand and waggled the other at him. It was necessary to cut him off; the Red Baron's discourses had been known to go on for hours. "And you're absolutely certain about all this? Sorry, but this may be important."

He shook his head. "This airplane," he said, holding up the framed photo in one hand, "and this one," he held up the color prints in the other, "are not the same aircraft. No way in hell."

I called Hondo Loomis from a pay phone near the Red Baron's place. "The guy I bought the club from?" he said. "Sure, I've got his name and address around here somewhere. Just a minute."

I waited. The clouds had blown away and the sun was out. It was the most pleasant day we'd had in weeks, but it was still no time to break out the shorts and the fishnet shirt. I looked up and down the quiet Tulsa street, but there was no sign of Shaw's gray compact or the green car. Or any other vehicles that didn't obviously belong here, barring my scabby old Camaro.

"Okay, I got it," Loomis said. "Even got his phone number, too, if you want that."

"Sure," I said. "Let me have it."

Mr. George Bennett, now a resident of Sand Springs, was more than willing to talk about the history of his ownership of the Flying Tiger Club. I had the feeling he talked about it a good deal, even to people who didn't necessarily want to hear about it.

"Poured every nickel I had and every dime I could borrow into that place," he said, not for the first time. "I must have been out of my mind."

He stopped talking long enough to cough wetly. "Damn flu," he said. "Can't seem to get shut of it."

His voice was that of a man on the far side of middle age, if not actually old. He had a depressing, rather whiny way of speaking, like Don Knotts on Quaaludes. Somehow he didn't come across as a person who belonged in the entertainment business. Of course a man could change a lot in two or three years, especially if he'd run into financial reverses.

"Nearly pulled it off, too," Bennett went on. "I had that place looking so beautiful it still hurts to think about it. All but the outside, and I'd have had that restored to original too if the bastards at the bank hadn't cut me off at the knees."

I said, "About the—"

"Everybody told me," he went on, rolling over me. "Don't get in so deep, they said, get the place into the black before you do all that work on it. But I always believed anything worth doing was worth doing right."

I tried again. "Mr. Bennett, about the airplane—"

"Oh, yes. Yes, that was one of the things I had to do," he said. "The original plane had sat up there in the sun and the wind for around forty years, and it had had almost no maintenance— you couldn't even make out the markings, the paint was so faded, and rust had almost eaten through the landing-gear struts. Then the last few storms had done a lot of damage. Part of the tail was simply gone. I would have liked to have it restored, but I didn't know where I could find people who'd know how to do the work. So I replaced it."

"With the one that's up there now?"

"Yes, that's right. It wasn't easy finding another one, you know. Finally one turned up in a barn near Enid. Never did find out the whole story on that, you know. Fellow who owned the farm didn't know much, except that his father had picked it up for nearly nothing in a surplus auction back in 'forty-six."

Bennett laughed suddenly, a not very hilarious laugh. "Boy, we turned some heads when we trucked that thing down the road. We should have shot a video. I could have sold it to one of those TV shows."

I took a deep breath. If I'd been Catholic I might have crossed myself at this point.

"And the original aircraft," I said, "what became of it?"

190

"Sold it to a man with a salvage yard," Bennett said. "He hauled it off in one piece, didn't cut it up on the spot, so I guess he wanted it for whatever it was worth in its own right, not scrap metal."

"Do you know where the place is? The salvage yard?"

"Oh, sure. My son and I went down there to help them unload the plane. Great huge place, spread out over half of Okmulgee County. Got wrecked cars and trucks and motorcycles, even boats and trailers, lying around in the weeds. Got a few more airplanes, too, or did," Bennett said. "I remember we went up this dirt road through a stand of pine trees and there they were, and that's where we left that old Curtiss. Looked kind of peaceful lying there."

"But you wouldn't know if it's still there."

He made a snuffling sound, like Harry. "No, but it wouldn't be much of a trip to go look for yourself. I don't remember the man's name, but I can tell you how to get there. You go south on 75, like you're going to Okmulgee, and right after you cross the county line there's this turnoff—"

He gave me detailed directions, and then he went over them again from the beginning, though I hadn't asked for a repeat. "I bet it's still there," he said at the end. "Why would anybody buy it? You couldn't fly it, and I don't think there's any market for parts on something that old."

"Thanks," I said.

"Don't mention it. Are you working for that fellow Loomis?"

"In a way."

"Well, tell him I wish him better luck than I ever had. I'm telling you," Bennett said, "you ask me, there's just no money in that place."

By the time I was done with Bennett the shadows were growing long and the air was turning colder. I dialed Hondo Loomis's home number, and then the club. There was no answer either time. Then I tried to call Rita, but she wasn't in either. Still at Tommy's, no doubt. I started to call there, but changed my mind. Whatever was going on, they didn't need an interruption from me.

I went back to the parked Camaro and sat in it a few minutes, thinking. My first impulse had been to share what I'd learned with Hondo Loomis, who could surely use some encouraging news. Now I wondered if that was a good idea. Why raise hopes that might be false? Maybe I ought to check it out on my own first. I couldn't see that the job would call for two men.

On the other hand, it would be nice to have somebody along when I did go looking for that old P-40, if only for company and to stand watch while I poked around. And—though I didn't like to admit it to myself—I wasn't one hundred percent certain that I trusted myself alone with that kind of money. I didn't *think* I'd yield to the temptation to screw Hondo Loomis and take it all, but then I'd never been in a situation like that before. . . .

Well, it wasn't a matter that called for an immediate decision. I wasn't going to accomplish anything more today, anyway. It would be dark before I could get halfway to the Okmulgee County line, let alone go prowling around enormous country junkyards. No doubt I could find a place that big even at night; and, if there was a good moon out and the flashlight batteries held up, I was fairly sure I could locate something the size of an airplane, going by Bennett's detailed directions. But why? If the money was still there, it wouldn't go anywhere overnight, and if it wasn't, I was in no hurry to be disappointed.

So at last I started the Camaro and drove down the silent street toward the expressway, meaning merely to go home. But when I got to the interchange some stray impulse took hold of me, and I turned onto the westbound ramp instead. Minutes later I was crossing the river. Might as well make one last pass by the club, in case Loomis had gone there for some reason. It was my only chance, since I couldn't talk freely over my home phone and I didn't know where Loomis lived.

I knew it was highly unlikely that he'd be at the club, but after all, it wasn't far out of my way. Then I could go home by way of Sapulpa and Glenpool, which would give me a better chance to check for following vehicles. On the Tulsa expressways at this hour on a Sunday afternoon, I could have the Batmobile on my tail and never spot it.

I was just turning off the Turnpike onto Route 66 when I saw the column of smoke.

I wouldn't have thought you could have a fire that big in a concrete building.

Of course the concrete part wasn't what was on fire; the walls still stood, obscuring the worst of the blaze within. But the interior of the Flying Tiger Club was obviously well and truly alight. A great pillar of rolling black smoke rose into the darkening sky, where the evening breeze carried it eastward in an ugly plume to join the rest of the pollution over Tulsa. At the base of the column, long red spikes of flame flickered above the low parapet of the roof. Occasionally there would be a sudden eruption of sparks and taller flames as something collapsed or exploded inside the dying club.

The Flying Tiger Club was once again surrounded by official vehicles; this time, of course, the gathering was dominated by the big red beasts from the fire department, and the hustling figures of fire fighters in their bulky suits. There were plenty of others too, though, including a couple of cars from the sheriff's department. A uniformed deputy was out on Route 66, directing traffic around the congested scene.

I drove on down the road a little way and parked the Camaro on the shoulder. When I walked back to the club a deputy tried to turn me away, but I flashed an ancient press card at him and he let me pass.

Close up, the fire was even more impressive. Whatever was burning inside the club—ceiling materials, furniture, carpeting, I had no idea what might or might not be combustible—it was producing some serious flame and smoke. The painted sign on the front of the club was already blackened to unreadability by the heat that was coming through the concrete-block wall. It must have been like a furnace in there. The tarred roof would have ignited right away, I supposed; obviously it had collapsed by now, wholly or in part. The flames licked under and around the old P-40, which was so hot some parts seemed actually to be glowing.

The firemen were dousing the fire with water, in a perfunctory sort of way, but it was obvious from their manner—if it hadn't already been obvious from the sight of the fire itself—that this was a terminal blaze. The Flying Tiger Club was history. As was anything burnable that might have been on the premises; anything, for example, made of paper. . . .

I looked around and spotted Hondo Loomis's blue van, and then Loomis himself. He was standing off to one side of the action, talking with a man in a fire-department uniform. Deputy Ellis stood nearby, watching the fire. He was dressed in ordinary street clothes, so I guessed they'd called him at home. He didn't look happy about having to spend a Sunday afternoon this way. One way or another, this place certainly seemed to have played hell with his off-duty time.

I walked toward Loomis, who turned and saw me just as I was about to speak. "Roper," he said. His face looked very bad. "You believe this shit?"

"What happened?" I asked.

"We don't know yet." That was the fireman. He was an older guy, with a long serious face; for all I knew he might have been the chief. "Plenty of possibilities in a situation like this. We'll have to investigate after the fire's out." He gave me a thoughtful look. "What's your connection, if any?"

"He works for me sometimes," Loomis said, saving me the trouble of lying. "He's okay."

The long-faced man nodded, as if to say he'd keep that in mind, and walked slowly away, toward the nearest fire truck. Deputy Hill, I noticed, was looking my way now. I thought he might come over and ask questions, but he didn't.

"Were you okay for insurance?" I asked Loomis.

"Oh, Christ, yes. That's the trouble." He waved his hand at the blazing building. "You think I mind having the damn place burn down? It was getting to be such a pain in the ass, this is almost a relief... but I was carrying a shitload of insurance, and these guys are already suspicious."

"They think you torched it? Or had it done?"

"Hey, it's not that easy to set a building of this type on fire. The wiring was in top shape—I had it inspected when I bought the place—and the kitchen's all electric, no gas lines. So you can see why they might figure this little barbecue had some help."

I glanced around, but nobody seemed to be close enough to eavesdrop, not with the noise from the fire and the various rackets being made by the fire fighters and their equipment. I said, "It may have, you know."

"Don't you think I've thought of that? All the shit that's been going down, all the crazy people running around—"

"Except that anybody looking for the money would hardly

burn the club, not if there's any chance Wilburn did hide it there."

"Yeah? What if somebody did find it, already? And torched the club so everybody would think the bread got burned up, and quit looking?"

He had me; I hadn't thought of that, damn it.

I said, "Actually, I've got some new information—"

"Well, let's not talk about it here and now. Too many official ears flapping in the breeze, you dig? Anyway," Loomis said, "I don't feel like thinking about a lot of complicated shit at this point. I just want to stand here and say oh, fuck. Repeatedly."

Deputy Ellis did amble over to join us then. "Evening, Roper," he said. "Keep running into you here, don't I?"

"He's been doing some work for me," Loomis interjected.

"That right?" Ellis tilted his head toward the flaming building. "Don't suppose you know anything about this."

"No. I just got here. Didn't even know the place was on fire till I saw the smoke."

"Right. Well, if I need to ask you any questions, I know where to get hold of you, don't I? See you around."

He walked unhurriedly away, hands in the pockets of his short quilted jacket. The handle of some sort of revolver protruded from his back pocket. "Suspicious mother," Loomis murmured.

"He gets paid to be that way," I said.

Loomis snorted. "Oh, shit, Roper, don't start one of those support-your-loco-police routines, okay? I get so tired of that crap. So cops have a tough, dangerous job—when they're not riding around on their asses in patrol cars, which is most of the time, but never mind that—so fucking what? So do construction workers and salvage divers and oil-field hands, and you don't see them strutting around like their shit don't stink. Look at these firemen, for God's sake, work ten times as hard as cops and risk getting roasted alive, and they don't seem to think that gives them a license to act like assholes."

He was certainly in a state. Not, of course, that he could be blamed for that, under the circumstances. I shut up and left him alone; and after a little time, I walked back down to the Camaro and sat in it, watching the smoke still rising into the evening sky. Off to the west, beyond Route 66 and the Turnpike, the setting sun mirrored the colors of the flames that were eating the heart out of the Flying Tiger Club.

It was completely dark, and most of the official vehicles had left, when Hondo Loomis's blue van came rolling out of the lot and turned down 66. A minute later it pulled to a stop beside me and the window came down. "Roper?" Loomis called. "You want to come over to my place? You said you had something to tell me."

I waved acknowledgment and waited while he U-turned the van. I did the same with the Camaro and followed his taillights back up Route 66 toward the interchange. The flames appeared to have died away inside the burned-out shell of the Flying Tiger Club, and it was too dark to see the smoke. There were still quite a few lights around the building, though, as various people continued to do whatever they did when a building burned.

Loomis, it turned out, lived in a small frame house in West Tulsa. As we went in he said, "Lifetime of living in apartments, man, my first time to have my own house. Well, it's not my own, I'm renting till I can find something to buy—" He grimaced. "The hell am I talking about? I'm not gonna be buying a damn thing. Soon as they settle the claim and give me that insurance check, I'm severely outta here."

The living room was almost as messy as the Red Baron's. Or mine. "Sorry," Loomis said, "I'm not usually this much of a slob. Only I been kind of down lately. Hard to make yourself care about the details when you're bummed out. I imagine you know how that is."

"Don't I?"

"Yeah . . . Julie split," he said, with no particular emphasis or expression in his voice. "Made the gig last night, then after the second set she sort of disappeared. Never came back for the last set, never came back at all. I got home, she was gone and so was all her stuff."

"Sorry."

"Don't be. I wouldn't be, if I had any brains. You ever hear B. B. King sing 'A Woman Makes You Stupid'? Only I don't think they do. I think they just work with what men already got."

He made a half-strangled attempt to laugh. "Help you realize your full stupidity potential, give meaningful development to your natural talents, huh? Never did find out how she got here from the club, or how she left here. Got some horny fool to drive her, I bet. She's good at that."

He looked around. "I'd offer you a drink, only she didn't leave with just her own stuff. Quite a few odds and ends missing around here, it seems. One of the things she liberated was most of the booze supply. There's some beer in the box, is all. Want one?"

"I better not. My stomach's pretty near empty."

"Come to think of it, so's mine. Let's see what we've got."

In the kitchen, he made a couple of big sandwiches from cheese and rye bread and unidentifiable but spicy cold cuts. He worked one-handed with great speed and precision. "Worst thing," he said, slicing cheese, "the bitch took some records I really cared about. Like my original seventy-eight of Johnny Hodges blowing 'Passion Flower,' the hottest bedroom record ever made. You could seduce a marble statue with that one on. And she doesn't even know what it's worth."

He led the way back into the living room, sandwich in his

hand, beer tucked between elbow and ribcage. "So," he said, "what's this big news you wanted to spring on me? Hope to hell it's the good kind."

I said cautiously, "It may be. I don't know yet."

I told him about the switched airplanes. Before I was half through, his face had begun to change. By the time I got done, he was damn near glowing.

"Hot shit," he said in a reverent whisper. *"Hot* shit. You found it. You fucking found it."

"I haven't found a damn thing yet. All we've got is a fresh possibility, and it may check out to zero. We don't even know for sure that it's all that fresh. Somebody could have found out about the switched planes by now—"

"Yeah, yeah, yeah. And tonight the little guys from Uranus could land and turn us all into Quarter Pounders and then we wouldn't need the money. Quit being such a bringdown, will you?" Loomis slapped his thigh. "Hot shit . . . little unwarranted optimism never hurt anybody, man. Does wonders for your circulation, you ought to try it."

He picked up his beer and drained half of it. "Wish we had something serious to drink right now," he said. "Go get you one of those brews, man, we gotta drink some kind of a toast—"

There was a knock at the front door. We looked at each other. I thought suddenly of the .380 Colt, its clip filled with lethal hollow-point loads, its action freshly cleaned and lubricated only a few nights ago. It was outside in the Camaro, tucked safely away in the glove compartment, and it might as well have been in a bank vault in Novosibirsk, Siberia, for all the good it was to me right now.

Hondo Loomis, however, had reacted with an entirely different assumption. "Julie?" he called as he crossed the room and twisted the doorknob. "Is that you, Julie?"

Without waiting for an answer, and before I could object or warn him, he pulled the door open. "Julie?" he said again.

"No, asshole," Freddie Manzano said in his face. "And it ain't Betty Lou or fucking Peggy Sue, either." He leaned slightly to one side and looked around Loomis. "Hello, Roper. Thought you might be here."

He walked forward, not waiting for an invitation. Behind him rose the alarming bulk of Danny. The bodyguard's right hand was out of sight inside his suit jacket. I didn't think he was adjusting his undershirt.

Loomis stepped back—it was that or get bulldozed—and Manzano and his gorilla came into the living room. Danny closed the door with his heel, not taking his eyes off me, ignoring Loomis. I'd made a mistake, all right, telling Manzano about taking Shaw's gun away from him.

But it was Freddie Manzano, not Danny, who came striding swiftly across the room and grabbed the collar of my unzipped field jacket. I must have had fifty pounds on him at least, but the surprise was enough to put me off balance, and I fell back hard against the wall, while he pushed his face up toward mine.

"All right, you smart bastard," he said, "what the fuck are you trying to pull?"

The next few minutes were a little on the tense side.

Usually my reaction to being grabbed and shoved is to knock the grabber/shover on his ass, or at least make a damn good try at it. That didn't seem a good idea under the present circumstances, particularly since Danny had his gun out now.

I said, "Freddie, what the fuck are you talking about?"

He was still hanging on to my coat, and now he gave me a little shake. "Don't play stupid, you lying sack of shit. You think I don't know what's going on?"

This was going nowhere, if not to hell. "Freddie," I said, keeping my voice carefully calm, "we can yell at each other all night, or you can have Danny work me over or kill me, if that's what you came here for. Or you can tell me what's eating you and maybe I can give you some answers. Call it."

His face didn't get any less angry, but he did appear to be thinking. After a second he let go my jacket and stepped back, breathing hard. "You found Wilburn's stash." He was still staring at my face, but he made a quick gesture in Loomis's direction. "You two shitheads found that half a mill, somewhere, some way. So you torched the club, to make everybody think the money got burned up. Figured you could cut me out, didn't you?"

Hondo Loomis started to speak, but Manzano said, "Shut the fuck up, piano man. I'll get to you later." He looked over his shoulder at Loomis. "I don't get some answers around here, maybe I'll let Danny do some work on that hand of yours."

He turned back to me. "And after your buddy runs out of fingers, you got a full set of ten for Danny to play with. You any good at writing with your toes?"

"Freddie," I said, trying to keep my voice steady, "Freddie, you've got this all wrong. In the first place—"

It took a little talking to persuade Freddie Manzano that we hadn't deliberately set fire to the Flying Tiger Club, and a little more to get him to believe that we hadn't been planning to shut him out if we found the money. He was definitely skeptical when I told him we still didn't have it. "Don't bullshit me," he kept saying, and other utterances to that effect.

And all the time Danny stood there, his big lumpy face totally without expression, nothing moving but the opaque eyes that swung restlessly from side to side, watching Loomis and me, while he waited for orders from the boss. The gun in his hand wasn't pointed at either of us; he held it up in a sort of Ready on the Right position, muzzle toward the ceiling, but I had no doubt that would change in a very tiny fraction of a second if anyone made a move, or at a word from Freddie Manzano. The gun was one of those blocky high-tech automatics that everybody had started carrying lately. I couldn't see the hole in the barrel well enough to estimate the caliber. I had absolutely no desire to have the angle altered.

Loomis didn't take much part in the debate at first. He stood beside the couch, watching and listening, his face registering nothing. But finally he spoke. "For Christ sake," he said.

He didn't raise his voice at all, even though Manzano and I were shouting at each other; but he was Hondo Loomis, and that voice cut through our yelling like a cathedral organ drowning out a couple of squabbling mice. We both shut up and looked at him.

"This is all a bunch of unnecessary bullshit," he went on. "We can settle the whole thing right now. Jesus, Roper, tell this guy about the airplanes."

And he was right, of course. It was the one infallible way to show Freddie Manzano that we hadn't been trying to screw him; and we were going to have to deal with him anyway, if the money did prove to be hidden in the junkyard P-40. I don't know why I was so reluctant to tell Manzano what I'd learned. Maybe, deep down, I *was* harboring fantasies of finding some way to cut him out.

I told him the story, then, about the switch and how I'd found out about it. The rage left his face at once, to be replaced by a mixture of fascination and fervor. Curiously, I didn't get any impression of overpowering greed; he seemed excited, almost childishly so, by the process of search and discovery in itself, as if this were some sort of game. I remembered Wiley Harmon's remarks about Manzano's obsession with treasure hunts. Maybe, if we did find the money, the thrill of success would be enough for him; maybe he wouldn't feel the need to kill the two of us and keep the whole pile for himself. Maybe.

"Son of a bitch," Manzano said finally. "So that's the answer. The plane we all been looking at is the wrong fucking plane. What a kick in the ass." He was grinning now, moving around the room in little aimless excited steps. "You guys were right. The money wasn't at the club after all."

"We don't know that yet," I pointed out. I didn't want Manzano building up any false hopes; disappointment might make him really nasty. "It's just a possibility."

"Yeah, but a hell of a good one. I been thinking about that all along," Manzano said, "trying to put myself in Jimmy Wilburn's place. He's out there on 66 in the dark, hanging on to a suitcase full of money, and he's gotta stash it fast, so he can go into the nearest town—"

"Actually, Oakhurst would have been the nearest town," I said. "I think he went down to Sapulpa because he knew it better."

Manzano waved an impatient hand. "Whatever, who cares? Point is, he couldn't fuck around, he needed to move quick for once in his life. And he wasn't planning on stashing the loot for ten years, you know what I'm saying? He just wanted a place to hide it for however long it took him to go steal another short. So I never could see him busting into that boarded-up building, or digging a hole and burying the take, or anything like that. Not with that fucking old airplane up there on the roof, big as shit. Easy for him to find when he came back for it, too."

He nodded, agreeing with himself. "All along, I knew it had to be the airplane. Nothing else made any sense. Only nobody could find anything in it," he said, "and now you tell me it's because we were looking in the wrong damn plane. How about that?"

Loomis cleared his throat. When Manzano looked at him, he tilted his head in Danny's direction and raised an eyebrow. "Oh, yeah, sure," Manzano said. "Danny, put the rod up. It's gonna be okay." He grinned at the big man. "You're gonna get to come along on a little late-night operation, Danny. I'll see to it you get a piece of change out of this, buy yourself a suit that fits."

"You want to go look for it right now?" I hadn't expected that.

"Shit, yes. Why not? You got a hot date lined up with that Indian broad, or something?"

"It's cold out there, boss," Danny objected mildly. "Dark, too. We could see better in the daylight—"

"Yeah, and somebody could see us, too. Some redneck, owns the junkyard, liable to show up with a shotgun and a couple of Dobermans. Or that crazy guy, what's his name, Shaw. Fuck that," Manzano said decisively. "I didn't get where I am today, dicking around. You got something you want, you go after it, right then. Let's do it."

"I've got a flashlight in the car," I volunteered. The flash was in the trunk, but it might be possible to fake these two out long enough to get that .380 out of the glove compartment. "You want me to get it?"

Manzano shook his head. "I got a big battery light I keep in the trunk, case of a flat or something at night."

"Well, a second one might come in handy—"

"Forget it," he said, a little irritably. So much for that idea; I hadn't had much hope for it anyway. "Let's go."

Outside, there was no sign of the black limo. A dark-colored BMW sat in the driveway behind Loomis's van. Freddie Manzano must have noticed my surprise. "Sometimes the limo's too conspicuous," he said, "so we use this little Kraut roller skate. Come on, everybody in. I want my hands on that half-mill before the sun comes up tomorrow."

The drive south took under half an hour. Traffic was light on Highway 75 and Danny kept speeding up, until Manzano told him to back off. "Last thing we want right now is to get stopped by some cop. Stay under the double nickel," he told Danny. "It ain't that far."

He turned to look at me. We were sitting in the back seat, Manzano on the left, me on the right. Loomis sat up front beside Danny. He hadn't spoken since leaving his place.

"You do know where this place is, Roper?" Manzano asked. "I mean, you can find it?"

"If the directions are any good."

"Huh." Manzano made a scornful sound. "These shitkickers around here can't give directions, you oughta know that." He was visibly edgy now, shifting frequently in his seat, tapping his fingers restlessly against various parts of the car's interior. "Hey," he said to Danny, "can't you go any faster?"

"But you said—" Danny made a put-upon sigh and shut up. I couldn't tell if he actually did anything to alter the car's speed.

The turnoff was perhaps a mile south of the Okmulgee County line, a narrow but paved county road running off to the left, crossing a stretch of open farmland and then diving into a patch of woods. A few miles along, following Bennett's directions, we turned onto a reasonably good gravel road and headed approximately south. The trees were close to the roadside now, creating a tunnel effect. A deer jumped out and sprinted across the road in the headlights, causing Danny to hit the brakes and Manzano to curse. "Jesus Christ," Manzano grumbled, "you sure this is the right way? Looks more like fucking Africa or something."

"Something coming up, boss," Danny said, slowing the car. "On the right."

Bennett had been right; you couldn't miss the place, even at night. Beyond a high barbed-wire fence, the shapes of automobile bodies showed clearly in the moonlight, ranks and troops of them, stretching off into the darkness. "Drive ahead slow," Manzano ordered. "Let's case the scene a little, you know what I mean?"

The BMW rolled on at little more than walking speed, its tires crunching softly in the loose gravel. More cars appeared beyond the fence, and a few assorted trucks. Most seemed to be missing large components—doors, hoods, fenders—but it was hard to see much detail. Freddie Manzano said, "Roll your window down, Roper . . . damn, I can't see shit, can you?"

"Look there," Danny said. "That oughta be the main gate."

There was a big wide break in the fence, and a dirt driveway. Danny turned the BMW into the drive, just enough to let the headlights illuminate the scene. A solid-looking gate barred the entryway. It appeared to be made of welded-together lengths of heavy iron pipe. Beyond the gate was a small frame building, painted white. A big sign on its roof read HENSLEY'S SALVAGE YARD. Another legend, painted directly on the wall of the structure, announced that WE BUY—SELL—TRADE. The gate bore a sign of its own: CLOSED.

"Shut off the lights," Manzano said. "Everybody be quiet."

Danny hit the switch and the headlights died. The little white building was dark, no light showing in the windows. The only sound was the soft purr of the BMW's idling engine. "The motor too," Manzano said. "I wanta listen."

We sat and listened for a few minutes. There was nothing but an owl hooting, off in the woods on the other side of the road. "Okay," Manzano said finally. "Nobody here and no dogs. I was worrying about dogs. They got some really big mean-ass mothers in some of these country junkyards, you know what I'm saying?"

"I don't hear no dogs," Danny said.

"That's what I said," Manzano told him, "and I know it's a big disappointment to you, but the rest of us would just as soon not get our nuts bit off, you know? Let's go. This ain't the place we're looking for."

According to Bennett, the entrance we wanted was a secondary gate, about half a mile down the road from the main gateway. Danny backed the BMW out of the drive and drove on. Now there were more trucks than cars beyond the fence, not just pickups but full-sized trucks and a couple of school buses.

Most of them were resting on blocks or the ground, their wheels and tires gone.

"There," Loomis said, speaking at last.

The gate was a simple farm-type gate of metal beams. A sign warned NO TRESPASSING. The headlight beams showed a chain and a big padlock holding the gate shut.

Danny turned off the engine and the lights and got out and went around the car. The trunk opened and Danny reappeared, walking toward the gate. There was the distinctive sound of a set of compound bolt cutters in action, ending in a sharp snap. The trees flanking the gate blocked most of the moonlight, but Danny's dark bulk was visible as he walked the gate open. A moment later he came back past the car. Something thumped in the trunk, the trunk lid closed, and Danny got back in the car. The whole operation had taken perhaps two minutes, no more.

Once the BMW had cleared the gate, Manzano said, "Close it, Danny. Might be somebody, come down the road, notice it open." And, when Danny had come back from closing the gate, "Use just the parking lights till we get out of sight of the road. I think it's light enough, if you go slow."

Danny drove the BMW cautiously along a one-lane dirt track, across a broad field covered with wrecked vehicles. The moon was high now, and three-quarters full, its cold white light glinting off shattered windshields and twisted chrome. There was no difficulty in staying on course; the rows of dead cars and trucks formed almost a solid wall on either side of the dirt lane. "Spooky fucking place," Manzano muttered. "Like some kind of a graveyard."

Suddenly the lines of wrecks ended, as the road disappeared into a dark wall of thick-growing trees. "I can't see," Danny said.

"Use the lights, then," Manzano said. "Oughta be safe, we're a good way from the road—"

The headlights revealed a dense stand of pines, not very old. "It shouldn't be far," I told Manzano.

It wasn't. A few minutes later the track emerged onto another open area, smaller than the first. "God damn," Manzano said, his voice a full octave higher. "Look at that!"

The clearing was full of wrecked airplanes. At least that was the initial impression, though I don't suppose there were actually that many. I saw a single-engine light plane of some sort lying on its belly, an old Stearman biplane trainer with the engine and the top wing missing, and a big helicopter, like the ones we had in Nam, with no rotor.

"This has to be the place," Manzano said. His voice was back down to its normal tuning, and softer, almost awed. "Damn, I never really believed it. You ever see anything so fucking weird?"

Danny shut the car down and we all got out. Here, the moonlight was strong, throwing the shiny airplanes into sharp-contrast lights and darks. Now I thought I saw something bigger, with two engines, off near the line of trees.

"Get the light," Manzano said, and Danny went back and opened the trunk again and came back carrying a big boxy hand-held lantern, the kind outdoorsmen carry. "Don't turn it on yet," Manzano told him. "Once you do, we can only see where you're pointing it. We need to look around first."

We all started walking up the dirt lane together in a loose little group, all of us looking around in the moonlight. Another airplane appeared, this one so mutilated it was impossible to tell what it had been or even which end had been which. "Holy shit," Danny said. "Wonder if anybody got killed—"

And then, by God, there it was.

It lay on its belly, off to the left of the road and a little away from the other planes. Brush grew high around it and a baby pine had grown beside it, obscuring part of the tail. There was no doubt as to what it was, though, no mistaking that long sharklike shape.

Freddie Manzano said, "I'm a son of a bitch."

I wouldn't have argued with him on that point at any time, certainly not now. I said, "Unless there's a third Curtiss P-40 lying around northeastern Oklahoma, which I doubt, this is what we've been looking for."

"Yeah," Manzano agreed. "Now to see if it's holding a little present for us. Come on, Danny, let's get that light on it."

Danny switched the big lamp on and we began walking toward the old fighter. The ground was rough, rutted by truck tires, and a little muddy from the recent rains. Weeds and brush crunched underfoot and grabbed at feet and ankles. Manzano tripped over something, caught himself, and cursed.

Even lying on the ground, the P-40 was an impressive object in the sudden strong light. The paint had faded to an overall dull brown and the shark-face markings were no longer recognizable. The vertical rudder was missing and the horizontal stabilizing fins in back were bent and twisted. The propeller and the spinner cap were gone. The panes of the cockpit canopy had been starred with numerous small-bore bullets: local boys practicing with .22's, maybe, or drunk hunters. And yet the wreck retained a certain derelict dignity, like the body of a beached killer whale.

"Okay," Manzano said, "let's get started. Danny, go back to the car and get the toolbox outta the trunk."

He rubbed his hands together. "Yeah," he said. "Gonna tear this fucker apart if we have to."

We must have made a weird and memorable sight, the four of us, scrambling over the carcass of that old P-40 in the moonlight, hands and faces now and then illuminated by the glow of the hand lamp. It was bitter cold and our breaths made big white plumes in the night air.

"Start there," Freddie Manzano said, "in the, what do you call it, where the guy sits to drive this thing."

"Cockpit," I said.

"No shit? Make a good name for Drummer's, wouldn't it? Anyway, that's where I'd put it, I was in Wilburn's shoes."

The cockpit canopy turned out to be jammed shut somehow. Even Danny's enormous strength wasn't enough to move it on its tracks; all of us had to pitch in and heave and strain, even Loomis with his one arm, before we could budge it. "Hell,"

Loomis said, gasping, "Wilburn couldn't have opened this thing by himself."

"No," Manzano agreed, "but maybe it wasn't stuck then. Could be something that happened when they moved it down here, fucked it up."

When the opening was big enough, Freddie Manzano wiggled through and Loomis passed him the light. We waited while he poked about in the cockpit. This plane had been stripped even more thoroughly than the other one; there wasn't even a seat.

"Fuck that idea," Manzano said at last, crawling back out through the narrow opening. "Not a thing in there, except a shitload of broken glass. Cut my hands all to hell, ruined this new suit."

He kicked the side of the fuselage, making a hollow booming sound. "I wish we had a torch. Open this tin can up."

"Burn the money up, too," Loomis remarked. "Half a million bucks' worth of ashes, just what we need."

"I know. I sure would like to cut this fucker up, though. This is starting to turn into work. Okay, Roper, you oughta know your way around these things by now, what next?"

Actually the layout of this plane was considerably different in many ways from the one I'd searched on the roof. It did, however, have the same big access panel in back of the cockpit. Or rather it had a similar opening; the panel itself was lying on the ground beside the fuselage.

"Anything in there, somebody'd already have found it," Manzano grumbled. "Still, we better check it out—"

He took the light from Loomis and put his head and shoulders into the hatch. Light shone through various small holes as he swung the lamp this way and that inside the fuselage. "Jack shit," he said eventually, emerging from the access opening. "I didn't expect to find anything, not with it already standing open like that. Where else is there?"

I looked over the ruined airplane. "Most of the remaining access panels take special tools to get open—"

"Which Jimmy Wilburn fucking-A didn't have. But remember, he was a hot car man, already boosted one short that night and he was planning to go rip off another set of wheels. So he'd have had some simple-ass tools on him, anyway, enough to get into a car and hot-wire it." Manzano spat on the ground. "Anything he could get into with what he had, we can get into with what we got."

Then, for the next little while, the job got nasty. The aluminum was incredibly cold in the freezing night and none of us had any gloves. Soon our hands were numb and clumsy, and then bloody from various accidents with sheet metal and improper tools.

And all we found were wasps' nests. "Good thing it ain't summer," Manzano said. "Get stung all over, that would just about make the nut."

He leaned against the vertical fin, which bore a pattern of holes where some jackass had tried out his shotgun. "Well, hell," he said tiredly, "nothing left but the wings. Any places in there?"

"The gun bays," I told him as we walked out onto the starboard wing. "That's all, if this one is anything like the other one."

"Then we'll know pretty soon, one way or the other," Manzano said. "Gun what? Where's that?"

Loomis shone the light on the battered upper surface of the wing and Danny and I went to work on the gun-bay access panels. This model evidently had mounted only two guns per wing, and they must have been of smaller caliber, because the space within was considerably smaller than in the plane on the club roof.

It was, however, just as empty.

We straightened up and looked at each other. "What the

hell," Loomis said. "Things are always in the last place you look. Everybody knows that."

"I don't know," I said as we walked around the tail to reach the port wing. "This one looks to have mounted smaller guns, and the gun bays are laid out differently. I can't see that there's room enough in there for a suitcase."

"Yeah, but we don't know that the bread was still in the case," Manzano insisted. His voice was developing undertones of strain and frustration. "Anyway, we're gonna look everywhere there is to look."

Bending over the panel, struggling with the seized-up fasteners, I heard Manzano's heavy breathing behind me. He grabbed the light from Loomis's hand and shoved it toward the opening as the panel came free.

The light shone on aluminum and dull green zinc chromate paint. That was all.

"Fuck," Freddie Manzano said after a moment. *"Fuck."*

He bent down and groped about aimlessly in the gun bay with his fingers, muttering to himself, while Danny stood in helpless attendance. Loomis looked at me. "Long way to go to find the store closed," he observed.

Manzano straightened up and stepped back off the wing and went over to the side of the fuselage. I thought he was going to start kicking the plane again, but instead he bent down suddenly and stuck his head into the access hatch again. Then he pushed his narrow shoulders into the opening too, farther than before, until he had most of his upper body inside the plane. The light shone through the little holes and cracks again and there were clattering sounds; he seemed to be pawing and scrabbling around in there.

The punch line of an old joke ran through my mind: "I got me a Shetland pony in here if I can dig him out." I didn't think it would be a good idea to tell it right now.

Frddie Manzano was making strange little inarticulate

sounds, muffled by the metal of the fuselage. Loomis said quietly, "This cat's on the edge. We better be ready to move fast."

I looked around. It was a long fifty yards or so to the edge of the woods, but maybe we could make it—

"Hey!" Manzano's voice came suddenly sharp and loud from inside the rear of the P-40. "The fuck's this?"

He wiggled his ass briefly, freeing himself from the opening, and his head and shoulders emerged. "Come take the light, Danny." He straightened up, holding something in his right hand. "All right, look what we got here."

He was holding what looked like a scrap of paper. "Look what I found," he said, "stuck in behind part of the bodywork in there. Put the light on it, Danny."

I jumped off the wing and went over and had a look. It was a rectangular piece of paper, covered with elaborate designs. Benjamin Franklin's cheerful Quaker face looked back at me in the harsh light.

"A bill," Freddie Manzano said, "a fucking hundred-dollar bill! Now what was that doing in there?"

"Damn," Danny said, staring at the bill. "You mean the money's in there after all?"

"No, you ape-shape moron, the money *was* in there. Somebody got here first. That's why the cover was off." He kicked at the access panel with the toe of his muddy shoe. "Either they opened the case up to check it out and dropped a bill without noticing, or maybe Wilburn dropped it some way when he put it in there. Way it was stuck in that crack, I wouldn't have seen it myself, I hadn't felt it with my fingers."

He held the bill in front of his face. "Half a fucking million and that's all that's left. A lousy yard."

"Wonder when it happened," Loomis mused. "Could have been a long time ago, before it was ever brought here."

Manzano was bending over, pushing the access panel aside and touching the ground with his fingertips, then running the fingers of his other hand over the inside surface of the panel. "Bullshit," he said after a moment. "It rained off and on, Friday and Saturday. Didn't quit till early Saturday evening. The ground's wet underneath this piece of tin, just as wet as the ground around it. And the metal's dry on the inside of this panel." He looked at me. "All you Oklahoma assholes are supposed to be part Indian, so you tell me what that means."

"Whoever opened the hatch did it after it stopped raining."

"Damn straight. Saturday night, no sooner."

He folded the bill between his fingers, staring at me. "I'm getting this real interesting picture in my head, know what I mean? Oh, you're cute, you're cute. You nearly pulled it off, too, if you'd only stopped to put that thing back in place."

I started to ask what the hell he was talking about, but he was going to tell me anyway.

"When did you do it?" he asked. "Saturday night, huh? Came down here late and grabbed the cash, then next day you torched the club so I'd think it was all over."

His voice was getting higher and the words were coming faster. "Only I figured out the scam and came after you and called you on it. And then, cool as shit, you came up with this little soft-shoe number, and I bought it. So we all come down here in the woods in the middle of the night and work like a bunch of niggers, and all the time you know there's nothing in it. So when it comes up empty you can stand there all wide-eyed and stupid, surprise, surprise. I gotta admit, it nearly worked. You were inches away from walking off with that half-mill, clean and clear."

He turned to Loomis. "Were you in on this, piano man? Or was this son of a bitch getting ready to dog-fuck you, too? Wouldn't surprise me, he was gonna rip you off same as me."

"Freddie," Loomis said calmly, "if shit was music you'd be the Mormon Tabernacle Choir, anybody ever tell you that?"

Manzano stared at him for a moment. "All right, if that's how you want it." He looked back at me. "I'm trying to make up my mind about something, Roper. I'm trying to decide whether I want that half a million bad enough to keep you alive till I can make you tell me where it is."

Danny had the light in his left hand now, and his gun was in his right. He'd made the move so fast I hadn't even seen him do it.

"That could be fun, all right," Manzano said, "watching Danny take you apart little by little, till you're screaming, begging me on your knees to let you tell me where you hid it. Or maybe I could have some guys snatch that redskin bitch and let you watch while we work on her. Lotta possibilities here, you know what I mean?"

His hand went inside his jacket and came out holding a short-nosed revolver. "But what I'd really like to do is just go ahead and burn you. You probably got that money stashed at that trailer of yours, or at this geek's house, something half-assed like that, we could find it. If we don't, way I feel right now, it might be worth it."

He held the gun out at arm's length, like a target shooter, aimed at my face. "I think it might be half a mill worth of satisfaction, shoot you in the guts and watch you crawl around on the ground a little before you croak. Maybe leave you here, let the wild animals finish you off." He swung the gun to point at Loomis and then back to me. "Both of you, get down on your knees and beg, you fucks—"

There was a quick flat bang, not terribly loud, and then another. Freddie Manzano didn't react; he had suddenly stopped moving altogether. A pair of big dark overlapping stains had appeared in the middle of his chest.

Danny was even faster than I'd realized. He turned, the light in his hand probing at the line of trees and his gun coming up to firing position, before the shots came out of the darkness and slammed into him. This time there were four bangs, very fast.

218

Whoever was doing the shooting wasn't taking any chances with Danny.

Freddie Manzano was still on his feet, but I think he was already dead. There was a look of mild puzzlement on his thin sharp face. The gun fell from his hand and clattered sharply on the metal access panel at his feet, and then he collapsed on top of it. A moment later Danny's big body toppled backward and sprawled across the wing root. The hollow aluminum structure of the wing reverberated with a brief low-frequency boom.

The light lay on its side by the trailing edge of the wing, still burning. I picked it up and started to aim it toward the trees, where the shots had come from, but then I reconsidered and switched it off. The shooter might not care to be illuminated.

The moonlight was still strong, though, and I had no trouble recognizing Shaw as he came striding across the clearing, holding something long and dark in one hand. I couldn't make out his facial expression, if any, but his step was downright jaunty.

"Hello, Roper," he called. "We meet again."

He came around the nose of the P-40 and stopped, looking down at the bodies that lay across the wing. "Both dead, I take it? Good."

I saw now that he was carrying a military-style rifle with a long clip, what the media persist in calling an "assault rifle." I didn't recognize the make; maybe an AK-47.

"Haven't done any serious night shooting in a long time," he added. "Nice to know you've still got it . . . well." He looked at us. "Took a chance, close as you were, but I wasn't sure what this dirtbag was about to do. He seemed right on the verge of shooting you."

So now I owed my life to Shaw? That wasn't at all a comfortable thought.

"Thanks," Loomis said. I couldn't tell if there was any sarcasm in his voice.

"My pleasure. And believe me, I use the expression sincerely."

He kicked lightly at Manzano's body. "Asshole. They're all assholes, these underworld types. Irrational as women and ignorant as pigs. That's why I was against getting mixed up with them, trying to use them, but nobody listened—" He stopped and looked around. "A few trees and bushes, so the asshole thought he was out in the fucking wilderness. Didn't occur to him that he might have company."

I said, "How did you do it? Find us, I mean? I know Freddie and Danny were watching for a tail, all the way down the highway. And there weren't any lights behind us on those back roads."

Shaw smiled. At least he showed some teeth. "As I said, Manzano was an asshole. Never occurred to him that somebody might have planted a beeper on his car."

He sounded as close to happy as I'd ever heard him. His dark eyes were very wide and shining in the moonlight. Whatever he was on, he was flying now.

"I saw you at the fire, you know," he said to me. "You didn't see me, did you? Nobody did. I borrowed a fireman's coat and hat off one of the trucks and walked around and nobody paid me any mind. Then I followed you to Loomis's place, and while I was waiting for you to come out, Manzano showed up. So I put beepers on all three vehicles. Didn't know which one I might want to follow."

Loomis said, "What do you want with us now? I don't think you came all this way just to save our asses."

"Oh, come now." I couldn't see the sneer, but I could hear it, as much as you could hear anything in that flat voice. "This fool already spelled it out in detail, before I wasted him. If a clown like that could figure it out, do you think you can bullshit me?"

The weapon came up suddenly to cover us. "Couldn't have him killing you before I could interrogate you, but that doesn't

221

mean I won't shoot you myself if you try to run. I can bring you down without killing you. I only need you alive and able to talk."

My insides felt very loose. As if they were trying to become my outsides.

"I tell you what," Shaw said, "I'm tired of freezing my ass off out here. Let's cut the dancing around."

The rifle snapped up, butt to his shoulder. He was aiming at Loomis now. "I'm going to count to ten," he said. "No, fuck that, five ought to be enough. A count of five, that's how long you've got to tell me where you're keeping that money. On five, I shoot Loomis through the hand."

He laid his face to the stock, taking careful aim. "One," he said. "Two—"

The voice that came from the woods behind him was so loud and clear and crisp that I thought at first it must be amplified. *"Gilette!"* it called. *"Sanford Gilette! Put down that weapon and place your hands on top of your head!"*

Shaw's head came up and around. His face was very white in the moonlight. The muzzle of the rifle wavered through a small arc. "No," he whispered. "No, God damn it, not now."

"Put down the weapon," the voice repeated. *"Now!"*

Shaw turned his upper body, the rifle swinging almost ninety degrees off target. That was good enough for me. I hit the ground in a sliding dive, weeds and brush crackling under me, little twigs stinging my face. Out of the corner of my eye I saw Loomis do the same.

"Give it up, Gilette," the voice blared.

It was a time to hug the ground and breathe mud, but I couldn't resist turning my head to watch. Shaw was still standing there, holding his weapon. "No," he said again, this time louder, and then in a wild shout, "No, you bastards, I finally found it, you can't take me out now—"

"Last chance," the voice called. *"Weapon on the ground, hands on the head. You know what to do, Gilette."*

Shaw's shoulders heaved briefly. "Fuck you!" he screamed, and spun around, the rifle still at his shoulder. The muzzle flashed quick flame, a short full-auto burst, perhaps half a dozen rounds. He had to be firing blind, without any real chance of hitting anybody, but I think by then he didn't care.

There was a single flash among the trees. Shaw bucked violently backward, dropping his rifle, and fell. The sound of the shot echoed briefly among the wrecked airplanes.

I got up, after a long minute, and went over and looked down at Shaw. His right hand was still groping for the fallen rifle. I kicked it gingerly out of his reach. It was an AK-47, all right. I hadn't seen one since Nam.

Shaw's eyes stared up at me. His mouth opened and his crooked lip lifted. "Told you," he whispered. "In over your head. No idea who you're fucking with."

I waited, but he didn't speak again. He wasn't ever going to speak again. I looked around as Loomis got to his feet. "They get him?" Loomis asked.

I nodded. "Good," Loomis said. "No, on second thought, I better wait to see who they are. Been kind of a tendency for things to go from bad to worse lately."

A couple of men came out of the woods and walked across the open ground toward us. I didn't recognize either of them. They were both carrying rifles. I stayed still and kept my hands in sight. They walked past me, without looking at me, and stood for a moment over Shaw's body. One of them bent down and picked up the AK-47 and slung it over his shoulder. I noticed that his own rifle was fitted with a large, complicated-looking gadget above the barrel, like a huge telescopic sight. Some kind of starlight sniperscope, I guessed. I'd heard about them but never seen one.

The other man came back and looked at Loomis and me.

"Roper and Loomis?" We both nodded. "Right," he said. "What I want you to do, you go over to that BMW and get in the back seat and stay there. All right? Don't get out for any reason until I tell you to."

"Then you better wait a minute," Loomis told him, "because there's something I need to do first. Been needing to do it real bad for the last few minutes, you dig?"

"Me too," I put in. I hadn't noticed until Loomis spoke, but now I felt ready to explode.

The two men looked at each other. The one with the sniper-scope grinned. "Sure," he said. "Understandable under the circumstances."

"When you're done," the first one added, "go wait in the car. Please."

Loomis and I sat in the back seat of the BMW for quite some time, while the two men did whatever they were doing. It was very late by now—I didn't know how late; my cheap watch had gotten smashed while we were working on the P-40—and very cold. I realized suddenly that I hadn't had anything to eat since lunch. I hadn't even had a chance to take a bite of my sandwich at Loomis's place. Somehow, though, I still didn't feel hungry.

The two men came walking up the dirt track, carrying something large and dark between them. They went past the BMW and stopped. After a moment one of them came back and opened the driver's door and reached in and got the keys from the dash. He closed the door without speaking. A minute later the trunk opened. There was a soft thump and the rear of the BMW seemed to settle slightly.

They did that two more times. By the time they got the third body into the trunk, the back end of the BMW was definitely riding a little low. I wouldn't have thought you could get three full-sized human bodies into a BMW's trunk. And Danny was considerably more than full-sized, although Freddie Manzano's slight build would perhaps compensate for that. BMW ought to look into it as an advertising gimmick.

The two men disappeared again. Loomis and I looked at each other briefly, but neither of us spoke.

Finally one of the men reappeared out of the darkness, coming toward the BMW. He didn't seem to have his rifle any more. He opened the door and got in behind the wheel. The light fell on his face for a second before he shut the door. He had a long nose and a slightly receding hairline. "Hey," I said. "Weren't you driving that green car—"

He turned around and looked back at me. It was dark inside the car and I couldn't make out his expression. "No, Roper," he said. "You've never seen me before in your life. In fact you don't see me right now."

He turned back around and started the engine. It took a little low-speed maneuvering to get the BMW pointed back up the narrow dirt lane. He did it all without using the lights, and he drove all the way back to the road without turning them on. The gate was standing open. I couldn't see any sign of the other man, or any vehicle except the endless ranks of wrecked ones.

"Right back," he said, when we were out on the gravel road. He got out and closed the gate. I wondered why he bothered. Maybe he grew up on a farm. Maybe he just liked things neat. That would be a useful quality in a member of a clean-up crew.

He didn't speak again until we were back on the pavement. Then, without turning his head, he said, "Nothing happened back there. Even if it had, you wouldn't have seen it, since you were both at home all night, weren't you?"

He didn't wait for an answer. "You've never seen me or my partner," he went on. "Or the man you knew as Shaw. Does anyone know that either of you had dealings with Freddie Manzano?"

"Several people," I told him. "Including one cop."

"Then you don't know what happened to him." He glanced back, then, for a second. "Am I making myself clear?"

"As Bombay gin," Loomis assured him.

"Good." He faced forward again. The headlights illuminated an armadillo crossing the road and he swung the car slightly to miss it. "Understand this: nobody will be asking you any questions. This will be seen to, you follow me? I'm merely cautioning you against, you might say, volunteering information. Loose talk, exciting stories over drinks. Your discretion will be required."

He paused. "Maybe I'd better emphasize that for you, Roper. Seeing that you've been a journalist, you work as a writer now, and you're involved with a woman journalist—"

"There won't be any stories in print," I told him. "Not even fictionalized ones."

"I know there won't, Roper," he said gently. "That's another thing that will be seen to, if necessary. I'm merely advising you not to make problems for yourself and others."

"Who the fuck are you guys?" Loomis asked him. "CIA or what?"

"We're people who don't exist," the long-nosed man said. "That's who we are, Loomis. I thought you'd grasped that by now."

The county blacktop ended in a stop sign. The long-nosed man swung the BMW onto Highway 75. When we were rolling northward Loomis said, "What about the money?"

"What about it?"

"Aren't you going to try to find out if we got it, or know where it is? Or warn us not to try to get it, or any of that stuff everybody else lays on us?"

The long-nosed man turned his head again to look at Loomis. "We don't care about the money," he said. "This wasn't about the money."

"Then what the—oh," Loomis said. "You guys came to take

226

Shaw out before he blew the gig. Before he did something that might get people to digging into that business ten years ago, because it might make trouble for somebody up top. That about the size of it?"

"Naturally," the long-nosed man said, "I don't know what you're talking about. Or wouldn't know, if I existed in the first place.... No, we're not after the money. But," he added, "if you do have it, I suggest you take it somewhere and set fire to it, and make sure there's nothing left but ashes. You see, there's no way two people like you can spend that kind of cash without attracting the attention of certain official agencies, and they'll want to know where you got it. I don't think you'll be able to satisfy them with any story you could concoct."

He raised a hand from the steering wheel. "And of course, if any investigation were to turn up the *real* story behind that half-million, then we *would* be forced to take an interest. I hope you understand me."

"We don't have it," I told him.

"It doesn't matter," he said calmly. "As long as it doesn't make trouble for us, we don't care who has it. If it does threaten to cause problems, the problems will be dealt with. If necessary, the people will be dealt with too."

I had a sudden mental picture of Shaw lying on the ground, looking up at me: *In over your head. No idea who you're fucking with.*

We rode for a little while in silence. As we went through the outskirts of Glenpool, the long-nosed man finally spoke again.

"Listen," he said, "you two live in this area, right? So what's a good place to get Chinese food?"

My old city editor used to say, "You can sweep anything under the rug if you've got a big enough broom."

The days that followed saw a first-rate demonstration of what might be called the Big Broom Principle. No bodies turned up anywhere, nobody found a BMW with bloodstains in the trunk, nothing.

Freddie Manzano's disappearance couldn't be simply overlooked, given his status in the area; but the official theory— Wiley Harmon told me this, when he finally started speaking to me again—was that this had been an assassination within the organized-crime scene.

"It ain't like the little turd didn't have plenty of people that wanted him outta the way," Harmon said. "Anyway, it looks like there's not gonna be any heavy pressure to investigate."

He looked at me with hooded eyes. "I might even say that I get this feeling there's some kind of pressure *not* to check too hard into the disappearance and possible demise of this sterling fucking citizen of the fine state of Oklahoma. I might say that if I was the kind of asshole to go around saying things like that. If I hadn't had so many people telling me lately I gotta learn to watch my mouth."

"Bradshear's on your case again?"

"When did Birdshit ever get off? Not to mention I had this kind of a hallucination," Harmon said, "where this spooky suit with a nose like a bottle opener came to see me and told me I should forget anything I might have picked up helping you. Turned out he wasn't really there, though. Told me so himself."

He slugged at his beer. We were sitting in the Copper Bottom, where we'd gone to discuss a new piece of business, never mind what. "Well," he said, "fuck 'em all in the ear. As Aunt Jemima not infrequently observed to Uncle Ben."

All that was later, though. For the first couple of days after the junkyard massacre, I didn't talk to anybody—except once on the phone to Rita, who called to say she was taking Tommy to Tahlequah to stay with their family—and I only went out to buy the basic necessities of life. At the time, these came mostly in liquid form.

I kept feeling I ought to call Hondo Loomis, but somehow I couldn't get myself to pick up the phone. He must have felt the same way; he didn't call me either. Not until Wednesday morning, when he rang me to ask if I could come over and help him with something. He didn't elaborate and I didn't ask questions. It was going to be some time before either of us felt easy about talking on the phone.

When I got to his place he was already standing in the yard, next to the blue van. He looked older, I thought, and tired; the red around his eyes, and the color of his face, suggested that I hadn't been the only one who'd needed some bottled help getting through the last couple of days.

His voice was steady, though, and his tone reasonably cheerful, as he told me what was on his mind. "It's Doris," he said. "You remember Doris, don't you? I've got her last paycheck ready, only I can't find her. I mean, I called that worthless brother of hers and he said she hadn't been there since the weekend. I couldn't get anything out of him. All he was interested in was trying to get me to give the check to him. Claimed she owed him."

"You think she went back to Roy Dolan?"

"It's possible. If she did, there's nothing I can do about it. But I still need to give her the check. I already paid everybody else off." His mouth twitched at the corners. "Except Julie, and she didn't leave a forwarding address . . . what I'm sort of worried about, though," he said seriously, "what if Dolan, you know, took her with him against her will? What if he's got her down at his place, like his prisoner?"

"Would he do something like that?"

"I don't think so," Loomis said, "but damn if I can be sure. Crazy as he is, who knows what he might do? Specially if he's drunk. Hell, you saw him that night."

"So what do you want to do?"

"I don't *want* to have anything to do with it," Loomis said. "But I think I better drive down and see if she's at Dolan's place. Give her the check if she wants to stay, go get the law if she needs help. If she's not there maybe he knows where she is. Good chance he would, the way he follows her around."

"And you want me along for backup?"

"If you don't mind. No heavy action, dig. Just like to have somebody along."

"Sure." I nodded toward the Camaro. "Want to take my car?"

"Fine with me. That van gets about half a mile to the gallon and it handles like a pregnant cow in a crosswind."

We started toward the Camaro. "It's not far to Dolan's place," Loomis said. "He lives down on the other side of Sapulpa, a little way off 66."

Route 66 wound southwest from Sapulpa, crossing underneath the Turnpike below Kellyville. It was a little more prosperous-looking than the stretch above Sapulpa, but there were still signs of a long-faded golden era: a deserted gas station with its pumps gone, a gone-to-grass lot with the foundations of an extinct motel still visible amid the weeds.

We didn't talk much on the way. At the start, as we rode past the burned-out wreck of the Flying Tiger Club, I opened my mouth to say something, but then I saw Loomis's face and decided to keep quiet.

As we left Sapulpa, he said suddenly, "I wonder what they did with his car."

"Whose car?"

"Shaw's. Gray compact job, wasn't it? He got down there some way, at least. And there were only two of them, and they had their own wheels, and Freddie Manzano's Krautmobile to get rid of. So what happened to Shaw's heap?"

"My guess," I said, after thinking about it for a minute, "would be that it's still down there. Christ, you saw that place, cars by the acre. All they had to do was run it in among a lot of junkers and chances are nobody'd notice it was there. Not for a long time, anyway, and if they did, what difference would it make? You can bet Shaw saw to it nobody could trace it to him."

"Sounds reasonable." He was quiet for a long time. Then, all at once, he turned to face me and said, "Jesus, Roper, they killed him!"

"He was getting ready to kill us," I pointed out. "I don't know about you, but I've got no complaints."

"Yeah, but that's not why they did it, man. You know that." His face was as strained as his voice. "They weren't down there

231

to save our asses. It was because he was starting to worry some people, somewhere, that he might do something to *embarrass* them. They killed him for that."

He looked out the window at the passing landscape. "I thought I knew the score, Roper," he said. "Didn't think anything could blow my mind any more. Looks like I wasn't as hip as I thought."

Roy Dolan lived in a smallish frame house beside a really bad blacktopped county road, not far from Heyburn Lake State Park. The yard was littered and rank with dead weeds. The white paint was peeling and yellow with dirt and neglect. An old three-quarter-ton pickup truck sat in the yard. It had been painted with rust-red primer and left at that. A crudely-made overhead rack, welded up from iron beams, extended from over the bed to above the cab.

"He doesn't have a job?" I asked Loomis as we got out of the Camaro.

"Roy Dolan? I didn't know you were a comic too."

We climbed the concrete-block steps and stood on the warped little porch while Loomis knocked. After a minute or so the door opened. "Hello, Mr. Loomis," Roy Dolan said. He looked at me with absolutely no sign of recognition. "Y'all come on in."

He held the door open and stood aside for us. He was wearing grease-stained jeans and a green work shirt with *Roy* stitched above the left breast pocket. He had on the mesh-backed Red Man cap he'd worn that night at the Flying Tiger Club. His face looked even longer and sadder than I remembered. As I passed I caught a whiff of rancid long-term booze breath.

Inside, the place was even filthier than I'd expected. Dust lay deep on everything, the floor was littered with beer cans and wine bottles and crushed-out cigarette butts, and there was a smell to make your eyes water. It wasn't the sort of what-the-hell mess you might find in, say, a rowdy fraternity house after a big party. This was a place so steeped in blank despair that it was impossible to believe anyone would ever care enough to clean it up.

Roy Dolan, however, was smiling, after a dogged fashion. "Heard your place got burned down, Mr. Loomis," he said. "Sure sorry to hear it."

Loomis thanked him and asked about Doris. The answer was immediate and negative.

"I ain't seen her," Dolan said, "I ain't heard from her, I dunno what's become of her. I thought she was still at her brother's." He wiped his nose with the back of one finger. "I went by there looking for her Sunday afternoon, but that son of a bitch run me off."

He looked at Loomis with the eyes of a dog that doesn't understand why he's been kicked. "She ain't never gonna come back, is she, Mr. Loomis? I finely come to see it. She don't wanta be my woman no more."

"I'm afraid that's it, Roy," Loomis told him. "Better for both of you if you can accept it."

"Yeah." It was more a sigh than a word. " 'Scuse me, I'll be right back."

He disappeared into the next room. I heard the rattle of a bottle cap being unscrewed.

Loomis and I looked at each other. I said softly, "Jesus, Hondo."

"I know," he said heavily. "What the hell do you say?"

I walked over and looked out the window, mostly as an alternative to the view inside the dirty little house. The old truck appeared to be leaking oil; the ground beneath it was black and wet-looking. The rack on top was heavily spotted with rust—

I said, "Oh, my God."

"What?" Loomis came over and looked out the window. "What's the matter?"

I took a deep breath and looked around. Roy Dolan still hadn't returned from his pitstop.

"The truck," I said. "Dolan's truck, remember? You had the kitchen help drive him home, because you didn't want him driving drunk. But when I came by later, when Wilburn's body turned up, there were no vehicles at all in the parking lot."

"So?" Loomis's forehead creased in confusion. "You mean—" Then he got it. "You think he came back for his truck, later that night? And ran into Jimmy Wilburn?"

There was a soft shuffling sound behind us. When we turned around Roy Dolan was standing in the doorway, looking at us.

"I killed that man," he said sadly. "I never meant to, but it was me killed him."

His voice was even more blurry than before; he was drunker than I'd realized. At the moment, however, that wasn't my main interest. I was paying more attention to the shotgun in his right hand. It was a weathered old single-barrel, outside-hammer job, the standby of generations of poor farmers and country pot-hunters. It was about as crude a weapon as anybody still manu-factured, and this one was in bad shape, its barrel streaked with rust and its stock wrapped with friction tape at the wrist.

It was, however, perfectly capable of blowing a big hole, or a lot of small holes depending on the load, in a human body at short range. Say across a small living room.

"Roy," Loomis began, "put down the gun, now—"

"I never meant to kill him," Dolan said again, and snuffled. "I come back to get my truck. Walked down to 66 and hitched me a ride with some high-school boys in a fast car. They made some fun of me but it was all right, they was just kids, drunker than I was. They let me off in Sapulpa and I walked out to your place, Mr. Loomis, and there he was with my truck."

He pointed out the window with the hand that wasn't holding the shotgun. "He had my truck over by the back wall—I guess he pushed it there, I didn't have it locked good—and he was up on top of it, using it to climb up on the roof, you see. He was standing on the rack when I seen him. I yelled, 'Hey, you get down offa there!' and he looked around and seen me."

"And he fell off?" Loomis asked. "It's not your fault if—"

"No, no." Dolan wiped his nose again. "He just said some stuff, cussed me out, you know, told me to get out of there. Acted all pissed off and excited." Dolan shrugged. "And I was still about half drunk, I thought hell, I don't hafta put up with no shit like that offa some sneak thief. So I went up and got in the cab and started her up and threw her in reverse and backed out of there."

He shrugged heavily. "I only meant to make him get down, but I guess it made him fall, some way. All of a sudden he come sailing down with his arms out and his legs kicking, and then he lit on his back and I knowed before I got out and looked that he was dead."

"And you put him in the dumpster?" I hadn't meant to speak, but I was fascinated past the point of good judgment.

He looked at me and something went across his face, a vague flicker of not-quite-recognition. "It didn't seem right," he said, "to go off and leave him there like that, out on the ground. I could tell it was fixing to rain. I couldn't think of nowhere else to put him where it wouldn't rain on him."

Loomis cleared his throat. "Roy, you didn't do anything wrong. It was an accident. You tell the sheriff what you told me, you'll be all right." His voice was low and soothing. "You don't know it, but that man was a criminal, people were looking for him—"

"It don't make no never mind," Dolan said with bitter finality. "It's all done gone to hell. Ever'thing just keeps on caving in on me. And I don't give a shit, anyway, if Doris ain't coming back."

He hoisted the shotgun and thumbed back the rusty hammer.

Loomis said, "Roy, for God's sake," but Dolan wasn't listening to anybody any more.

"It's done over," he said. "I said all I got to say."

He began turning the shotgun around, so clumsily that I thought surely it would go off, and I got ready to jump him if it did. But he got it reversed and put the muzzle where he wanted it. It was a long reach to the trigger, but he had long arms, and he made it.

I turned my head at the last instant, not wanting to see it happen. But after the deafening blast I turned back to look, ears ringing, and it still wasn't a sight anybody should have to see.

Deputy Ellis put his notebook in the pocket of his brown uniform shirt and said, "It's getting to be a little too much, gentlemen. I'm trying to be very professional and legal and all that, but I don't have to tell you that a lot of law enforcement officers in my position would have hauled you in by now, just on general principles. Or at least made you get out of my county and stay out."

I said, "Christ, is it against the law to witness a suicide?"

Ellis gave me a dark impassive stare. "As far as I know, neither of you has broken any laws, which is the only reason you're not in a cell right now. But you have to admit, you do keep showing up at the scenes of nasty events." He looked at Loomis. "Are you planning on rebuilding and reopening that night club?"

Loomis shook his head. "I'm not even staying around this part of the country, once the insurance money comes."

"Good. Because I'd feel I had to recommend to the licensing board that you shouldn't be allowed to run a night club in Creek County. Maybe nothing that happened was your fault, but it adds up to a pattern. And if you'd called us that night Dolan came to the club," he said, "we'd have taken him in, and both men might still be alive."

236

I wanted to bet against it, at least in Jimmy Wilburn's case, but I kept still.

They were coming out of Dolan's house now, carrying the body on a stretcher. They'd covered him up, including the head, or what was left of it. My memory saw right through the material, though, and I fought down a brief dry retch. Ellis stepped back, but he needn't have worried about his shiny uniform shoes; all the contents of my stomach had departed before he and his men had arrived.

"As it happens," Ellis went on, "I did need to speak with you two anyway, about another matter." He folded his arms and stared at Loomis. "We caught the person who set fire to your club."

"How'd you do that?" Loomis didn't sound particularly interested. He and Ellis were definitely failing to establish a warm relationship. "Dust the ashes for fingerprints?"

"Several things," Ellis said, ignoring the bait. "A man at the truck-driving school down the road saw a car speeding away at the same time smoke began to appear above the roof of the club. A gas station attendant in Oakhurst remembered a customer who'd filled several gallon cans with gasoline, and paid with a credit card. And a young man showed up at a hospital emergency ward with bad burns on both arms and no clear explanation of how it had happened. The kid wasn't exactly careful about covering his tracks."

"Kid?" I said.

Ellis swung his stony eyes toward me. "A teenage boy from Oakhurst," he said, "with a history of problem behavior. He told us all about how he set fire to the place, as soon as we brought him in. Used gasoline all over the interior, soaked the carpeting and so on, then tossed an emergency flare in the front door. Wonder he wasn't blown to bits." Ellis shook his head. "Very surprised, too, when he found out his mother wasn't going to be

237

able to come get him out immediately. He got pretty wild then. Amazing, the vocabulary these kids have nowadays."

He looked at Loomis again. "According to his confession, he was also responsible for the threats and vandalism you reported earlier in the month. Are you going to want to press charges?"

"Not unless the insurance company makes me."

"No point in it, really. He's a juvenile and he's obviously in need of professional help. At least it's going to look obvious to the judge, you can bank on that." Ellis shifted his weight and suddenly turned to face me, square-on. "One little thing, though. The boy told a pretty strange story about running into a man one night at the club. Said the man beat him up with a baseball bat, tried to kill him. Claims the same man went to his home and assaulted his mother. You wouldn't have any idea what that's all about, would you?"

I shook my head. Ellis sighed. "Of course not. Anyway, you're not nearly big enough to fit the description the boy gave us. He said the man was bigger than me. And when we interviewed the mother, she denied that she'd been attacked by anyone at all."

The men were closing the ambulance doors now. A deputy came out on the porch, carrying Dolan's old shotgun.

"At least this lets us close the file on Jimmy Wilburn," Ellis said in a slightly less hostile tone. "Poor bastard, he finally ran into somebody who was an even bigger loser than he was."

"Can we go now?" Loomis asked.

"Go? Oh, Christ, yes, do that." Ellis let out a snort like a bull buffalo. "Of course you'll have to come in and make statements for the official record, but we'll get in touch with you about that. Right now, you're free to go. Please do."

We started to walk toward the Camaro. A young man in a brown deputy's uniform, coming the other way on some errand, looked at me and then ran over to Ellis and began talking to him in a low voice. I heard Ellis say, "Horse shit," very loudly, but then he nodded and waved his hands in a shooing motion and the young guy took off toward one of the parked patrol cars.

"The hell was that all about?" Loomis asked as we got into the Camaro.

"Who knows? These county cops seem kind of—"

"Sir?" The young deputy had appeared beside the car. I'd almost closed the door on part of him. "Are you Taggart Roper?"

I nodded warily. "Oh, good," he said with a big smile. "It's a real honor to meet you."

I couldn't think of anything to say but "Thanks."

"I just bought this, while I was on my lunch break," he went on, "and I haven't had a chance to read it yet, but I know I'm going to like it. It looks like the kind of book I really enjoy." He was digging in his uniform pocket for a pen. "Would you be willing to autograph it for me?"

And he held out a copy of *Steel Spurs*.

Next day was Thanksgiving. God seemed to be in one of His ironic moods this month.

Rita was out of town and I didn't feel any enthusiasm for cooking for myself. I took Harry down to the hamburger place, the only thing open in Yuchi Park that day, and we sat in the car and ate burgers and fries and agreed that we were thankful for that. Since it was a special occasion I let Harry have cheese on his.

Back at the trailer, Harry stretched out on the couch and went to sleep, and I sat down beside him with the harmonica and tried to play a little. I slogged doggedly through "God Bless the Child" and did some criminal things to "Ain't Misbehavin'." While I was slapping the spit out of the reeds and trying to think what to assault next, a vehicle pulled up outside, and when I went to look I saw Hondo Loomis getting out of his van.

"Gobble, gobble," he said, coming up the steps as I held the door open for him. He had a brown bag under his arm. "Wondered if you'd be home." He came in and looked around the place. "Hey, you got anybody here, you're about to go somewhere, anything like that, I can split."

"No," I said, closing the door, "no, it's just me and Harry."

Harry was already awake again, raising his head to look at the new arrival. "This is Harry, huh?" Loomis said, sitting down in the old chair by the coffee table. "Nice dog."

Harry jumped off the couch and headed toward him, sniffing. I got ready to grab him, but to my amazement Harry merely walked up and laid his head, very gently, on Loomis's lap. He closed his eyes as Loomis scratched him behind the ears. Only the flailing of his tail showed his joy.

"So," Loomis said after a couple of minutes, "you had your big Thanksgiving dinner yet?"

"Such as it was."

"Yeah, by yourself, huh? I'm in the same bag myself, man, only I guess yours is coming back. Anyway," he passed the brown bag over to me, "I thought we might share something appropriate."

The bag contained a bottle of Wild Turkey. I said, "I'll get some glasses."

We sat and had a few, not enough to get seriously or even legally drunk, only an unhurried warming-up inside.

"You got any sides, man?" Loomis asked. "You know, records, tapes, anything?"

"Not even a player. Want to try the radio?"

"Why not?"

I flipped the radio on and tuned it to the first station I found. A boompa-boompa rhythm came from the cheap speaker. Elvis Costello began singing "Watching the Detectives." Loomis and I looked at each other and broke up. "Cat's good, you know," Loomis said as the song continued. "Most of the modern crowd don't know shit, but this guy's got some ideas. Him and Tom Waits."

We listened to the rest of the song. After a lengthy series of commercials, a Fleetwood Mac number came on. We both lunged for the knob but I got there first. "So much for that," Loomis said. "It ain't so much that there's a lot of boring shit around, you know, there's always been that. It's that nobody seems to know the difference any more. Even when people listen to somebody good—Roy Orbison, Jerry Lee Lewis, Dylan—half the time it's not because they actually dig what the cat's doing, they're just into a nostalgia trip."

He reached for the Wild Turkey and poured himself a refill. "My last, man, don't let me take another. I gotta drive home and one wipeout was enough." He glanced down at his pinned-up left sleeve. "Too fucking much, in fact."

He sipped at his whisky. "Yeah, everybody's hung up on the past. People came out to the club because it was on Route 66, or because there was a World War Twice airplane and a picture of John Wayne. Or because the star act was a genuine living legend, it said so in *Rolling Stone.*"

He tilted his glass and made the contents swirl around and around. The Wild Turkey kept climbing almost to the rim of the glass but he never quite let it escape.

"That's what all that shit was about," he said quietly. "All these people who had it figured that there was somewhere in the past that they'd fucked up, or life had fucked them up, or something. And if they could just find a way to fix it, everything would be cool. Like Roy Dolan. Poor son of a bitch had it in his hillbilly head that if he could get Doris to come back to him one more time, they'd turn into the all-American happy couple. Or like all of us silly bastards chasing around after that money."

"You lost me there." I was topping up my own glass. I didn't have to drive anywhere. I was sitting on the couch; I didn't even have to make it to the bedroom.

"Man," Loomis said, "haven't you seen it yet? That's what everybody wanted with the money. We all had this idea it would let us fix the stuff that had gone wrong." He set his drink down, raised his hand, and began folding fingers down one by one. "Jimmy Wilburn ripped it off in the first place because he thought it would turn him from a punk to a big-time operator, and he came back for it and got himself killed for the same reason—only by then he had ten years in the slammer to make up for, too."

He folded down another finger. "Shaw thought he'd recover the loot and it would wipe out the big disaster of his spook career, the night he got taken off by some half-assed Okie hoods. Me, I had this picture of all this shit I was gonna do, where I wouldn't have to be up on a stage any more with everybody looking at the living proof of where *I* fucked up."

He looked at me and grinned. "As for you, I don't guess I know enough to say, but—"

"Oh, sure." I admired the color of my drink. "I see what you're saying."

"And it was all bullshit," he went on. "If Wilburn had gotten the money back, he'd still have been a punk, and if Shaw didn't kill him for it somebody else would have. If Shaw had scored, he'd still have been a cuckoo clock, and those two scary bastards or some others like them would have snuffed him sooner or later. And all the hundred-dollar bills ever printed wouldn't grow me an arm back, or bring back the old talent . . . you know, I haven't written a song since I lost the arm."

Harry put his head in Loomis's lap again, asking to be scratched. Scratching, Loomis said, "As for you, like I say, man, I dunno."

I swallowed some bourbon and shrugged. "Maybe I had some idea I could finally escape the consequences of having gone into a line of work where it's statistically impossible to succeed."

"Right. It's all bullshit, man," he repeated. "Dolan, Wilburn,

243

Shaw, you and me, we're all the same. Our lives are fucked up because we're fuckups. Or were," he added. "Now they're all dead but the two of us. Here's to all us losers."

"I'll drink to that," I assented. And did.

"Even Freddie Manzano," Loomis said after a moment. "I don't know whether there was anything in the past that was eating him, but he sure was trying to live there. I mean, all that old-time gangster act of his, threads and dialogue like a heavy in a Bogie movie."

He made a face. "Julie, now, that's another story. The Julies of the world never look back. That's why they beat everybody else's brains out."

He finished his drink and stood up. "Well, Roper, it's been a stone gas. Sit still," he added. "I'll let myself out. Harry, see you around."

When he was gone I sat for a little while finishing my own drink, thinking about what he'd said. He might, I decided, be on to something. Maybe, if I cared to pick things apart, it might even explain what caused me to write stories about events of the distant past, or other people to read them.

"So we beat on, boats against the current, borne back ceaselessly into the past." Thus F. Scott Fitzgerald, winding up the tale of Jay Gatsby, another loser.

As usual, Fitzgerald almost got it right, and, as usual, he blew it. The current runs the other way; and we paddle frantically against it, searching for that eddy that might let us work back upstream and start the trip over on a new line, *get it right* this time . . . and all the time the river pulls us steadily toward the cataracts of an inscrutable and ultimately terminal future.

The last time I saw Hondo Loomis, it was the third week in December. I was just finishing a few revisions to the final chapter of the new manuscript when Harry began barking, and I looked out to see the blue van in the yard.

"Sorry," he said when I came out to meet him, "but I don't have time to come in. Got a meeting with the guy from the insurance company in a little while. They're finally gonna settle. I already got my stuff packed and loaded in the van, here."

"Where will you go?"

"Back to Chicago, I guess. For now, anyway. Cat up there says I can have my old club job back."

He reached back and took an envelope from his back pocket and held it out. "Reason I came by," he said, "I thought you might like to see this."

The envelope was addressed to Hondo Loomis, 29 Mocoso Road, West Tulsa. It bore a large, bright-colored stamp from a country I'd never heard of, something vaguely Caribbean-sounding.

"Read it, man," Loomis urged.

I took out the enclosed letter and unfolded it. It was written on high-quality stationery from a hotel with the same name as the country. The handwriting was large and childish but clear:

Dear Mr. Loomis,

I know I am taking a chance writing to you but you were always kind to me and I wanted to tell you what happened and that I am all right.

I heard you and Mr. Roper talking that night. I was coming to tell you we needed to order some more Wild Turkey, because you and Mr. Roper had drank it up, and I could hear you thru the door. I know it was wrong to listen to a private convorsation but I could'nt help it.

I knew that Mr. Bennett had changed the airplane. I was there when the man came to get it. I knew where his place was too, because my brother used to sell him car parts. I said to myself I bet that money is in that old

245

*airplane. Saturday night after I got off work I drove down
and climbed over the fence and found it. I was lucky, the
money was in almost the first place I looked.*

*It is real nice down here and the people are so friendly.
I have met this real nice man, only a little older than me,
who is here because of some kind of a misunderstanding
about some stocks and bonds. He says I can live on the
island for the rest of my life on that much money and the
government here never sends anybody back. He and I are
thinking about getting a little house down by the beach.*

*I am sorry to run out on you and I guess it was a sin
to take money that was not mine, but Mr. Loomis I
couldn't take any more living with my brother and his
wife and I sure wasn't going back to Roy.*

> *With best wishes,*
> *Doris*

*P.S. I think I had one more check coming, if so you can
give it to Roy. He'll drink it up but I guess I owe him that
much.*

I looked up at Loomis. "Holy shit," I said. "Doris got it. Doris."

"Yeah," he said happily. "Ain't it a gas?"

We both began laughing then, barnyard cackles at first and
then great bellowing guffaws, slapping our legs and pounding
our fists against the side of the van, tears running down our
cheeks in the freezing wind. Harry began dancing around, barking agreement with whatever the joke was, making little rushes
at our feet, while we stood there in the chilly light of the
end-of-the-year sun, laughing like madmen.